A carpenter and joiner by trade, Geoff McQueen worked abroad for many years before he began writing five years ago. His first real success came with an episode of *The Gentle Touch* which was screened in 1982, and more recently he wrote the popular series *Give Us A Break*.

He lives in Hertfordshire and is married with two sons.

Also by Geoff McQueen

GIVE US A BREAK

Geoff McQueen

BIG DEAL

Novelisation by Angus Wells

Futura

A Futura BOOK

Copyright of novelisation by Angus Wells © 1984 Futura
based on material Copyright © 1984 by Geoff McQueen

First published in Great Britain in 1984 by
Futura Publications,
a Division of Macdonald & Co (Publishers) Ltd
London & Sydney

ISBN 0 7088 2636 9

Photoset in North Wales by
Derek Doyle & Associates, Mold, Clwyd.
Reproduced, printed and bound in Great Britain by
Hazell Watson & Viney Limited,
Member of the BPCC Group,
Aylesbury, Bucks

Futura Publications
A Division of
Macdonald & Co (Publishers) Ltd
Maxwell House
74 Worship Street
London EC2A 2EN

A BPCC plc company

CHAPTER ONE

Smoke hung trapped in the blue-white frostiness of the floodlights that exorcised shadow from the oval of the stadium. In the centre, grass glowed like neon astro turf, ringed by the low fence containing the track. Beyond that, a second fence stood higher, holding back the watchers from the objects of their enthusiasm. Behind the fence ranks of wooden benches climbed in stepped layers to the glass frontages of the enclosed areas. Over the benches and behind the glass faces watched. Nervously; cheerfully; indifferently. Cigarettes and cigars were lit or ground out. Glasses were raised in toasts, or to steady nerves; form cards rustled softly; voices hushed, then fell silent. A bell rang: electric warning in an electric atmosphere. A ragged shape, vaguely similar to a hare, flew from its stationary position to run a solitary circuit of its pre-ordained path. There was a susuration of inhaled breath as the lifeless dummy completed its circle. A second, louder clanging of the bell, accompanied by the clatter of opening traps. And a great, echoing shout from the onlookers as the dogs burst forth.

Long, lean shapes in multi-coloured waistcoats exploded into action, necks craning forwards in hopeless pursuit of the lure as stick-thin limbs propelled the greyhounds around the track. Tails stretched out, bodies flattening as the dogs raced round, oblivious to the bellowing of the spectators, intent only on the chase.

The shouting grew louder as the animals came into the final bend, the punters seeking to lend their chosen dogs extra speed with lung and will-power. The drone of the lure, the furious thudding of paws on dirt, all was lost

5

under the roar of the crowd as the racers blurred into the final straight. On the terrace level with the finish line a man with curly black hair showing the first sprinkling of grey punched the air and yelled encouragement, his excitement flapping the worn sheepskin coat he wore. Beside him, a pretty blonde woman with a mouth designed for smiling alternated her attention between the dogs and her boisterous companion.

The dogs crossed the line and the man's eyes closed, his amiable features screwing into an expression of exaggerated despair as he ripped his betting slip to small pieces that drifted carelessly to the ground.

'Which one won?' asked Jan Oliver.

And Robby Box answered, 'The lousy four dog,' in a tone that succeeded in combining disgust with resignation as he shook his head and turned to glance up at the blank-faced man standing a tier above. 'Terrific, Chas! Just terrific.'

The man's shoulders lifted and dropped like a body-builder's grateful to set down the weights. Robby shook his head some more, sniffing. Jan said, 'I've just won £2.80.' Pleased with herself and her luck.

Robby sighed, staring as his form card. 'Had two hundred and thirty sovs going on that flea-ridden mutt.'

The way he said it, it might have been his life savings or nothing at all: just one more minor set-back.

Jan's wide mouth spread in a smile that lit up her face. 'Come on, I'll buy you a beer to cry in. I'm a fiver up on the night.'

Even if Robby Box was the kind of man to cry over spilt milk or lost pounds – which he wasn't – that was the kind of smile to make a man forget his troubles: he grinned as he said confidently, 'I got a dead cert going in the last race.'

Jan's smile faded slightly, taking on an element of resignation as she murmured, 'You always have,' and followed him up the walkway in the direction of the bar.

Coming up the steps, Robby halted as he swung the door open, holding it for Jan as he stared at the mob assaulting the counter in search of celebratory good cheer or solace.

'Oh, look at that mob.'

Businesslike, Jan pushed past him, 'I'll get them.'

Robby grinned in a way that said he knew she would and suggested, 'Give us that fiver, then. I'll go an' stick the bet on.'

Jan's long blonde hair fluttered about her oval face as she rummaged for the note, smiling as she said, 'I'm the only dead cert you've got tonight!'

Genuine appreciation showed in Robby's eyes as he took the money and headed for the betting windows, waving over his shoulder as she added, 'And we're fifty-fifty on that one.'

There was a queue at the glass-fronted openings ranged along one wall, and as Robby joined it he glanced back to watch Jan working her way into the press of bodies lining the bar counter. Confident that he was not observed, he eased his sheepskin open and reached down to fumble at the inner stitching, where the leather turned up. From a carefully-stitched slit, he extracted a small wad of brown ten pound notes that he shielded with his hands as he counted them: six. After a moment's thought he tugged a single note loose and slotted the remainder back in the hideaway pocket, shuffling forwards to present a total of fifteen pounds to the ever-waiting window. Then, pocketing the slip, he pushed back to find Jan standing with their drinks beside the glass observation wall.

'Did you bet the whole five pounds, Robby?'

'The whole lot, Princess!' Eyes opening wide in mock disbelief. 'All of it!'

Smiling as she shook her head, Jan said, 'You've no respect for money, you.'

Robby took the glass she offered him without replying. The statement was perhaps a little closer to the truth than he cared to admit. Or perhaps his expression of fond exasperation summed up his attitude to money. Either way, it didn't matter because the loudspeaker system announced the commencement of the last race and Jan's attention was caught by the runners parading around the tracks towards the traps.

'Oh!' she said. 'I like that one's coat.'

'That your system, is it?' Robby chuckled. 'You bet on the colour of the covers?'

'Listen.' Jan feigned superiority. 'I'm a fiver in front of you.'

Robby's answer went unspoken as a man a few years younger, but somehow managing to look older, appeared out of the crowd. Slightly balding, Gus Hayes – known with a certain degree of inevitability as Gabby – was the kind of man genteel old ladies would mistrust on sight. Gabby always managed to appear in need of a shave and a bath, wearing clothes that were starting to go out of fashion when he bought them five years ago. He said, 'I thought that was you up at the window, mate. How you doin'? All right?'

Robby grinned. 'Wotcher, Gab. How's your luck?'

'Let you know after the last race. You havin' a result?'

Robby glanced at Jan before replying, then said, 'Yeah, you know me, Gab ... Ain't doing bad.' Jan looked away, and he added, 'Oh, this is Jan. Jan, Gabby's an old mate from school days.'

'Hallo,' Jan said, looking as though she was surprised Gabby didn't smell the way he looked. Robby had a habit of surprising her with his acquaintances.

'Always did have good taste, him,' Gabby leered, nodding at Robby. 'Nice to meet you, girl.'

Jan winced and Gabby performed a swift variant of the softshoe shuffle as he realized that he had said something wrong. Robby just went on grinning, amused at Jan's loathing of the term *girl*.

Embarrassed, Gabby muttered, 'Yeah. Well. I'd best be shootin' off. See you later. Ta-ta, mate.'

Gabby sensed he had managed to say the wrong thing again and shuffled some more, like a sand dancer looking for a practice tray. 'Right. See you around. Ta-ta, girl.'

The sand dance turned into a backwards movement as he caught the expression on Jan's face, then transformed into a swaying pirouette as he turned and scurried into the shelter of the crowd. Robby watched him go, reluctant to face his girlfriend.

'Later?' she asked, ominously.

'Well, yeah.' Evasively. 'By *later* he means around, like … Any time.'

Jan's expression said there was an explanation needed, and it had better be a good one. Robby was grateful for the respite offered by the loudspeakers and the massed shout of encouragement.

'Oh! They're off.' He swung to peer out through the fingerprinted glass as the greyhounds came surging out of the traps. 'Go on, my cocker!'

'But what goes on round Bernie's later?' Jan was not to be put off so easily.

'C'mon my beauty!' Robby didn't take his eyes off the runners, wishing Jan would forget about the future and concentrate on the present. 'A million this 'un, Princess. Go on, my cocker!'

Jan sighed and shook her head, thinking, *Robby Box, you and your gambling. I hope it never comes to a choice between that and me.*

The bus moved slowly through the departing traffic, inching its way from the stadium towards the heart of north London. Robby and Jan sat in silence, he staring fixedly ahead, rigidly upright in the seat, hands thrust deep in the pockets of the sheepskin coat, mouth clamped tight shut. The big red vehicle lurched to a reluctant halt as lights glinted red before it and Robby sighed.

'Why is it the dead certs always blow out?' Jan asked.

'It was nudged off its line.' Robby's voice was as tight as the line of his mouth. 'Should've been an objection.'

Jan said, 'Oh,' as the conductor made his way down the aisle to halt by Robby's shoulder with his fingers drumming on the ticket machine. Robby looked up at the man.

'All right?'

'So-so.'

'Terrific.'

Robby went back to his study of the traffic, folding his

arms morosely across his chest as the conductor went on waiting. Jan opened her bag and began to search for change, passing over coins as she gave their destination. The conductor issued two tickets and pulled a face as he handed them to her, ignoring the silent figure staring through the dirty window. Jan glanced sideways at Robby, opening her mouth then closing it again as she decided against speaking. There were times it was best to leave Robby to his own thoughts, and this felt like one of them. He would, she knew, snap out of it soon enough.

He had by the time they reached her front door. She turned the key and swung the door open, leading the way inside the small terraced house.

'Debby won't be back 'til late. Gone to a disco.'

'Makes me tired just thinking about it.' Robby yawned as he closed the door. 'I'm knackered.'

Sensing the change of mood, Jan smiled.

'What's the matter? Getting past it?'

'Past it an' on me way back.' Robby patted her bottom affectionately. 'Get in there!'

Curtains shut out most of the light coming from the street lamps, obscuring the familiar details of the bedroom as Robby moved on tiptoe around the double bed hunting for his clothes. Jan lay with her golden hair fanned over the pillows, the continental quilt drawn up to her chin. Her breathing was soft in the darkened room, and Robby was taking pains to move without disturbing her, clutching his jumbled clothes against his naked body as he hunted for a missing sock. Gingerly, he went to her side of the bed, freezing with breath held as she murmured in her sleep and turned over, outflung arm touching the indentation on the pillow where he had lain. Then, when she remained asleep, he let a silent sigh ease out and decided to forget the sock. Still on tiptoes, he opened the door and stepped into the darkened hallway wearing only his underpants, clothes still bundled against his chest as he tugged the door gently closed and crossed to the bathroom. With the light switched on, he began to hop on one foot as he pulled on his solitary sock.

10

'New dance?'

'For Gawdsakes!' Robby's heart performed an unhealthy jump as the laughing voice cut through his concentration. 'Debby! What you doin'?'

Jan's daughter was a smaller, younger version of her mother. The generous mouth and laughing eyes were the same, as was the blonde hair, cropped fashionably short. She wore a mini-skirt and a huge grin as she leant against the door frame watching him.

'They was all doing that down the disco tonight.'

Robby crossed his arms modestly. 'Shush. Don't wake your mother up!' He eased into his trousers and regained some dignity. 'Anyway, you're late. Twelve o'clock, you was supposed to be in.'

'Yeah.' Debby nodded solemnly. 'I'll go tell her.'

'No!' Robby's dignity was short-lived. 'No, don't do that.'

Debby's eyebrows rose in an unspoken question and he added, 'All right, smart-arse, I won't tell.'

'You going out?' she demanded, casually.

'Well. Er, thing is, babe ...' It was hard to be commanding wearing only one sock. He zipped his fly. 'Thing is, it's Saturday tomorrow. Jan's lie-in, like. An' I gotta be up and about early, see?'

'Kip here.' Debby's smile was wry. 'You often do.'

'Er, no.' Sockless, Robby fidgeted. 'Can't. I um ...'

'Oh, you liar,' Debby giggled. 'You've got a card game!'

'Well ...' Robby grinned back, finding it difficult to stay serious with the teenage girl.

Debby seized the advantage. 'I'll say you looked really creased an' you needed your own bed.'

'Left about quarter to twelve, didn't I?' Robby winked conspiratorially.

''Bout then,' Debby agreed. 'Oh, and Rob? You're going to fat.'

'What? Fat?' Robby looked down automatically, and when he looked up she was gone. 'Cheeky monkey! I ain't getting fat. Never. Fat? Me?'

He slipped his shirt on, then paused, sucking in his

stomach as he turned to the mirror. In the bright glow of the overhead light he could see a softness around his midriff. Not too much, but a slackening of the muscle that spoke of too many hours spent sitting and too many hurried, greasy meals. For a moment his naturally good-humoured face got despondent, then he shrugged and buttoned his shirt as his innate optimism overcame the momentary depression to convince him that Debby was only joking. He finished dressing and left the house, shivering slightly in the post-midnight chill. Across the street a taxi squealed to a stop, light spilling across the pavement as the passenger disembarked. Robby grinned, congratulating himself on his luck as he moved towards the open door.

'Must be my lucky night. You geezers are like gold dust.'

'Hold on, mate.' The cabby did not share his would-be-fare's enthusiasm. 'Where you goin'? I was just off home.'

'It's just off Kingsland.'

'All right, hop in.' The cabby re-set his meter reluctantly. 'I been on since this mornin'.'

'Keeping you busy, then.' Robby settled back as the taxi lurched from the kerb.

'Not many!' the cabby did the trick all cabbies do: turning to speak over his shoulder whilst somehow still keeping his eyes on the road. 'Still, shouldn't really complain, eh? So many poor bastards outta graft these days. Immoral, innit?'

'Yeah, ain't it just?' Robby nodded, studying the interior of the vehicle as he crossed his legs. He saw a bare ankle and remembered the missing sock: swapped legs. 'Your'n is it? The cab?'

'Yeah – will be next month. Last payment!'

Robby lounged back, a thoughtful expression on his face as he continued his perusal of the taxi. Like a man studying the face cards in a game of stud poker. The driver fell silent, concentrating on the darkened streets as he steered for his fare's destination.

They arrived and the taxi pulled in to the kerb alongside

12

a tall, nondescript block of flats. Robby climbed out and moved around to the side window, reaching into his coat.

'Three-fifty, mate.'

Robby passed a fiver over. 'Must do all right on the old tips an' all, eh?'

The cabby looked at him, misinterpreting this interest in his finances. He said, 'Sometimes,' with a heavy hint in the word.

Robby nodded, pocketing his change and the cabby's expectant look turned into one that didn't need any translation: *You tight git.*

CHAPTER TWO

The room was furnished discount warehouse style: more discount than style, with overladen ashtrays providing a blue haze that did a lot for the decor. As Bernie Long ushered him in, Robby glanced automatically at the players. Gabby Hayes and two men he knew only as Len and Sid grinned at him from over lager glasses. They were both around Robby's age and both dressed in a casual style that isn't found in the pages of fashion magazines. The fourth man was younger and sharper, not quite a medallion man, but getting there. He looked as though he was doing his best to look bored. Robby frowned as he saw him, card player's memory a fast print-out in his mind: *Tony Cannon. A genuine smart-arse.*

'All right, lads?' Robby took the seat Bernie indicated. 'How's yer luck?'

Cannon lounged back in his chair, animosity written all over his cold smile: the would-be gunfighter eyeing up the old hand.

Gabby tried to lighten the mood. 'That bird of yours layin' on your shirt-tails was she, Rob?'

'It weren't me shirt-tails, Gab.' Robby grinned.

Cannon put a *let's play poker* expression on his loosely handsome face and Gabby did a stationary sand dance as he said, 'Oh, sorry. Right! We all set?'

'Yeah.' Bernie pulled up a chair. 'First jack deals.'

'Len. Sid.' Robby winked at the two men, ignoring Canon.

Gabby said, 'Jack's alive. My deal.' He hauled in the cards.

15

Cannon said, 'Thought it was way past your bedtime, dad.'

Robby said, 'You'll know when I'm ready to turn in, son. You'll be walkin' home potless.'

'You reckon?' Cannon sat forwards, lips curled in an expression midway between a sneer and a snarl. 'You got a big shock comin' your way.'

'Not from your quarter I ain't sonny,' Robby said, casually. 'Now I came here to play poker. OK?'

'Now, now, chaps. Let's keep it nice and friendly, eh?' Bernie interceded sternly. 'I told you, Tone: no aggro, all right? Let's all just play some poker.'

Cannon smiled, still playing the Cincinnatti Kid, 'That's my game.'

'King the bet.' Sid quashed any further argument. 'I'll open with a little nicker.'

He lifted a note from the pile at his elbow and dropped it beside the card Gabby had dealt him. To his left, Gabby said, 'Yeah, I'm there.' And matched the opening bet.

Bernie was next around the table, going with it. Then Robby, who said, 'Yeah. And up a nicker. A deuce the bet.'

Lenny, on Robby's left, nodded. 'Called.'

'Called,' echoed Cannon. Then grinned and added, 'And up another one.'

The others went with the raise and Gabby dealt the next card. The game was stud poker: three cards to show, two in the hole; high card to bet and money with the mouth every time. Cannon got an ace of Spades to go with his four of Clubs. He was still grinning as he said, 'Right. Let's sort out the men from the boys. Blue one the bet.'

A five pound note joined the three oncers in front of him.

'Uh-oh, testin' us out on the first, eh?' Sid checked his hole card. 'Yeah. I can live with that.'

Gabby matched and so did Bernie. Robby said, 'Called and raise. Five and five up.'

'Oh, turn it up!' Lenny threw his cards down, shaking his head. 'No way on them.'

'Like it,' said Cannon succinctly, tossing a second fiver down.

One by one, the remaining players folded until Robby and Cannon faced one another across the table. Gabby dealt the fourth round, giving Cannon a pair of aces showing, Robby a nine of Hearts to match his nine of Spades. High pair displayed, Cannon nodded appreciatively.

'Well now, a pair of bullets has gotta be worth a little flutter. A score the bet.'

Two ten pound notes fell like a challenge. Robby picked up his cards and looked at the third nine. The one Cannon couldn't see. He let his eyes flicker over the cards already out, calculations running at computer speed through his mind. The fourth nine was showing, as were two of the other tens. With three nines and the ten of Clubs in his hand he needed that missing ten to make the full house. Without it, he had nothing – and it could be one of the five hole cards. There was a strong chance Cannon had his third ace in the hole, which would marginally increase his chances. It wasn't worth it.

He shrugged, stacking his cards as he conceded, 'Yours.'

'Bottle job, eh?' Cannon was smug as he raked in the pot. 'What was you sayin' about us walkin' home?'

Sneering, he flipped his cards to show two pairs, aces over fours.

Robby said, 'The night is young,' expressionlessly.

'You went a score on a pair of bullets?' Gabby stared disbelievingly at Cannon. 'Jesus!'

'Yeah,' Cannon grinned unctuously, 'I made dad, there, think I had the third one in the hole. That's what poker's all about, pal. Right, dad?'

Robby stayed cool and unruffled as he said, 'If you say so, sonny.'

The game grew older with the night. The ashtrays were emptied and got filled again. The empty beer cans began to outnumber the full. Gabby's nervous shuffling got worse as the tension between Robby and Cannon grew. The others ignored it, more interested in the game. It was developing into a duel.

'Called and raised.' Robby pushed a blue note across the table. 'Up another five.'

Cannon frowned, his cocksure confidence fragmenting. 'Well now ...' He studied the dead hands. 'I'll call.'

Robby's face stayed deadpan as the cards were turned. Cannon showed two pairs, tens over eights. The drop outs watched tensely, waiting for Robby to show. The cards turned: tens over nines: a winning hand.

Cannon said, 'You lucky bastard!'

Robby shrugged, 'If you say so, son. That's poker.'

He caught Gabby's grin and winked. Cannon saw the exchange and scowled.

'Just good friends, are we?' Ominously. 'I was only one out, dad. Only one.'

'Two, sonny,' Robby murmured. 'You called me, remember.'

He picked up the deck and allowed himself a slight smile: things were looking up. There was money in front of him now, enough to give him some room for manoeuvre. He shuffled with an expertise born of long years of practice and began to deal the hand.

'Here we go, you lucky lads. A nice lady for you, Siddy. Your opener.'

In another part of town Jan Oliver woke as a cistern flushed, rising on one sleepy elbow with the awareness that she was alone in the bed taking its time to register. She saw a lonely sock on her pillow and muttered, 'Oh, charming.' Then, as the door opened, 'Robby?'

Debby shook her head sleepily, yawning from the doorway.

'It's all right. Only me, mum.'

'You all right, love?' Jan asked.

'Yes.' Debby yawned hugely. 'Tired, though. Night, mum.'

'Good night,' Jan replied automatically, yawning herself as Debby went out. She looked at the sock on the pillow beside her, then around the room, slowly realizing that Robby's discarded clothes no longer decorated her carpet. She leaned across the bed to lift the alarm clock from its place on the side table, bringing the illuminated dial close

18

to her sleepy eyes. The hands showed four in the morning. Frowning, she set the clock down and looked again at the empty floor. Then at the solitary sock. She picked it up as the realization dawned on her: Robby was gone.

Furious, she hurled the sock across the room.

Back in Bernie's flat the game was following the pattern established earlier. All the money on the table sat before Robby and Tony Cannon, the others nursing what little they had left. And again it was a stand-off; a two-hander.

'Last cards, gentlemen,' Gabby said.

Robby ignored it, drinking water from a paper cup and yawning hugely. He looked tired now, eyes reddening and lines showing across his forehead. Cannon was swigging beer straight from the can, still intent on needling Robby.

'We keepin' you up, dad?' Macho-man, he crushed the empty can and wiped a hand across his curled lips. 'Called an' raise another score.'

'You ain't keeping me up, son.' Robby aped Cannon's actions, mimicking Richard Dreyfuss in *Jaws*, elaborately crushing his paper cup before wiping his own mouth. 'Yeah, I'm there. Forty the bet and up another score.'

He sat back, trying not to let his tiredness show, keeping his face deadpan. Cannon sat forwards, his mean eyes ugly as he glared at Robby, then down at the cards. In front of Robby the three, seven and ten of Spades showed; Cannon had kings in Diamonds and Hearts, and the ace of Clubs. He flicked his eyes over the stacked hands.

'I reckon you're full of crap, Box. You're on a bluff.'

'Sixty sovs'll find out,' Robby said evenly.

'Yeah, that's right,' Cannon rasped, throwing the money down. 'Sixty. An' up another score. You ain't hit the flush.'

Watching the raise, Gabby let out a gasp that matched the low whistles from Len and Sid. Bernie stifled a yawn, his bloodshot eyes fastened on Robby, who just sat there, his features expressionless, showing only fixed concentration through the exhaustion.

'Wakey, wakey, dad!' Cannon sneered. 'I called your

19

bluff. Put up or pull out.'

Robby sighed. 'You got to learn to keep your mouth shut, son. So ... Eighty the bet, and raise another score. A oner down to you.'

He permitted himself a small smile as shock registered on his opponent's face. Cannon's hands clenched and unclenched as doubt showed clear in his frown. He was in deep now, in terms both of finance and face. His gaze made another nervous circuit of the table, locking on Bernie as the tired man let out a yawn, then returning to Robby.

'Called,' he husked, tossing one hundred pounds onto the table.

'No raise?' asked Robby innocently.

'I'd've said so, wouldn't I?' Cannon snapped. 'I've called the bet. OK?'

'Just wanted to give you the chance.' Robby stayed calm.

Reluctantly, Cannon turned his cards: two pairs, aces over kings. Five pairs of eyes switched to Robby. The only man in the smoke-heavy room to doubt Cannon's full house. Deliberately, Robby turned his own cards. The three Spades were already on display: the first hole card was the ace in the same suit; the second, the king. Ace high flush: a winner.

Cannon let out a soft oath. 'You're one right lucky face, dad!'

'Name of the game, son.' Robby scooped the pot to his side of the table. 'The name of the game.'

'Right, that's my lot.' Gabby climbed wearily to his feet. 'I done me dough — home to kip.'

'Yeah,' Bernie agreed. 'Knock it on the head.'

Len and Sid rose from the table. Robby began to stack his winnings and pocket the notes. Cannon just sat there with fury blazing in his eyes, glaring at the disappearing money.

'You play a good game, son.' Robby tucked the final notes away and stood up. 'Except that you drink too much and you should never go gunning for one man.'

Cannon's chair pitched over as he sprang to his feet, a tic pulsing violently on his temple. Bernie stepped forwards.

'Now hold tight!'

'All right, Bern. No problem, mate.' Robby met Cannon's

furious glare. 'No problem.'

The younger man's voice was hoarse as he said, 'When I want your advice, grandad, I'll ask for it. Right? Until then, shove it!'

He wheeled around, snatching his jacket from the pile on the sofa and tugging it on as he stalked out with no further comment. Robby grinned at the slamming door.

'He walkin', you reckon?'

The hamburger stall either stayed open late or got started early. Light was showing in the dull sky above the houses as Robby and Gabby satisfied their hunger, and somewhere a lonely bird was playing alarm clock to the morning.

'Wish I'd ordered one o' them now.' Gabby indicated the steak sandwich fast disappearing into Robby's mouth. 'Smells great.'

'Handsome.' Robby wiped grease from his chin.

'You had a bit of a result tonight,' smiled Gabby, speaking around a mouthful of burger.

'Started with a fifty,' Robby shrugged, 'So I'm about a twoer up on the night. Needed more, though, Gab. Got a biggy comin' up tonight at Danny Macgrath's.'

'Yeah?' Gabby sounded interested.

'Seven card stud,' Robby nodded. 'A monkey to sit down, though.'

Gabby whistled. 'Five hundred sovs? Any room?'

'If you got the dough, I suppose. None of tonight's lot'll be there. Be too heavy for me unless I can pull a result on the card. You got anything you can put us on?'

'There's a cert goin' in the one o'clock at Newbury,' Gabby shrugged. 'Mongo. A million.'

'Mongo, eh? I'll have some of that.' Robby nodded, then yawned hugely. 'Coo, dear.'

'You're gettin' past it, son,' Gabby opined.

'Ain't we all?' countered Robby.

Gabby looked at him, dawn and the street lights bright enough that the redness in his eyes showed, and the tired lines on the easy-going face. 'Listen,' he said seriously, 'I can remember a time you'd have done that wally up like a kipper in the first hour.'

'Who? Cannon?' Robby hauled a paper tissue from the counter and wiped his mouth and hands.

'Yeah, Tony bleedin' Cannon,' agreed Gabby. 'He nearly had you.'

'Leave off!' Robby protested. 'I knew what I was doin'.'

'Yeah, of course.' Gabby didn't sound so sure. 'Tell you what, son ... If you get a result on that nag an' make the game tonight, get some kip in first. You won't stay the course if you don't.'

'What are you?' demanded Robby. 'My quack, or somethin'?'

'Just a pal markin' your card.' Gabby took his companion's plate. 'Want some more?'

'Yeah,' Robby nodded. 'Ta.'

He stared thoughtfully at Gabby as the smaller man went up to the counter. There was no denying the truth of his words, not if Robby was honest with himself. He was forty-one and he had to admit the night had taken its toll. He could feel it in his smarting eyes and the dull ache in his back. All right, he had taken Tony Cannon in the end, but like Gabby said, there was a time he would have stitched up the loud-mouth a whole lot faster. And come away feeling a whole lot fresher. Maybe it was time to settle down – Jan would like that. And, Lord knew, he wouldn't mind spending the whole night in her bed instead of more than half the time creeping out like a burglar. Trouble was, he didn't know any other way to make a living: cards and dogs and horses were his life. Maybe he couldn't do anything else.

His pessimistic musing was interrupted by the arrival of two cabbies. They were drinking tea, laughing over a joke, with bulging wallets jutting from their pockets. Robby studied them the same way he had earlier studied the taxi that brought him to Bernie's flat. Maybe ...

'There you go, son.'

He turned as Gabby came back with two big steak sandwiches that did a lot to cheer him up.

*

The milkman was clattering bottles as he arrived home, accustomed to seeing Robby going in when most people were going out. He grinned as he said hello, then added, 'You look shagged out, mate.'

'Oh, thanks a bundle.' Robby watched him walk away, whistling like a happy canary. Indignantly, he put his key in the lock, thumbing the cap of the bottle and drinking deep as he went inside. 'Cheeky bastard!'

It was home, but not his house. Most of his life had been lived there, and when his father died the insurance policies had ceded the property to his mother, Vi. Somehow, he had never quite got around to finding a place of his own. There had never seemed much point. Nor did his money seem to stay with him long enough to organize such tedious details as a mortgage. Which, anyway, would have required a whole lot of details he couldn't supply. Like a regular job or a guaranteed regular income. He was a kind of stateless person; unregistered; officially non-existent. He went into his room and glanced at his face in the mirror hung on the wall above a small table set with a chess game. The sight wasn't too impressive, but it wasn't too bad, either. And he was too tired to worry much about it.

'Ain't that bad,' he murmured as he threw himself thankfully on the bed. 'Not considering ...'

Considering what got lost in a yawn as his eyes drooped closed and he fell asleep still fully clothed. Save for the missing sock.

Not long after her son's arrival, Vi was up and bustling about her kitchen. She was one of those big, jolly women who radiate comfort and accept whatever comes their way with good-humored equanimity. It helped, having a son who used the place like rented digs. For most of the morning she pottered about the kitchen, indulging in her habit of talking softly to herself as she worked, her low muttering a counterpoint to the radio.

A dee-jay was announcing that the time was twelve forty-six and Vi was making a pot of tea when she heard the front door bang shut. A moment later her boyfriend walked into the kitchen with a copy of the *Sun* in his hand. Tommy was the same age as Vi, a grey-haired man with scalp showing through the strands and a smile as gentle as hers was generous. Retired now, he mostly tended his allotment, making a little extra on the side by selling the produce at their local pub, the Railway Arms.

Vi smiled at the sight of him and said, 'Smelled it as usual.'

'Always had good timing, me.' Tommy settled himself at the kitchen table and opened the paper to page three, pulling a face at the girl displayed there. 'Seen more fat on a jockey's whip. Rob up?'

'You're joking.' Vi shook her head. 'Been banging on his door for the last half hour.'

Tommy shrugged. 'He likes to get down the betting shop a bit sharpish on a Saturday.'

'Saturdays ain't no different where that boy's concerned,' Vi grumbled half-heartedly. 'Dunno why he don't go an' live down the betting shop.'

Tommy smiled at the familiar complaint, standing as Vi poured tea. 'Here. Gimme his an' I'll go give him a shout.'

'And see if he's nicked me milk again while you're at it.' Vi raised her own cup. 'The lazy sod should be out gettin' a proper job. Gawd knows where he gets it from.'

Tommy left the kitchen with the words washing over him only half-heard. Robby was all right in his book: they got along nicely, which was just as well considering Tommy's relationship with Robby's mother. He eased the bedroom door open and saw Robby stretched on the bed sound asleep and still dressed.

'Robbo? You awake, Robbo? C'mon Maverick: tea's up.'

The announcement was greeted with groans from the supine form. Tommy set the tea down beside the chess board and yanked the curtains open. Then he returned to the board and studied the placement of the chessmen, a thoughtful expression spreading over his ruddy face. Robby lifted a heavy head from the pillow and blocked the sunlight with an upraised arm.

'Turn it in, Tommy,' he complained, falling back on the bed. 'Gawd! What's this?'

He tugged the empty milk bottle from under the small of his back and dropped it on the floor. Tommy said, 'Your mum's been lookin' for that. Got the right hump with you, she has.'

'So what's new.' Robby made his legs follow the milk bottle to the floor and rubbed his face. 'What's the time?'

"Bout a quarter to one.' Tommy went on staring at the chess board. His bishop was threatened by Robby's knight. 'Maybe a bit later.'

'Oh, no!' Robby came off the bed like a greyhound starting after the hare. 'Why didn't you wake us earlier? I got a dead cert goin' in the one o'clock.'

'You look like a pile of old bagwash,' remarked Tommy, conversationally. 'An' why you only got one sock on?'

Robby stared down, then shook his head as he remembered his furtive hunt for clothes. That would be something he'd need to explain to Jan – he doubted she'd take too kindly to his disappearing in the middle of the night. He yanked off his shoes and fetched a clean pair of socks from the dresser beneath the window. Tommy moved pawn to queen three.

'Reckon you've missed the one o'clock, old son. You should've let us know.'

'Bloody hell!' Robby pulled the clean socks off. 'I may as well get cleaned up proper.' Then, brightening, 'Maybe it won't come in. Was only Gabby told me.'

Tommy chuckled and nodded towards the chess board. 'See what you make o' that. I gotta cuppa waitin' for me.'

Robby slid out of the sheepskin coat and began to unbutton his shirt as he stared at the board. After a moment's thought he moved his bishop to Tommy's king's knight five. Then he took off his trousers and, smiling to himself, headed for the bathroom.

As he dressed, he could hear Tommy and Vi talking in the kitchen and his good humour left him for a moment.

'That's it!' Vi was saying. 'You side with him. You're all the same, you men. He should be thinking about the future.'

'He's only a youngster,' Tommy answered. 'Plenty of

time for that later.'

'He's nearly forty-one, you silly old sod.' Her tone was as serious as Robby had heard it. 'He should be married and settled. Not hanging around with villains an' gamblers an' getting home at all hours.'

Looking smarter and feeling fresher, Robby entered the kitchen with a sly grin at Tommy.

'Naggin' again, you old sexpot?' He pinched his mother's ample backside affectionately. 'Talk under water you would, Mum.'

'Get away from me.' Vi wriggled her shoulders as Robby put his arms around her. 'You're a sod, you are, Robby.'

'Yeah?' Robby looked hurt.

'Yes, you are.' Vi was emphatic. 'An' it's no good you trying on all the old soft soap with me. It won't work.'

'Nah?' Robby ducked forward in a mock yosser and planted a kiss on her cheek. 'Course it won't. Here.' He drew a twenty pound note from his pocket. 'Go buy yourself a new hat. Now stop naggin' and where's me breakfast?'

Grinning, he sat down opposite Tommy and snatched the newspaper.

'Make you go blind you know, Tom.' He folded the sheets over from page three to the racing page. 'At your age.'

'Yeah?' Tommy mimed a blind man looking for the paper.

Despite herself, Vi began to smile.

CHAPTER THREE

Gil's betting shop was one of those establishments found around a lot of corners in a lot of cities, but especially in the outer reaches of London. There'll be a few shops, one inevitably a small supermarket and one a newsagent's, perhaps a greengrocer's; and the betting shop. The basic necessities. It wasn't the kind of place big bets got laid, but as it catered pretty well exclusively to the local inhabitants, that didn't matter: there was a nice, regular turnover. The decor was standard: cream and green, with the form pages from a few national newspapers tacked up alongside the photoprints of winning nags and champion jockeys. Gil's office was out back, beyond the glass-fronted counter that protected his sole employee – whom everyone knew as Juicy Joan – from the more personal attentions of the patrons, whose standing joke was that Juicy Joan was the only dead cert Gil ever offered.

And like any back-street betting shop, Gil's had its regulars. And around mid-day on a Saturday they were guaranteed to be there. Like pigeons homing on the coop.

There were Kipper and Geordie and Black George and Ferret. And Ferret's dog, a stringy greyhound with an anorexic look and a knack of clearing itself a space by the simple expedient of farting. Standing slightly apart was Irish, a man with a face that looked like life had carved some hard memories on the sallow skin and a cough like a stalling lawn-mower.

Kipper, several years junior, with a cheerful face as plump as Irish's was etched, asked solicitously, 'You all right, Irish? You're coughin' well today.'

Irish waved some fingers that looked as if they had been dipped in nicotine-coloured paint and went on coughing as he nodded.

Ferret said, 'He don't half look rough, don't he?'

Ferret himself would never grace the pages of a health magazine. Except, perhaps, as the first half of a before-and-after feature.

'He's looked like that for years, mun.' Geordie was trim. As a jobbing builder with a wife and child to support, he didn't have much time to get fat and couldn't afford to get ill. 'He'll see you an' me away, I bet.'

'How much?' asked Ferret quickly, face serious.

'You're immoral, you,' Kipper remarked. 'Suppose you'd like odds an' all.'

As usual, Black George said nothing, just grinning amiably at the exchange and nodding as though on the point of adding something that would never quite get uttered. They all looked towards the door as Robby came in, dressed neatly enough, but still looking in need of sleep.

'All right, lads? Who won the one o'clock at Newbury?'

'Mongo.' Geordie supplied. 'Three to one.'

'Shite!' Robby pulled a face. 'Was gonna bet on that.'

He grabbed Kipper's *Sporting Life* as the others exchanged the kind of looks that said they'd all heard it before: the big one that got away. It's easy for a gambling man to be wise after the event.

'Day of the faves, mun.' Geordie had a lilting accent to match his name. 'All the rest are donkey meat.'

'I gotta do something.' Robby studied the paper intently. 'Gotta pull at least two an' a half by tonight.'

'You got some chances,' Kipper said doubtfully.

'You in bovver then, Rob?' asked Ferret.

Geordie chuckled and said, 'I'll lay odds it's a big spieler. Right?'

'Yeah.' Robby nodded thoughtfully. 'Danny Macgrath's gaff tonight. I'm short on the sit-down money.'

After a while he handed the paper back to Kipper, shaking his head as he said, 'An' that ain't gonna help.'

'Have a sub off Gil,' Ferret suggested, drawing looks of

blank amazement from his friends.

Robby hauled out a wad of notes and stared thoughtfully at the odds board, then shook his head again and turned to Geordie.

'Too iffy. You got your motor outside, mate?'

Geordie sighed and led the way to where his battered old Thames van was parked. 'I'm a fool to meself,' he grumbled as he turned the key in the ignition.

'Yeah?' Robby grinned, settling on the worn vinyl of the passenger seat.

Geordie nodded, 'How come I always end up running you all over town?'

'Must be 'cos we're pals, eh?' Robby's voice was innocent as his face.

'Pals!' Geordie snorted. 'It's all right for you, mun. I got responsibilities, though! Work to do – a family to keep.'

'I know,' agreed Robby, with feeling. 'Just get us to Jan's, eh?'

'Be just your luck she says *no* this time,' Geordie murmured.

And Robby said, 'Never!' Confidently. 'I'll use my charm on her.'

They reached the row of houses and Geordie halted the aged van, watching his friend with a mixture of long-suffering resignation and more than a little affection as Robby went up to the door and opened it with his own key.

As he went down the hall, Robby could hear Jan speaking on the telephone, guessing she was talking to her boss, Henry Diamond, as he heard her say, 'I'm grateful Henry. Really. Matter of fact, he's just coming in now, so please tell Mr Cook we're both looking forward to seeing him tonight.'

'Am I?' Robby asked.

Jan glanced at him, her eyes cool as she said, 'See you this evening, then. 'Bye Henry,' before transferring her full attention to Robby and saying, 'You've got a nerve.'

'Princess,' Robby placated.

'Glad enough to climb into my bed, weren't you?' Jan's

voice was cool, too. 'Couldn't you be bothered to say goodbye?'

'Don't be like that,' Robby asked. 'I couldn't sleep ... didn't want to wake you.'

Jan cut the apology short. 'I was hoping – just hoping you'd come round to apologize.'

'Yeah, well,' he protested, aggrieved. 'I am doing, aren't I?'

'Are you?' Tersely.

'Who's this Cook I'm looking forward to meeting?' Robby changed the subject adroitly.

'You don't deserve it,' Jan mellowed a little, 'but I've fixed things with Henry for him to bring this accountant round. Tonight.'

The word *accountant* had the kind of effect on Robby that *dentist* has on people, or *police* on a villain.

'Look, you,' Jan continued firmly. 'Henry thinks of himself as my friend.'

'I know.' Robby's voice was sour, the two words full of unspoken meaning.

'But he is my boss!' she continued. 'And it isn't easy to get favours out of your boss. Especially ...'

She broke off, not sure how to finish the sentence. Robby did it for her. 'When it's for me?'

Jan shrugged wearily. 'All I'm saying, Robby, is it wasn't easy.'

'All right, all right,' Robby agreed, reluctantly. 'I'll be here. Early though, isn't it?'

'About nine-thirty.'

'Terrific.' Unenthusiastically.

'You wanted it,' Jan said. 'You asked me, Robby.'

'I know,' he nodded. 'I know.'

Exasperated, Jan said, 'Any man who hasn't paid any tax for years needs an accountant.'

'What I need, love,' Robby replied, 'is the necklace.'

An expression in which disbelief and anger mingled in equal quantities showed on Jan's pretty face.

'What?'

'I gotta pop it again, Jan. For tonight. It's a big one.'

'No!' Jan folded her arms resolutely, staring at him with anger outweighing the disbelief.

'Eh?' Robby was surprised by her determination.

'No, no, no!' she repeated, voice rising. 'All these years you've been a gambling man. Done what you like when you like, how you like. But can't you see, Rob? It's over.'

'Oh, Jan.' Hurt.

'For your own sake, Rob. Not mine. Can't you see? It's not working any more.'

'You think I'm finished?' he demanded. 'Over the hill?'

Jan said, 'Yes.'

And Robby spun round, stalking towards the door with anger hunching his shoulders. Jan moved after him, clutching at him with tears moistening her hazel eyes.

'Don't go, Robby! I'm not giving you any ultimatums. I love you! For what you are — nothing else matters. But what good will it do talking to Henry's accountant if you're just going to carry on the same?'

Her concern broke through Robby's anger. He halted, turning to face her, putting his hands on her arms as he looked into her pretty, tearful face.

'Jan,' he said, earnestly, 'Jan, all I need is a big one. And tonight's the night. I can feel it. Trust me, Jan.'

'Why should I?' she questioned. 'I've got Henry Diamond pestering me morning, noon and night.'

'Plum,' Robby sneered.

'Maybe.' Jan shrugged, folding her arms. 'But he can offer me something. Not much, but something. What are you offering, Robby?'

It was Robby's turn to get serious. Gabby, Vi, even the milkman. Now Jan was telling him he was past it. 'Listen,' he said, 'all I need is to get enough together to start something of my own. I dunno what. Something. And the only way I'll do that is doing the only thing I know — gambling. I'll talk to Henry's bloke … Let him start on the tax rubbish. But let *me* sort out our future, Jan. Now trust me?'

He pulled her close, folding his arms around her as he felt her relax against his chest. Softly, he said, 'Look, I ain't got much time. Just for a couple of days, Princess. It's important.'

Reluctantly, Jan extricated herself and crossed the neat room to the sideboard, opening a drawer from which she took a flat, rectangular box in dark blue imitation leather. Taking out a heavy gold necklace, she passed it to Robby.

She was shaking her head as she said, 'I'm a fool, Robby Box.'

Late afternoon sunlight glinted on the three brass balls that announced the function of the small, wire-windowed shop as Robby hurried down the street. A small man with a head as shiny as the emblems of his profession was about to draw down the heavy shutters as Robby aproached, greeting his customer with a familiar smile. Robby grinned back and they went into the pawnshop together.

'This must be a record, Robby,' chuckled Sammy Cohen as he went behind the counter. 'Almost a month since your last visit.'

'Tryin' to mend me ways, Sam.' Robby took the necklace from his jacket pocket. 'Two an' a half this time, OK?'

'Sure it's OK.' Sammy agreed. 'Have more if you want. Then maybe I stand a better chance of keeping it.'

'Nah.' Robby shook his head. 'Just the two an' a half, ta, Sammy.'

Sammy shrugged and put the necklace in a drawer, taking notes from another. Chuckling, he asked, 'Tell me, Robby. When you purchased this for your lady, did you ever get to give it to her?'

'Very funny that, Sam.' Robby feigned outrage. 'Very funny. Anyway, make the most of it. With luck, this'll be the last time.'

'Oh, and you one of my best customers,' Sammy protested. 'Don't say things like that.'

Robby laughed, pocketing the notes.

'Meshugana, Sam.'

Back home, Robby was getting dressed for the evening as

Tommy pondered the chess board. He seemed uncomfortable, as though something preyed on his mind that he wanted to talk about, but wasn't sure just how to put. After a while he lifted a pawn to king's rook three and grunted to himself, like a man coming to a decision.

'Rob?'

'Tom?' Robby looked away from the reflection of his tie. 'What's up, mate?'

'Can I ask you a serious question?'

Robby heard the concern in the older man's voice and left off his dressing. 'I don't see why not.'

'The thing is, son, me an' your mum have been seein' each other a long time now.' Tommy paused, still nervous. 'Well, you see ... when you get to our age, you need someone. A companion, like.'

'Yeah?' Robby encouraged.

'Yeah,' Tommy nodded. 'Look, I know you'll think I'm a daft old fool, but I want to ask your mum to marry me.'

The last few words came out in a rush. Like a confession. Robby blinked, taken aback.

'Marry?'

'I know you might think it's daft at our age.' Tommy sounded embarrassed and defiant at the same time. Robby was quick to put him at ease.

'No. No, I don't, Tom.'

'Would you mind?' Tommy asked earnestly.

'Me? Mind?' Robby's mouth stretched in a big smile. 'I don't mind in the least, mate. Good look to you. Tell you what, we'll make it a double wedding!'

'Oh, great! I ain't asked her yet,' Tommy said, relieved. Then, as Robby's words sunk in, surprised. 'A double? What, you an' Jan?'

'Well.' Robby prevaricated. 'Like you, I ain't asked yet. Won't until I got myself sorted out. Soon as I have though ...'

'Well, I'll be blowed,' Tommy chortled. 'You!'

'Keep that under your hat.' Robby spoke urgently as the telephone in the hall began to ring. 'OK?'

'Yeah, no risk,' Tommy agreed. 'Cor, Mum won't half

be chuffed, son. Straight up. Shall I?'

He nodded in the direction of the trilling phone. Robby said, 'Ta, mate.' And carried on with his preparations.

Then Tommy put his head around the door and said, 'For you, Rob. Geezer name of Macgraw or something.'

'Macgrath?' Robby hurried to the phone. 'Danny Macgrath?'

Jan had spent time getting her place ready for the impending visit, which – naturally enough – she saw as important to her future with Robby. If there was any future there. Right now, she wasn't sure. And she was very angry.

'But you promised, Robby! You *promised*!'

'I know, Princess.' Robby fidgeted awkwardly, uncomfortable with the knowledge that he was letting her down, but unwilling to change his mind about it. 'I know I did. It's not my fault Danny brought the time of the game forward. Last minute phone call ...'

'The game,' Jan said bitterly.

'Look,' Robby pleaded, 'can't you put them off?'

'No, I can't!' Jan snapped. 'You know I've already confirmed it. Henry went to a great deal of trouble ... This man is one of the best in his field. You won't get another chance like this!'

'Oh, leave it out, Princess.' It was Robby's turn to sound hurt now. 'How was I supposed to know, eh? Look, love, I'm trying to do this for us.'

'This meeting tonight is all about *us*!' Jan countered. 'All about getting you sorted out. Ready for *our* future!'

Robby's expression was like that of a schoolboy caught out in some misdemeanour he doesn't understand: *what have I done wrong*? 'Princess,' he said, plaintively, 'a spieler like this one don't happen every day.'

Jan shook her head, torn between anger and weariness. 'Oh, Robby, but they do, love. Can't you see? There'll always be another big spieler. Another big deal where you're concerned. You can't keep away.'

That touched a raw nerve. Robby got angry. 'I can!

34

Can't you understand I'm trying to do this for us? I gotta do it my own way.'

'All right, Robby.' Jan's voice held a fatalistic note. 'Go.'

'Oh, c'mon, Princess.' He ignored the door she held open, knowing that if he walked through it there would be little chance of walking back into her life.

'I mean it, Robby.' Her voice had that brittle quality of angry tears only just held back. 'This time I mean it! You prove you can by being here by nine tonight.'

'Now that ain't fair and you know it,' he complained.

'Do I?' Jan asked. 'Do I? Make this meet tonight, Robby, or you and I are through. Finito! It's your last chance, gambling man. Us or the big deal. It's up to you.'

Not waiting for an answer, she went through the door and hurried up the stairs. Robby heard the bedroom door slam closed and shut his eyes, letting out a long, slow sigh.

Debby appeared from the direction of the kitchen and leant against the door frame, her teenaged face concerned. 'I think she means it this time, Rob.'

'Yeah,' was all he could think of to say as he moved to the hall door. 'Yeah, I think she does.'

Some people like silence when they have things on their mind. Others like music that matches their mood. Robby Box liked Mantovani. Full stop. Any time. The orchestra was playing now, high volume strings echoing lushly around the four walls of Robby's room as he sat slumped in the armchair, deep in thought. Vi eased the door open and stared at her son, then went in to lower the volume.

Robby said, 'Wotcher, sexpot.' Absent-mindedly.

'What's the matter, son?' Vi's plump face was concerned.

'Nothing.' Robby shook his head. 'Thought you an' Tom were goin' out.'

'We are.' Vi perched precariously on the arm of the chair. 'Is it Jan?'

'I'm all right, girl.' Robby smiled wanly, his expression belying the words. 'Stop fussing.'

'You're just like your father was, you are.' Vi stood up. 'You share your happiness, your money ... Everything but your troubles. You love this one, don't you?'

'Do I?' said Robby dully.

'I reckon.' Vi bent down to kiss his cheek. 'See you later.'

'Yeah, see you sexpot. Enjoy yourselves.'

Vi went out and Robby eased the volume back up as he concentrated on the chess board. After a while he moved his bishop to take Tommy's knight.

Two hours later he left the house and walked down the street to the corner occupied by the Railway Arms. A little farther on he spotted a cruising cab and flagged it down, giving Jan's address. Not long after, the cab pulled to a halt outside the little terrace house. Robby stared at the lighted windows and Henry Diamond's Jaguar parked on the yellow line outside. His lips pursed as a worried expression creased his face, then he took his hand off the handle and spoke through the open partition.

'Drive on, pal. Lea Bridge Road.'

The cabby shrugged, accustomed to dithering passengers. It didn't matter much to him: the punter was paying.

Danny Macgrath opened the door and ushered Robby into a room set up for a spieler. Three men were seated around a circular table, ashtrays at their elbows and a clean deck of cards in the centre. Six glasses were set out to hold the lager crated on the floor or the spirits on the sideboard. Robby knew only one of the players well – Peter the Ponce, so named for obvious reasons. The other two were passing faces, Roy Maggs and Terry Beale.

Peter the Ponce said, 'Wotcher, Robbo. How's yer luck?'

'Pete.' Robby nodded as he slid out of his sheepskin. 'How you doing, Roy? Terry?'

He looked as though he didn't hear their answers. There was an unfamiliar, worried expression on his usually-cheerful features. If expressions had names, this one would be called Jan.

'Anywhere you like, son,' said Danny, frowning at him. 'You all right?'

'Yeah,' Robby said in a tone that meant no. 'Terrific.

Time change caused me some aggro, though.'

'Sorry about that, Rob.' Danny apologized as he sat down. 'Couldn't be helped. Anyway, you're here now.'

'You know me,' Robby said.

Danny grinned, 'Yeah. Bloody addict, you.'

Robby shot his host a look that could have frozen a blowlamp. Maybe Jan was right. Maybe he couldn't give it up. But he made no move to leave.

'Right. Let's get started,' said Danny. 'Where's the kid got to?'

'Bog,' chuckled Peter the Ponce. 'Sortin' out his money belt.'

'Pullin' the spare aces out of his pants,' added Roy Maggs.

'That's all he has got down his pants,' said Danny.

Neither Terry Beale nor Robby said anything, Terry because he never did have much to say and Robby because he was still thinking about Jan's accusation and Danny's joking comment. Half in jest, whole in earnest? He was still deep in troubled thought as Tony Cannon ambled across the room like he owned the place. He caught sight of Robby and his lips curled in a sneering smile.

'Well, well, well. If it ain't the lucky grandad.'

Danny and the others glanced at him. Danny said quickly, 'You know Tone, Rob. Course you do,' and began to deal. 'First jack all right, Tone?'

'Yeah, sure.' Cannon was seated directly opposite Robby, staring at him like a man with revenge on his mind. 'The night's young.'

He sipped from a glass Robby noticed was filled with water. It hurt as the thought crossed his mind that maybe Cannon could learn, but he couldn't.

Then Danny Macgrath said, 'First jack to you, Rob. Your deal. Always a good omen, I reckon. But then you always was a lucky face, eh?'

Robby was suddenly aware that he was tensed up part-way out of his seat. As though he was about to leav
Or jump at Tony Cannon. He stared down at the jack and lowered himself as Danny stacked the deck in front of him.

'Yeah, I'll second that,' Cannon agreed. 'A right lucky face.'

Robby stared at him, all thoughts of leaving banished. Cold anger overtook him: he'd show Cannon. And show Jan, too; show her that he could do it his way. He picked up the cards and began to shuffle as Cannon sneered and said, 'For a minute there, dad, I thought you was gonna bottle out.'

'Wishful thinking, sonny,' he replied coldly. 'Wishful thinking.'

'He shouldn't be long,' Jan said, accepting the bubbling glass of champagne Henry Diamond offered her. 'He promised to be here.'

She ignored the look Debby shot her as she ignored the scorn showing on Diamond's face. Jeremy Cook, the accountant, sensed that something was wrong and filled the suddenly awkward silence.

'From what Henry's told me, this chap of yours has got one or two problems, Jan.'

'That's putting it mildly,' said Diamond, smugly, enjoying the chance to score off Robby. Hopefully scoring in a different way with Jan. 'Wine, Debby?'

'Just a small one, thank you Mr Diamond.'

The man smiled expansively as he filled her glass, delighted that Robby had failed to show up.

'Oh, come now. Call me Henry. After all, I'm practically family.'

Debby winced at his proprietary air, seeing her mother do the same. Jan worked as a secretary-personal assistant in Diamond's builder's yard, and her boss – despite a wife and children – was openly anxious to put more emphasis on the *personal* aspect. Debby took the glass with a coldly murmured 'thank you' and wished that Robby would show.

'I understand that Robby – Mr Box – has never paid any form of income tax or National Health contributions,' said Jeremy Cook. 'Is this correct?'

Jan nodded helplessly as Diamond smiled smugly.

The evening went on like that until it became obvious that Robby was not going to be present. Jan felt embarrassed and angry by turns. It was bad enough that he couldn't bother to turn up when she had arranged the whole thing for his benefit, hoping that Cook might somehow sort out the problems that must inevitably arrive when – *if* – Robby got some kind of regular work. That his absence afforded Henry Diamond the chance to rub in his unreliability made it worse. Finally, Cook glanced at his watch and begun to make noises about leaving. Jan apologized – which gave Diamond another chance to emphasize Robby's fecklessness.

'He's that sort of chap, isn't he? Unreliable.'

'There are plenty of them about,' Cook murmured cheerfully. 'It's how I make my living. Good night, Jan. Nice to have met you.'

Diamond added his farewells, kissing Jan on the cheek. 'Don't lose any sleep over him. He isn't worth it.'

Jan smiled without speaking and closed the door. Then she marched back into the lounge and hurled herself furiously onto the settee. Debby decided discretion was the wisest course and kept her mouth shut.

Back in Danny Macgrath's place, Robby and Tony Cannon were once again down to a two-hander. Danny was clearing ashtrays while Peter the Ponce snored noisily on the sofa and Roy Maggs and Terry Beale watched bleary-eyed as the game played itself out. Robby was looking haggard, late nights and heavy concentration showing on his face; Cannon looked fresh as the pile of winnings by his elbow.

'Called,' Robby said, huskily.

'No raise?' Cannon grinned. 'That's a shame.'

Robby refused to rise to the jibe, simply flipping over his cards to show a full house: queens over tens. Cannon went on grinning as he exposed winning kings over jacks.

'You can't win 'em all.' Robby's voice was expressionless: it was the final hand and he was cleaned out.

Cannon laughed out loud as he raked in the pot,

stacking his winnings in neat piles. Robby climbed stiffly to his feet and shrugged into his sheepskin like a man with a lot of hours sitting heavy on his shoulders.

'Cheers, Dan. See you around.'

He opened the door, then halted as Cannon said, 'Oy, grandad. Get yourself a cab.'

A fiver was tossed insultingly across the table. Robby watched it flutter in the smoky air, spiralling down to the carpet. Cannon's laughter rang loud as he shut the door and walked out into the night.

One way and another it hadn't been the best day of his life: Jan felt – rightly enough – that he had let her down, and he had failed to walk away with the stake he had hoped for. And to rub it in, it had been Cannon who took his money. No, not the best day by a long chalk. Shivering in the chill night air, he turned up his collar and thrust his hands deep in the pockets of the sheepskin as he plodded wearily past the blank housefronts. A black cab rattled past and he watched its tail lights swing around a corner, then realized the shape huddled in the cold shelter of a shopfront was a derelict, wrapped in an old coat and fresher newspapers.

A cold chill ran down his spine.

CHAPTER FOUR

Smoke and spielers go together like bubble and squeak. Set a few men down around a table with a deck of cards and before long a blue haze will fill the air. It probably has something to do with concentration and nervous tension: often enough, the cigarettes aren't smoked, just left to burn in the ever-present ashtrays, like incense lit at an altar of playing cards.

In the case of Max's spieler, a fair part of the fug came from his kitchen: Max the Greek owned a cafe with a back room that served as a regular venue for poker sessions to which Robby Box was a regular visitor. There was a session going on now, behind the drawn curtains that shut out the night and prying eyes. After all, the unlicensed playing of card games in which large sums of money are involved is against the law. And in this case, the pot was approaching £1,000.

Robby matched a raise of fifty and took it up another half century, his face showing no expression as he studied the five strangers around the dirty table. To his left the punter with the option studied his cards like a fortune-teller having trouble with the future. Beyond him, a character with the nickname of Lumps, and a face that explained it, looked impatient, urging the undecided player to action.

'Tell you what all the rush is, son,' he explained in a voice that didn't sound used to waiting. 'That lucky face there has got most of my dough in his sky.'

Robby went on looking expressionless and the punter went on looking worried. After some more deliberation he decided Robby was bluffing and called the bet. The next man stacked, and Lumps took his chance to speed things up with a call and raise that left Robby with two hundred to find. He found it and raised another hundred, putting a frown on Lumps' unhandsome features and a look of disbelief on the punter's.

'You're on a chancer,' grumbled the punter, with more optimism than belief in his voice.

Robby shrugged and favoured the man with a slight smile that gave absolutely nothing away.

'Four hundred notes an' you'll find out.'

The punter studied the money sitting on the table and the cards in his hand, then sighed like someone saying a last farewell to an old friend and folded his hand. The betting – and all the eyes in the room – turned to Lumps.

'Four hundred the bet.' His voice was slightly strangled; his glare said that it was Robby he wanted to strangle. 'And up another ton. How does that grab you?'

'Terrific.' Robby's expression didn't change. 'Called. And raised another ton.'

Lumps' angrily confident smile disappeared as his lower lip parted company with the upper and beads of sweat sparkled on his forehead. Close set eyes flickered in Robby's direction, then to the pot, and finally to the dwindling pile of notes by his elbow. The punter who had dropped out suggested, 'Call 'im, son. He's on a bluff – sticks out a mile.'

'I paid hard pound notes to get this far, pal.' Lumps' voice was as hard as his knuckles looked. 'You pulled out. So shut it. OK?'

A nervous tic fluttered his right eye as he glared at his cards. The punter closed his mouth. Robby waited. Finally, Lumps said, 'I can't call the bet,' and began to stack what little cash he had left as he muttered irritably, 'I had you, pal. You was well beat.'

'You reckon?' Robby asked.

'Yeah.' It was the punter, jumping in with both feet. 'Me an' all. You was on a right chancer.'

Robby was about to haul in the pot, but the comment

halted him, just as his words halted Lumps.

'Tell you what. What you short to call the bet? About a twoer?'

'About,' agreed Lumps.

'Here's your chance, big mouth.' Robby swung to face the punter. 'You make up the shortfall and I'll take it the bet's called. OK?'

The punter's mouth dropped open as he realized his feet were firmly inside. He began to stutter.

Robby stared at him. 'C'mon, pal. You was very sure a moment ago, when it wasn't your dough up on offer. C'mon – his cards against mine. Simple enough bet.'

The punter's lips writhed around his mouth like excited worms. He tugged at his already-loosened tie, not pleased to find himself suddenly the focus of attention. Lumps grunted a question, nodding at his cards, and when Robby shrugged his agreement, pushed them across to the punter, who picked them up and stared at them, seeing three nines and two tens making up a full house. A wet, pink tongue caressed the worms. Lumps smiled faintly. Robby said, 'You got five seconds, son.'

The punter glanced at him. Then at the cards again. Then at Lumps.

'What's in it for me?'

'Double your money,' said the hard-faced man.

'You gotta be jokin'!' The punter complained. 'Half the pot an' you're on.'

Lumps shrugged. 'All right.'

'Right!' said the punter firmly. 'Bet called.'

He peeled notes from a wad and threw the bundle onto the table. Robby reached out to touch his three hole cards. Showing, he had the ace of Spades and the jack of Hearts. The first hole card to turn was the ace of Clubs. It was followed by the jack of Diamonds. Lumps moved to go, shaking his head. Robby grinned, reaching for the pot.

And the punter said, 'Oy! Hold tight. You ain't won yet, mate. I wanna see that last card!'

Lumps was already at the door, disbelief in his sneer as he said, 'You don't reckon he was on that much of a chancer, do yer? The lucky bastard's filled it in, no risk.'

'I still wanna see it,' stuttered the punter.

'Yeah?' Robby turned the final card: the ace of Diamonds.

Lumps snorted and went through the door. The punter collapsed back in his seat, staring at the last card as though trying to change its design by psychokinesis. Robby raked in the money, a small, unsympathetic smile on his mouth. The punter made a noise midway between a groan and a snarl and stamped out of the room, slamming the door to emphasize his dissatisfaction. Two of the onlookers went after him, one pausing to murmur an apology.

'Sorry, lads. He's not the best of losers.'

Robby looked at the remaining players and got two shakes. The game was over. He pocketed his winnings and climbed into his sheepskin as the school broke up. Max opened the rear door elaborately, his moist eyes expectant.

Robby shook his head as he handed over cash.

'You're gettin' too greedy, Max. You're the dearest house on the manor.'

'Why you always complain, eh?' complained the Greek. 'You know before you sit down how much is the house cut.'

'Yeah.' Robby sighed, accepting the inevitable. 'You're a thievin' git, Max. A thievin', fat git.'

He turned away so that he didn't see the single finger Max waved at his back, tugging up his collar as he paced down the darkened back street. His pace slowed as he took out a pack of cigarettes and stuck one in his mouth, halting completely as he struck a match. The flame lit his face for an instant, and in its glare he saw a shadow. Turned, lifting an arm. Not far enough to stop the blackjack that knocked the arm down, the force of the blow watering his eyes. Not turned quite far enough to prevent the second blow landing on the back of his head, smashing him to the ground. After that, there was a sudden firework display that ended in blackness.

Tommy came into the room with a cup of tea in his hand and a smile on his face. Both got put down when he saw

44

Robby. He crossed to the window and snatched the curtains open, settling by the chess board as Robby groaned and began to sip the tea.

'Looks like you had some aggro last night. Or was it that lovely lady of yourn?'

The look he got told him he had said the wrong thing and he mumbled an apology. Robby grunted, 'What you doin' round here so early, anyway?'

'Me an' your mum are goin' down the market to do a spot o' shopping. We'll pop in for pie an' mash an' all. Fancy some of it?'

'Yeah. Full o' tricks, me.' Robby eased cautiously from the bed. 'Ouch! That hurts.'

Tommy watched him stand up like a paper clip unbending. 'Found the ace up your sleeve, did they?'

'I'll put an ace up you in a minute.' Robby groaned again as he straightened.

'You're gettin' past it, son.' Tommy shook his head knowledgeably. 'Too old and, by the looks of it, far too slow.'

Robby was too busy examining his bruises to do more than suggest Tommy take Vi out. Right away. Tommy chuckled and headed for the door, turning to nod in the direction of the chess board.

'Check!'

Robby took his tea cautiously over to the board and said, 'Oh, shit!' Then he looked at his face in the mirror and added, 'He's right. Far too slow.'

Villains like big cars and Frank Aldino was no exception. His was a brand new Jaguar XJ6 that matched its owner: expensively smart and looking capable of turning on the power. Aldino was lounged back against the plush leather of the rear seat, talking to his driver, Denny More, who had the same aura of groomed toughness.

'The last thing I need at this moment,' Aldino was saying, 'is aggro, Denny.'

'The guy's been good as gold in the past,' More replied. 'Always weighed out, no bovver.'

'Well he ain't no more.' Aldino frowned. 'An' he insisted on seein' me?'

'Yeah.' More shrugged. 'I didn't wanna get silly, like. Been dead quiet in the last year or so.'

'Yeah, an' that's just the way I want it to stay,' said Aldino. 'No aggro unless I say so. Right?'

Denny nodded: no one argued with Frank Aldino. Not for long. And never twice.

'Gordon Bennet!'

Robby grinned painfully as Kipper's mouth hung open. 'You should see the other geezer, Kip.'

'Come home and catch you, did he?' asked Juicy Joan from behind the window.

'I should be so lucky,' winked Robby. 'Is me main man in?'

'Yeah.' Joan nodded towards the office door. 'Out back crying in his beer.'

'Someone had it off, then?' Robby tried not to smile: it hurt his split lip.

'Monty,' smiled Juicy Joan, 'had a cockle on a fifty to one at Newmarket.'

Robby forgot about his lip as he thought of Gil parting with £1,500.

Gil Roach was a long, thin streak of balding middle-age, the concerns of running a betting shop showing on his lean face. Especially when he had to pay out. The sight of Robby's battered features cheered him up.

'Nice job,' he remarked in a conversational way as the bruises came into his office.

'Can fix you up for one if you like,' suggested Robby.

Gil chuckled. 'No, ta. I'll stick with what I got. So, you don't know which one it was?'

'I'll find out.' Robby shook his head. 'Listen, did you have a word with your accountant?'

'He says you've got problems.'

'Well, I know that,' snapped Robby. 'Don't I?'

'Look, mate,' Gil shrugged, 'he can't help you. The plumb's so straight he's immoral. Know what I mean?'

46

'Yeah.' Robby nodded, sighing. 'Gnomes in his garden?'

'With fishing poles,' Gil agreed. 'Dunno why I employ him really.'

'In your game you gotta know someone,' Robby said.

'Oh, steady on!' Gil stood on his dignity. 'This is the sport of kings. Anyway, I thought your lady was gonna get you a meet with her boss's book-cooker.'

'She was,' Robby confirmed. 'Or did. I couldn't make the meet.'

Gil looked at him with no surprise.

Frank Aldino's Jaguar smoothed its way to a halt outside a club with dead neon announcing it as the Slipper and Denny More opened the door for his boss. Inside, the club was large and empty, the worn patches on the carpeting and the faded patches of paint noticeable in the harsh light of day. Two cleaners looked up irritably as Aldino and his minder left footprints across the newly-polished dance floor on their way to the office at the rear.

Denny More knocked and Aldino smiled as the door was opened by a young, busty blonde girl. Beyond her, Phil Graves rose from behind his desk looking like a non-conformist scheduled for an interview with the Spanish Inquisition. Aldino smiled expansively as they shook hands and exchanged pleasantries that didn't sound sincere. The blonde poured them drinks and took Graves' hint to leave, closing the door carefully behind her.

'So,' said Aldino. 'What's the problem, Phil? Why you suddenly turned monkey on us?'

'I ain't turned monkey, Frank,' said Graves.

'So why send my lads away without a donation? So you've got fed up with a peaceful existence?'

The implicit threat hung in the air, kept company by the steady cracking of Denny More's knuckles.

'We had a deal, Frank,' said Graves quickly.

'*Have*!' Aldino snapped. 'We *have* a deal, Phil.'

Graves shrugged, looking hurt. 'So why start puttin' up the ante without chatting about it? Another two-fifty a week, Frank! That's not easy to find.'

Aldino's ugly smile got replaced by an uglier expression. His stocky body locked rigid, suspicion and rage glinting in his cold eyes.

'How much? How much did you say?'

'Two hundred an' fifty sovs puts my outlay up by fifty per cent,' answered Graves. 'A grand a month.'

Aldino glanced at More. Denny shrugged, face blank.

'Since when?' asked Aldino. 'When did I stick up the ante?'

'Since a month ago.' Incomprehension contorted Graves' features, slowly replaced by realization. 'Don't tell me ...'

The two heavies ignored him. Aldino was glaring at More, who was shaking his head and saying, 'Don't know nuffink about it, Frank. Straight up.'

'Well you bloody well should, Denny.' Aldino's voice was cold as his face was flushed. He took a deep breath, containing his anger. 'Right. Out! Phil, I'm sorry you've had aggravation. Leave it with me – I'll sort it. It's a monkey a week. No more, no less. A slight misunderstanding at my end.'

He controlled his rage very well as he led the way back to the Jaguar.

Inside the big car he gave free vent to his anger as it became apparent that one of his minions had been dipping greedy fingers in the till and Denny More had failed to spot the villainy. Given Phil Graves' news, the guilty party was easy to identify.

'I'm sorry, Frank,' Denny More was saying, 'I never figgered Lumps'd pull a stroke like that.'

'You dopy, no-good berk!' Aldino cut in. 'You know he can't keep away from a spieler.'

'I'll top him,' said More consolingly. 'I'll have his head off.'

'You won't, son!' Aldino was angry enough to get out of the car unassisted, putting his face close to More's through the open window. 'You've done enough. Now you just find him. Find the light-fingered bastard an' bring 'im to me.'

Without waiting for a reply, he marched towards the

imposing house across the raked gravel of the drive, his parting words floating back to Denny More like a curse, 'I'll give him a game of cards, the cowson!'

Robby came out of the betting shop with Jan on his mind and found Ferret propping up the wall with the anorexic greyhound semi-comatose at his feet.

'Again?' he asked.

'Yeah,' nodded Ferret. 'Old big knockers flung us out. I mean, all he did was bite Black George on the leg. I mean, he's always done that, ain't he?'

'Tried feeding him?' Robby grinned. 'Perhaps he's hungry an' thinks old George is a black pudding on legs.'

'Oh, very funny,' sniffed Ferret, folding his newspaper as he took a good look at Robby's multi-coloured facial decorations. 'What you been up to?'

'Fell out of bed,' said Robby. 'Seen Geordie on your travels?'

'Pointin' job just up the road,' Ferret supplied. 'Cutters Terrace.'

Robby found his friend up a ladder, just finishing. He helped him stow the gear in Geordie's old van and asked what was on his mind.

'You seen anything of Jan at the yard?'

Geordie could hear the concern behind the casual tone. 'Can't help seeing her, mun.'

'She said anything?'

'She wouldn't, mun,' Geordie shrugged. 'Not to me, anyway.'

'Not a word?'

'Nope. But she don't look very happy with herself.'

'Oh.' Robby steadied the ladder as Geordie lashed it down, reluctant to extend the enquiry. 'Old Diamond ...'

'Aye?' prompted Geordie.

'Trying his luck still?'

'He's persistent, I'll give him that,' came the unwelcome answer. 'Why he's good in business, I suppose.'

'He's got no chance with my Jan,' said Robby, defiantly.

Geordie stared at him, face serious. 'Diamond may be a

bunny merchant, but he's a well-off one, right? Money. A big house. Thinks the world of her.' He shrugged, all the banter gone from his voice. 'What you got to offer the girl?'

'Leave off,' Robby protested. 'He's married already.'

Geordie snorted dismissively. 'His set-up isn't a marriage. More an agreement.'

Under the bruises, Robby's face got serious.

'Give us a lift back to the yard?'

'OK.' Geordie agreed. 'Then you can treat me to some dinner at Maxie's.'

'Yeah.' Robbie touched the purple swelling beneath one half-closed eye. 'I wanna see that fat bastard, anyway.'

'You want to tell me about it?' Geordie asked.

Robby told him as they drove towards Henry Diamond's yard.

When they arrived Robby saw Jan by the window of the office building, fussing with a kettle. He crept up to the glass and tapped, ducking out of sight before she turned. He waited until she crossed the room and threw the window open, then popped into view. Jan's face radiated surprised pleasure, then shock as she caught sight of his damaged features. Then she hid all her emotions under a stern, unyielding brusqueness.

'Can we talk?' he asked.

'There's nothing to talk about.' She kept her voice cool only with effort. 'It's all been said. Said and said and said again.'

'Please, Princess. Hear me out?'

'No,' she said. 'Go away.'

'Will you just listen?' Anger sounded through the concern in his voice. 'We've got to talk.'

'You're good at that, Robby.' Jan was terse. 'But I'm not listening any more. Now go away – I've got work to do.'

'Look, Princess,' he pleaded.

'No,' snapped Jan, interrupting. 'You look, Robby! You made your choice! Me or the big spieler. I lost.'

Robby opened his damaged mouth to say something more, but then Henry Diamond put his head around the inner door, managing to look surprised and irritated and smug all at the same time. He began to apologize, making moves to leave until Jan halted him with two sentences that left Robby speechless.

'Henry ... about dinner tonight? Thank you – I'd like that.'

Smug became the chief expression on Diamond's face as he said, 'Oh, fine! Yes ... well, carry on.'

He ducked out of the room with a triumphant smile as Jan did her best to keep from crying when she saw Robby's angry, unbelieving stare.

'You were saying?' she whispered.

But Robby wasn't saying anything. He was too angry and too hurt. Beneath the discoloration of the bruises, his face was pale, his shoulders hunching in impotent rage. Without a word, he spun round and stalked away. Jan watched him go out of the yard and couldn't hold the tears back any longer. Her shoulders shook as she wrapped both arms across her chest and began to weep.

Geordie had seen the drama enacted from across the yard, and now he stepped up to the window, unsure what to say or do as he studied Jan's tearful face. He tried a simple, 'Jan, love,' but all she did – all she could do – was shake her head and turn away, hiding her grief. Geordie shrugged helplessly and went over to his van, where Robby sat staring deadpan through the windshield. He started to say something, but Robby cut him short. Geordie sighed and started the old Thames.

The cafe still smelled of onions and burnt fat, daylight taking the gloss from the faded travel posters pinned on the walls, so that the place looked like any other run-down backstreet cafe in need of redecoration and a new menu. Max was sitting at a table near the counter with a newspaper spread in front of his belly and a greasy smile on his face as they walked in.

'Your momma she belt you good because you get home so very late, eh?' he said by way of greeting.

'I won this with a full house last night, Max.' Robby

51

didn't smile. 'Twenty seconds after you let me out the back door.'

The smile went away from Max's face, replaced by alarm. He said, 'You kid old Max! You mean ...'

'That's right, son.' Robby's face stayed straight and menacing. 'Right outside your back door. I was well turned over.'

'Oh, Bobby, that's real bad luck.' Max came close to wringing his pudgy hands. 'How much you lose?'

'Every penny I won in here last night.'

Robby studied the obese Greek, trying to read the woe-begone expression on Max's face as the cafe owner said, 'I not know what's this place coming to, eh?'

'Who was that stroppy geezer, Max?' Robby stepped a pace closer. 'And the other face? The one I drew in.'

'Oh, Bobby! You know better than to ask.' The Greek shrugged elaborately. 'I fix up the school – you play; you don't play. I no have nothing to do with after. You know?'

Robby narrowed his eyes, doing his best to make his naturally easy-going features threatening. The way he had been worked over, that wasn't too difficult.

'Well, Max, I'll tell you – you got five seconds to give me a couple of names. Or I'm gonna get well out of order.'

Max looked at his expression and got worried. 'I can't help! I not know any names!' There was real fear in his voice and heads began to turn. Robby heightened the dramatic effect by grabbing hold of the Greek's shirtfront.

'I'll burn this grease factory down, Max!'

He was genuinely angry now, no longer needing to put on an act, and that got through to Max, who began to quiver like a jelly going out of control. Geordie saw the situation going too far and stepped in before real violence was committed.

'Steady on, Rob!' He took hold of Robby's wrists, turning to Max. 'Max, I've known this man for a long, long time. Do yourself a favour and tell him what he wants to know.' He eased Robby's grip loose, interposing himself between the two men. 'If you don't, he'll probably top you.'

The last few words were said with a big smile, as if that

52

was the most natural outcome and the only thing holding Robby back from a homicidal rampage was the chance he might get the names he wanted. Max's eyes got bulbous as a knot of genuine terror bubbled its way down his throat. He didn't see Robby looking at Geordie with amusement replacing the anger on his face. Or Geordie's wink.

'OK,' he agreed quickly. 'OK.'

Geordie's van pulled up outside a run-down pub in bad need of a coat of new paint and both men climbed out.

'Look,' Robby said, 'no point in you gettin' involved, mate. It could get silly, like.'

'I know,' Geordie grinned, a foot long length of stressed steel slipping magically from his sleeve. 'Be prepared. That was our motto in the Girl Guides.'

'Turn it in, son.' Robby caught his pal's arm before Geordie got inside the pub. 'That ain't necessary.'

'No?' Geordie's craggy face was serious. 'Take a gander in the mirror, Robbo.'

There was no arguing with that, and Robby shook his head helplessly as Geordie retrieved his arm and went into the pub. Inside, the paint work was worse than the exterior, cream and brown matching the peeling linoleum on the floor and the polish-free woodwork of the burned, scarred tables. It was nearly closing time and the landlord was behind the bar waving a dirty rag in the direction of some dirty glasses that he periodically dunked in a bowl of dirty water. Robby spotted the punter from the game sitting alone and walked over with a casual, 'All right?'

The punter frowned at Robby's newly redecorated face and said cautiously. 'Yeah. How about yourself?'

'Remember me?' Robby asked.

The punter studied the bruises, then said warily, 'Oh, yeah. 'Course I do.' Followed by, 'Cor! You did me up bad, I'll tell you.'

The landlord came over with a beer then and the punter said, 'Stick it on me tab, Sid?' And to Robby, 'Drink?'

'No, ta.' Robby saw the landlord raise his eyebrows and

heard the punter add, 'Don't worry, Sid. I'll square me slate. You know that.'

'All right.' Robby spoke to the landlord. 'I'll get it.'

'Cheers!' The punter raised his mug, nodding at Robby's face. 'Old lady one for ruckin', or what?'

'Yeah,' Robby agreed. 'Listen, d'you know who the big geezer was? The guy that drew you in on that last hand?'

'The moanin' git?' asked the punter. 'I don't know him exactly. More know *of* him.'

'Know where I can find him?' Robby asked.

The punter took a fresh look at the bruises, then said, 'That down to him?'

'Ain't down to you, then?' Robby countered.

'Me?' The punter sounded shocked. 'What you on about? What's this all about?'

'I got rolled last night,' explained Robby. 'When I left Maxie's drum.'

'Here, hold on a minute!' The punter gave vent to self-righteous indignation. 'It weren't me.'

'All right, all right.' Robby waved the man to calm down. 'You'd hardly be sittin' here havin' a beer on the slate if you had my two grand in your bin.'

'That's for sure.' The man nodded enthusiastically. 'Listen, I don't like losin' an' I don't go about pullin' strokes like that. Ask anyone round here.'

'I said I believe you,' Robby told him, leaving a question hanging between them.

The punter re-appraised the facial renovations then said, 'Know of a villain called Frank Aldino?'

'Who don't?' Robby confirmed.

'Right,' said the punter. 'Well, the geezer you're on about is one of his headbangers. Only know his nickname – Lumps.'

Frank Aldino had done well in his chosen line of business and it showed in his home. For a backstreet boy made good – or bad, depending on your point of view – he had taste, which also showed in the muted decor and the decorations. Aldino was watching the three-thirty from

Kemptown on a fifty-two inch Bang & Olufson when Denny More came in with an apologetic expression.

'Can't find the geezer nowhere, Frank.'

'What d'you mean?' Aldino demanded irritably. 'Can't find him? He can't just have disappeared, can he?'

'We checked out the boozers an' the clubs.' More waved his hands placatingly. 'Nuffink. Drew a blank all round.'

He exchanged a nervous glance with his driver as Aldino glowered. Then he added, 'Found out where he was last night, though. An' old Greeko's cafe.'

'A spieler. Right?'

'Yeah,' More agreed. 'Rolled a guy after the game by all accounts.'

'Anyone we know?' Aldino asked.

'Nah.' More shrugged. 'Just a mug punter. Find out if you like.'

Aldino thought for a few moments, then nodded as a small smile graced his mean mouth.

'Yeah. Find out the geezer's name. I'd like to have a few words. This could be interestin'.'

'What now then?' Geordie asked as he and Robby closed the door of Robby's room.

'Find this animal called Lumps,' Robby said. 'What else?'

'He don't sound like the kind of guy you deliberately go looking for,' warned Geordie. 'Least, not without a Sherman tank or three.'

'Got no choice, mate.' Robby flopped onto the bed, putting his feet up. 'It was more'n just money this time. That little bundle was my climb-out stake.'

'I've heard that one before.' Geordie was doubtful.

'I mean it this time.' Robby's voice was sharp. 'I want out. I want to join the system. Be normal. That animal stopped me.'

'The system stinks an' you know it.' Geordie studied his friend with curious eyes. The upset with Jan was affecting Robby a whole lot more than he was letting on. 'I've seen you blow what I earn in a week in one hour at a spieler. You're better off as you are.'

Robby climbed off the bed and went over to the table, studying the chess board.

'You reckon?'

'If I were single, you wouldn't catch me grafting for a living,' Geordie said fervently. 'You got it made! Your cards, the gee-gees, no worries.'

'No worries?' Robby looked up from the chessmen. 'Listen, son. Take a good, hard look at me an' learn a lesson. I'm forty-one. I got no trade, no prospects. I'm tired. Worn out. An' if I don't get myself sorted out double quick, it'll be too late.'

'For what?' asked Geordie, surprised.

'For everything!' answered Robby earnestly. 'Geordie, can't you see? If I don't get myself sorted out, there ain't gonna be any future for me an' Jan. All I got is me old mum, an' she won't be around for ever. Then what have I got? Nothing! Sweet f.a.! I'll end up like those poor old sods down the betting shop. With nothing to look forward to but the next race. Wettin' their pants when a five bob yankee comes off, 'cause it gives 'em a stake for the next meeting. Oh, mate! Do yourself a right good favour – don't even think about goin' down my road. It's a mug's game.'

It was a surprising speech and it took Geordie aback: he had never heard Robby express such dissatisfaction before. Not sure what to say, he said, 'Listen. If ... Well, if you're dead set on goin' straight, you've always got a job with us. Any time.'

Robby looked up from the chess board with a genuine smile on his battered features.

'Cheers, mate.'

From the kitchen, a kettle began to whistle. Suddenly embarrassed, Geordie was glad of the interruption. He went to make the tea.

Gil's betting shop was crowded as Robby came in with Ferret using him as a shield to hide the greyhound. He sidled away, doing his best to hide from Juicy Joan as Robby spotted Kipper.

'Had a result, Kip?'

'Only a silly five to one,' shrugged the younger man. 'Crown Prince at Haydock.'

'I was on that meself,' said Robby; pleased. 'What about the two o'clock at Thirsk?'

Joan heard him and supplied the answer. 'Banjo Boy walked it by six lengths.'

'Terrific!' Robby's smile got broader and he turned his head to call, 'Who won at Thirsk, then, Ferret?'

Joan's eyes followed his voice to where Ferret and the greyhound lurked.

'You better not have that stinky mutt with you, Ferret!'

'Eh, no. No, I ain't, luv,' Ferret mumbled. 'He's out in the street.'

Then he said, 'Oh, shite!' as the dog bared its teeth and began to growl.

'Out!' Joan bellowed, bosom heaving. 'I've told you before. Out!'

Muttering furiously, Ferret hauled the greyhound to its feet and shuffled from the betting shop. 'Sorry, mate,' Robby said guiltily. 'I forgot.'

'Pork pie on legs!' Joan snapped, loathing for the luckless animal written all over her face. 'Sodding thing ought to be put down.'

'The mutt?' asked Kipper innocently. 'Or Ferret?'

'Leave off,' protested Robby. 'This old manor wouldn't be the same without 'em.'

Gil must have heard his voice, because his head emerged from the office with a worried expression on the face and said, 'Robbo, you got a mo?'

'What's up, Gil?' Robby walked behind the counter to the office.

'You had a couple of visitors.' Gil sounded like he would have preferred not to meet them again. 'One of 'em was Denny More. Frank Aldino's oppo. Heavy, Robbo. Real heavy. I know – Aldino's an account client of mine.'

'Second time today that geezer's name's come up,' Robby said thoughtfully.

'That geezer, as you call him,' said Gil worriedly, 'wants to talk to you. The rubbish that rolled you last night ...'

'Works for Aldino,' Robby cut in. 'Charmin' character they call Lumps. Why's he wanna talk to me?'

'They just left a number to ring.' Gil passed over a slip of paper like a man losing incriminating evidence. 'The Denny character said to tell you it ain't aggro. Well, not for you, that is.'

Robby took the slip as an explosion of sound from the outer room deepened the lines on Gil's face.

'Oh, no!' moaned the proprietor. 'Not another outsider. I dunno why I'm in this business.'

In Frank Aldino's living room a tailor was doing his best to measure his client as the villain strolled the carpet waving his arms expansively.

'I hope the Slipper's the only touch-up, Denny,' Aldino was saying. 'Cause if there's anyone else …'

The threat hung in the air like a parachute bomb. More said quickly, 'I'll get round a few tonight, Frank.'

'No.' Aldino shook his head. 'I want you here.'

'I'm all done now, Mr Aldino,' said the tailor, nervously.

'Terrific,' Aldino said. 'I'll take one of each.'

Thankful to be done, the tailor began to collect his samples as Aldino crossed to the built-in bar and poured himself a drink.

'What's on tonight then, Frank?' asked Denny More.

Before his boss could answer, the telephone rang. Aldino lifted the receiver and said, 'Yeah?'

At the other end of the phone, Robby said, 'Denny More?'

'Who wants him?' asked the villain.

'I do,' came the answer.

'I ain't in the mood for funnies,' Aldino snarled. 'Who wants 'im?'

'Tell him it's Robby Box,' said Robby.

'Hang about.' Aldino looked at Denny More. 'Geezer name of Robby Box.'

'That's the punter you wanted,' said More.

Aldino went back to the phone. 'Listen, pal. You got turned over last night, right?'

'Who wants to know?'

58

'I do.' Aldino waved More off as the door bell rang. 'I wanna know.'

'You the Denny bloke then?'

'No, I ain't. You want a fair chance to get your loot back, be at the Slipper club at ten tonight.'

'And?'

'Just be there. Tell the guy on the door you're my guest.'

'And who are you?'

'Frank Aldino. Be there.'

Aldino put the phone down on the cradle as Denny More ushered Lumps into the room. More's face was impassive, waiting for his boss's cue to break bones. Instead of issuing the expected orders, however, Aldino smiled at his headbanger and said, 'Ah, Lumps me old mate, you like a bit of a spieler, don't you?'

'Love a spieler, Frank,' Lumps agreed.

'Terrific!' said Aldino cheerfully. 'We got one on tonight an' I stuck you in. All right?'

'Yeah,' said Lumps. 'Terrific.'

Tommy stared at Robby's knight threatening his own knight five and saw the glossy pamphlets scattered beside the chess board. They were all to do with taxi cabs: price lists and performance specifications, illustrations and maintenance lists. The old man frowned thoughtfully, forgetting the game as he reached for a leaflet showing the new Rover diesel taxi, his perusal interrupted by the hurried entry of his prospective stepson.

''Allo, son,' he grinned, gesturing at the board. 'Left us in a bit of bovver here, ain't you?'

'Nothin' you can't sort out, Tom,' said Robby. 'Where's Mum?'

'Over the Railway,' Tommy explained, 'having a drink with the bingo crowd. An' what's all this about?'

Robby glanced at the pamphlets and asked, 'What's it look like?'

'Taxi cab prices,' said Tommy. 'You can't even drive.'

'Well, then,' Robby grinned as he stripped out of his

shirt, 'you can give us a lift across to the Slipper club. Save us gettin' a cab.'

'Always bumming lifts, you,' complained Tommy good-naturedly. 'Why don't you buy yourself a motor?'

Robby buttoned the clean shirt as he said straight-faced, 'I may just do that, Tom.'

CHAPTER FIVE

'Where's the game then, Frank?' Lumps asked as the XJ6 glided smoothly through the north London night.

'The Slipper, mate,' Aldino said easily, prompting a nervous glance from the heavy.

'Fancy the Hammers on Saturday, Lumps?' interjected Denny More. 'Me bruvver's got a couple o' seats.'

'Yeah!' Lumps nodded enthusiastically. 'I'll have some o' that.'

'Wouldn't miss it for the world, mate,' smiled Denny, pleased with his diplomacy.

Silence reigned in the car as they completed their journey to the club, the Jaguar sliding to a neat halt to dispense the three men as Tommy's battered old Ford slewed to a precarious stop inches from the limousine's gleaming bumper. Robby climbed out, looking smart in a dark suit and quiet tie, the marks on his face dulling now. He waved his thanks to Tommy and crossed the pavement to the foyer, where a man looking like a distant cousin of King Kong despite his bow tie asked with polite threat, 'You a member, please, sir?'

'I'm a guest of Frank Aldino's,' said Robby.

And it was like Ali Baba saying *Open Sesame*: the bouncer even held the door open.

Robby followed him along a passageway that led to the rear of the building where a flight of stairs went up to a door that got opened by Phil Graves, who ushered him in like a honoured guest.

'Bobby Box, right?' said Aldino from behind Graves' desk.

'Yeah,' said Robby. 'Frank Aldino, right?'

'C'mon in. Have a seat. Drink?'

'Jack Daniels sounds good,' Robby agreed.

Aldino said, 'Same for me, Phil.'

'Nice place,' Robby remarked. 'Warm, though.'

'Yeah.' Aldino sat smiling like a crocodile watching someone drown as Graves got the drinks ready.

Robby said, 'Cheers,' when his arrived. Aldino said, 'Yeah, cheers,' and downed the sipping whiskey in one quick gulp. He set the glass down and came around the desk.

'Right then, son. Me an' you an' Phil here have all got somethin' in common.'

'That right?' said Robby; warily.

'I just said,' said Aldino. 'Phil, you, an' me have all been turned over by the same geezer. Lookin' at the state of you, I'd say you came off the worst.'

'I'll drink to that.' Robby sipped the whiskey.

'But then you're bound to take a hiding or two in your line. Right, Bob?'

Robby shrugged. 'Occupational hazard.'

'You're older than I figgered,' Aldino said. 'Old enough to know better'n to step out into a dark alley with a bundle in your bin.'

'I should've sussed he was bad news,' Robby agreed, still not sure where the conversation was taking them. 'The cards were doin' me proud – the flashing red lights went unnoticed. A bad mistake.'

'Costly an' all, I understand,' Aldino prompted.

'Very,' said Robby solemnly.

'How very?'

'Two grand very.'

'Tut, tut, tut.' Aldino chuckled. 'OK. Bobby-boy. I said on the phone I'd give you a chance to get your dough back. Right?'

'That's why I'm here,' Robby said.

'Notice I did say a *chance*,' Aldino warned. 'The way I see it, I ain't lost no dough, but what I lost was much more value to me. Loss of face. Respect, like. To me it means survival. My livelihood. Know what I mean?'

'Course,' nodded Robby.

'Phil here lost a grand,' continued Aldino. 'The trouble is, Bobby, Phil lost his bit before you did. That means the pound notes you won – an' then lost – all came out o' Phil's pocket.'

'But I lost two,' Robby argued.

'So you did,' Aldino agreed. 'So you did.' He nodded towards an inner door. 'Sittin' in the other room are three blokes all waitin' for us. One of 'em's Denny More, an' another is a friend of Phil's who just likes a game of stud poker. D'you know who the third one is, Bobby-boy?'

'Lumps,' said Robby. 'Right?'

'You got it,' smiled Aldino, crocodile becoming shark. 'Now, because I lost something that means much more to me than just a few grand, I get his bones. OK?'

'Can't I have just one good kick?' Robby asked.

Aldino laughed out loud. 'We'll see.'

'OK.' Robby shrugged. 'How do I get my money back.'

'You play poker,' Aldino explained. 'You play poker and hope the cards are runnin' for you. An' if you win, I'll personally see you get home safe an' sound. Now that's not a bad deal, is it, Bobby-boy?'

'What's the alternative?' Robby asked, knowing it was a pointless question.

'There ain't one,' smiled Aldino, reverting to crocodile.

'Put like that,' said Robby, 'it's a good deal.'

Aldino chuckled like a torturer examining some new equipment and motioned for Robby to rise. Not waiting to see if he was obeyed, he crossed the office and threw the inner door open, revealing three men seated around a card table. Robby recognized Lumps immediately, guessing the other big man must be Denny More because Aldino was busy greeting the third party as Laurie Woods.

'Bobby,' he said as they sat down, 'meet Laurie. That's Denny. An' Lumps I think you know.'

Robby nodded coldly as a blonde with less dress than bust put a fresh deck in front of Phil Graves.

'Gentlemen,' said the club owner, 'the game is five card

stud poker. There's no limit provided the bet is covered by cash. That's it. First jack deals.'

He began to flip cards across the table, first to Denny More on his left, then to Lumps, Laurie Woods, Aldino and, finally, Robby. The first jack went to Laurie Woods.

Lumps said, 'Didn't know you was a friend of the family, pal.'

Robby stared at the minder. 'Would it have made a difference, then?'

The way he said it left the question ambiguous. Lumps said, 'Nah. You'd still've beat us. That full house was a right fluke in the death, eh?'

'Won me more'n I bargained for.' Robby took his eyes off Lumps long enough to study his hole card. 'A lot more.'

'King's the bet,' Laurie said.

Denny More took the hint. 'I'll go a score on the king.' Twenty pounds went into the pot. 'Keep it nice an' friendly.'

'I'm in.' Lumps called the bet.

'Your score,' announced Laurie, 'and up a cockle.'

Aldino said, 'Called.' And thirty more pounds joined the mounting pile on the table.

Robby took it higher. 'Your thirty and up another score.'

Aldino smiled at the raise. It wasn't a pretty smile.

Laurie said, 'All there?' and began to deal again. Aldino got a five to go with his ten of Spades. Robby got a king of Hearts that didn't look much alongside the two of Diamonds he had showing, but was useful with the king of Diamonds in the hole. Phil Graves had the nine of Hearts and the ten of Clubs in front of him. Denny More had the two of Clubs and the king of Clubs. Lumps received a four of Spades alongside the five of Hearts. Laurie dealt himself the ten of Diamonds; he already had the four of Hearts. He said, 'Still the king to bet.'

Denny looked at his hand and shrugged as he threw it down. 'Out.'

Lumps said, 'Called,' and put fifty pounds down.

Laurie folded, but Aldino stayed with it and Robby took

it up another twenty, leaving Phil Graves to add seventy pounds to the pot.

'Right then,' said Laurie. 'Here we go again. Four runners.'

He gave Aldino the jack of Spades, making for a useful flush, while Robby got the two of Hearts, giving him two pairs, kings over deuces. Phil Graves got blown out with an ace of Spades, and Lumps got the ace of Diamonds.

'Three runners,' said Laurie. 'Ace high the bet.'

Lumps looked pleased with himself as he tossed money onto the table. 'Seventy the bet and up another thirty.'

'Called,' said Aldino. 'And up another fifty.'

£150 went into the pot. Lumps' smile faded a little as he stared across the table at Robby, still unsure of the stranger's position in the villainous fraternity. Robby said, 'I'm there,' casually, and added £150.

'Stayin' with us, Lumps?' Aldino asked innocently.

This time the thick-set man studied the cards showing before agreeing to the raise.

'Right, three runners,' said Laurie Woods, dealing the last cards face down. 'And the best o' British.'

Aldino looked at his cards, that final jack of Diamonds blowing out his prospective flush, and said, 'That's blown that.'

Lumps looked at Robby and said, 'You an' me again, pal.'

Robby picked up the new card without looking at it as he said, 'I came to play poker, dickhead. Not to listen to you.'

Outraged astonishment showed on Lumps' ugly face at the words and his body went rigid, only a cautionary glance from Aldino holding him in his seat. He picked up his own card: the ace of Hearts, giving him three aces. The cold smile came back to his face and he murmured threateningly, 'I'll let that remark go, pal. For the moment.'

'Just bet,' Robby replied.

'One an' a half,' grated Lumps. 'An' up another twoer. Three an' a half the bet.'

'Called.' Robby put money down. 'And raise. Up another one.'

Lumps stared at the cards fronting Robby, then at the diminished pile of notes. His smile became smug.

'You got problems,' he remarked. 'Remember last night? Well, the boot's on the other foot now, pal. The four an' a half an' up another twoer.'

He grinned at Robby's coldly set face, reaching for the pot. 'Shame. The first hand an' all. Like you said – it's a hard life.'

'Leave it be!' Robby's command froze the grasping hand. 'Don't touch that, son. I ain't done yet.'

'Put up or shut up,' snarled Lumps.

Robby glanced at the notes still left him. There wasn't enough in his stake to match the raise, but like all good poker players he was in the habit of thinking ahead. He turned to Aldino.

'You know Gil Roach?'

It was less a question than a statement, and Aldino nodded. 'Betting shop down King Henry's?'

'I had three big winners come in today.' Robby reached inside his jacket to extract an envelope that he passed to the chief villain. 'Gil hadn't the wedge in the till to weigh me out. Your account is well overdue.' He ignored the furious glare Aldino gave him as he added, 'The amount on that invoice is about what he owes me.'

'So what are you then?' Aldino snapped. 'His collector?'

'Check with him if you like,' suggested Robby.

'So what d'you want?' Aldino flicked the invoice with an impatient finger. 'This?'

'Just cover the bet.' Robby grinned at the gangster. 'When you get down to the bones of the matter, you can't really lose. Right?'

'The bones of the matter, eh?' Aldino's glare got replaced by a thoughtful expression. ''Course you're right. But what about you, Bobby-boy? I mean, you ain't even looked at that last card. An' what you got showing ain't exactly gonna set the world alight, is it?'

What Robby had showing was the king of Hearts, the

two of Diamonds and the two of Hearts: Aldino was right. Nonetheless, Robby smiled confidently as he said, 'That's my worry ... Frank.'

'Now this ain't right,' Lumps protested, staring at Phil Graves. 'You said to cover the bets in pound notes. No markers; just pound notes.'

'I got pound notes!' Aldino rasped, silencing the minder's objections with a stare that left Lumps speechless and confused. 'All right, Bobby, I'll cover the bet. Just for the crack.'

He kept his word and Robby said, 'Bet called.'

Sensing things were wrong, Lumps spluttered, glancing around the table at the suddenly hostile faces waiting for him to make his move.

'Look,' he gabbled, turning over his third ace. 'I got him beat.'

'Play the hand!' ordered his boss.

'I have, Frank! Look! Three of 'em. Three lovely bullets.' He turned to Robby again. 'You can't beat that, pal!'

Aldino stared at his minion with contempt in his hard eyes. He said, 'I hope he does you bad, son. If he don't, then I will. You've been sussed.'

The colour drained from Lumps' face as he swallowed. The reason for Robby's presence – the reason for the spieler – was suddenly apparent. And the realization was an ugly knot of pure terror deep in the pit of his belly. He seemed to crumple in on himself, all the bravado dissipating under Aldino's cold glare. Lumps appealed to Robby.

'Listen, mate. I got into a bit of bovver ...'

'You bet your arse you have, rubbish,' Aldino grated.

'Please, mate? I can pay it all back now. Straight up! Was only like a loan.' He turned back to Aldino, knowing that a whole lot of pain was riding on the hand. 'See, Frank, you can have all that. All what's in there.'

Robby felt a twinge of an emotion alien to the others: pity. The sight of Lumps squirming like a hooked fish was not pleasant.

Aldino said, 'You called it, son. Let's have a look at it.'

So far no one, not even Robby himself, had seen the final card. He touched it, facing Aldino.

'At least give him a chance on the turn of the card?'

Lumps looked hopeful. Denny More looked impatient, as though he wanted to get to work. Phil Graves looked like he would enjoy watching. Laurie Woods looked bored.

Aldino said, 'My bones, remember? Turn it!'

'That invoice,' Robby asked, not sure why he was doing it, 'the pot and what he's got in his sky for a chance.'

'What is it with you, son?' Aldino sounded surprised and confused at the same time. And unrelenting. 'He's rubbish! Look what he done to you. Turned you over like eyes are winkin'. He ain't worth it.'

Robby felt apprehension join the pity as he studied Aldino's face, but he stuck to his point. 'He wins, he walks away potless. You keep the lot.'

'Why?' asked Aldino.

And Robby said, 'Why not?'

For what felt like a long time Aldino glared at Robby, his teeth gritted like a guard dog making up its mind where to bite. Robby felt cold fingers prickling their way up and down his spine and wondered why he was chancing his arm. 'Why not' suddenly felt like a pretty poor argument.

Then Aldino grunted, shaking his head as though in amazement at his own generosity. His voice dripped loathing as he told Lumps, 'You got one chance, rubbish. The turn of that card.'

Robby swallowed and began to turn the pasteboard rectangle, but Aldino's hard, hairy hand clamped onto his wrist like a closing trap and the villain said, 'If that card's a winner you leave here with what's in there. No more! The bones are mine!'

Robby nodded and turned the card as a tense silence filled the room.

It was the king of Spades.

King of Spades; king of Hearts; king of Diamonds; two of Diamonds; two of Hearts: full house. Robby didn't know whether he felt pleased or sorry. Mostly he just felt empty.

'It can't be!' Lumps' chair went over as he jumped to his feet. 'He cheated! He must've done!'

Denny More rose with him, shouting for the two heavies who came in and grabbed Lumps by the arms as More sank a fist into his belly to quiet his yelling. Lumps still managed to protest noisily as they dragged him from the room. Robby didn't see him go. He just sat staring at the full house.

Aldino was benign again as he said, 'My bones.'

Aldino's Jaguar rolled to its customary smooth stop outside Vi's house. The rear door opened and Robby climbed out, pausing as the door closed and the window rustled down with electric ease.

'Right, Bobby-boy,' Aldino said, 'you got your wedge back an' I've got you home safe and sound. Now ain't I man of my word?'

'What will you do with him?' Robby asked.

'Got nothin' to do with you, son.' Aldino's voice was curt. 'Go home an' forget it.'

Robby shook his head, sinking his hands deep into the pockets of the sheepskin coat. Feeling the notes there. Crisp and valuable and bloody.

'That was one hand I really didn't want to win.'

'You're a bigger mug than I thought.' Aldino smiled from inside the luxurious interior. 'Win or lose, I'd've had his bones.' He glanced past Robby, nodding towards the dark housefront. 'Looks like you got company. See you around, son.'

'Not if I can help it,' Robby murmured as the Jaguar slid away from the kerb and he turned towards the house.

Then he halted, eyes widening in surprise as a smile of pure pleasure creased his lips. Jan was standing there, shivering in the early morning cold. Robby walked towards her, taking off his coat to drape it about her shoulders. Following the coat with his arms. There were tears in her eyes. He hugged her, not speaking, then fumbled for his key and went inside with her.

The night had a good ending, after all.

CHAPTER SIX

Yawning, Robby ambled into Jan's sunny kitchen and grinned at a sleepy-eyed Debby as she nibbled toast, ignoring the crumbs that fell onto her school uniform. Jan was bustling about, concerned that his early-morning arrival had made her late for work. Their disagreement was forgotten now, replaced by a fresh commitment on Robby's part to get his life sorted out, and a determination on Jan's to help him any way she could. He still played cards and bet the horses and dogs – it was, as he had pointed out, the only way he knew to make a living, but now definite ideas were taking shape to change that, though he remained as irrepressibly easy-going as ever. Jan had to admit to herself that his happy-go-lucky streak was one part of him she would not want to alter. Now, though, she had other things on her mind – like getting Debby off to school and herself to work.

The one accomplished, she and Robby hailed a taxi to deliver her to Diamond's builder's yard.

'Should've had the day off, Princess.' Robby smiled as he yawned. 'We could've spent it ...'

'Huh!' Jan smiled back, glancing at the cabby, who was paying them no attention whatsoever. 'In your condition? You'd have been dead to the world by half nine. Besides, it's Thursday – my busiest day. And you've made me late!'

'I ain't made you late,' he protested. 'I've got a busy day as well, you know.'

'A lot of meetings on?' Jan wondered, provocatively.

'Nope.' Robby grinned. 'Got an appointment with an accountant Dickie Mayor put us on to.'

'Turf, if I know Dick Mayor,' Jan replied.

'Oh ye of little faith!' Robby assumed an expression of hurt innocence.

'You will go, Robby?' Jan said it with feeling. 'Really, this time?'

Robby nodded, humming to himself and looking pleased. For a moment Jan stared at him, as though doubtful, but then she smiled, too, and snuggled against him as the cab moved slowly through the rush hour traffic. They reached the yard and Jan jumped out, ignoring Geordie's 'Afternoon' as she waved goodbye to Robby and hurried for the office. Robby wound down the cab's window, grinning cheerfully at Geordie.

'I thought you'd be involved.' Geordie ducked his head in Jan's direction. 'Henry's doin' his crust, mun.'

'Stuff Henry.' Robby refused to let Henry Diamond dull his good humour as he climbed out of the cab, the scowl Diamond sent his way producing only the cheerful response, 'Morning, Henry.'

Diamond ignored him, getting into his Jaguar as Robby turned back to Geordie to ask the usual favour.

Accepting the inevitable, Geordie motioned for Robby to get aboard the old van with his part-time helper, Irish, whose seamed face still looked like a worked-out pit. They drove to the pawnshop, Geordie and Irish waiting in the Thames as Robby hurried inside, emerging a little later with a cheery, 'When you like, Geordie.'

'I must be off my rocker.' Geordie shook his head good-naturedly. 'Look at the time! We still ain't done a stroke. And I'm payin' him day money.'

'And piss poor it is at that.' Irish winked at Robby as the van rattled into life. 'Now mind you be good.'

Vi was seated at her kitchen table busily marking a *Sun* bingo card. The radio was on and she was humming along with the sound, smiling her pleasure as she marked the numbers. Two cups stood on the work surface nearby and when the front door banged, she rose to lift the teapot, not sure whether to fill Robby's or Tommy's.

Her momentary indecision was resolved by Tommy's entrance.

'It's me,' he said, sounding nervous, which was no more like him than the smartly-pressed suit he was wearing or the bunch of flowers he was concealing behind his back.

'I can see that.' Vi poured tea. 'Ten to one if I'd jumped the gun an' poured yours, it'd've been Robby.'

Tommy came across the kitchen like a man walking on thin ice, extending the flowers.

'For you.'

Vi smiled with unfeigned pleasure, then frowned: surprised.

'What you after?' She noticed the suit; the tie; the clean shirt. 'All done up like a dog's dinner at this hour.'

Tommy fidgeted with the flowers until she took them from him, then took her arm and steered her to a chair. Confused, Vi sat down, staring at him.

'You're right,' he said, 'I am after something.'

'Tommy!' Alarm sounded in Vi's voice. 'Has something happened?'

'No. Nothin' like that.' Tommy was quick to reassure her, though still nervous as he took a small, square box from his jacket. 'We been seein' each other for a long time now, girl.' He opened the box to expose a ring: gold, with small diamonds. 'I just thought it was time we did things all proper, like. I want us to get hitched, luv. Before it's too late.'

The words came out in a rush, as though he was afraid she might hush him before he could finish. They took her by surprise, incomprehension clouding her face to be rapidly replaced by pleasure.

'What?' she said, for want of anything better. 'You silly old beggar.'

Tommy went on grinning, fingering the knot of his tie like any nervous suitor.

Vi was dusting Robby's room when her son came in, shaking her head as she caught sight of his weary face.

'You look like you could sleep for a fortnight.'

73

'Be the death of me,' Robby grinned, shucking out of his coat and opening his wardrobe to rummage inside. 'Any clean shirts?'

'If you put them in the laundry like you're supposed to.' Vi lifted a collection of dirty washing from the floor.

'You gonna start naggin' again?' Robby moved towards the chess board, but Vi headed him off.

'Er, Robby. Son.'

She sounded awkward, almost embarrassed. Robby heard the seriousness in her voice and turned to face her.

'You need some dough?' He began to pull notes from his pocket.

'No. I don't need money.' She plucked at the duster in her hands.

'Oh, I got it!' Robby put a mock-serious expression on his face. 'You're in the club. That randy Tommy!'

He broke off at the look on her own face, waiting to hear what obviously had to be important news.

'It's about me and Tommy, son. Well, you see, we … Me an' Tommy have had a chat.'

Robby recalled his own conversation with Tommy about the older man's intentions and guessed what was coming. Not wanting to spoil his mother's surprise, he said nothing, just waited expectantly.

'Yes, and …' Vi said, looking for the right words. 'Well, the thing is … Robby, I …'

At a loss, she lifted her left hand, the diamonds glinting. Robby assumed a shocked expression.

'Mother! You don't mean?'

He held the look as Vi nodded, trying to decide if he was genuinely upset. The look on her face made it difficult for him to keep up the pretence and a huge smile creased his features as he said enthusiastically, 'Fantastic! 'Bout time an' all!'

He folded her into a bear hug as she asked, 'You don't mind then?'

'Mind? Me? He eased her away, still smiling. 'I was gonna have words with that young Thomas about his intentions, anyway.'

74

'Oh, Robby. Son.' Vi went back into his arms, hugging him close with tears of pure joy moistening her eyes.

'Great!' he chuckled. 'Now listen, young lady, tonight we get drunk! All of us.'

It felt good: one way and another, everything seemed to be working out for the best.

A while later he wasn't so sure. The previous night's game was taking its toll as he walked along the street checking the numbers. The one he was looking for belonged to a doorway jammed between a delicatessen and a hairdresser's. There were several brass nameplates bolted to the wood, the one he was seeking announcing the premises of Symbols & James, Accountants. Robby studied the plate for a while before taking a breath deep enough to herald a dive into cold water. Then he pushed the door open and began to climb the stairs.

Edward Symbols was a garden gnome of a man, all ruddy, round cheeks and twinkling blue eyes as he listened to Robby's account of his life, taking notes on a small sheet of scrap paper.

When Robby was done, the accountant said, 'It's not a problem as uncommon as you may think, Mr Box.'

'So what's it all top up to?' asked Robby warily. 'How do I start?'

'You do realize you will have to pay?' Symbols smiled benignly over the tops of his half-frame spectacles. 'The Inland Revenue is not in the habit of letting chaps like you get off scot-free.'

'How much?' asked Robby, directly.

Symbols shrugged. 'Until I can make an assessment of your earnings for the past twenty years ...'

'How do we do that?' Robby could feel doubt like a dog worrying at the edges of his mind. It didn't feel like the straight life would be easy to achieve.

'It won't be easy,' Symbols confirmed. 'You do realize that once we start the ball rolling – make it official – it is then unstoppable? No turning back! Once the Inland Revenue have got their sharp little teeth into you, they won't let go until you bleed.'

He smiled as though his announcement should be taken as comforting. Robby looked the way he felt: worried. Symbols asked almost casually, 'Have you got access to a sum of around £10,000, Mr Box?'

The noughts danced in Robby's mind, drying his throat so that his voice came out hoarse as he gasped, 'How much?'

'Twenty years tax,' said Symbols cheerfully. 'Twenty years National Health contributions, penalties, my fees, etcetera, etcetera. That's just an educated guess – a sort of round figure – of what your final bill could arrive at. It may not be as much.'

'Listen,' said Robby in a strangled voice, 'can I think about it? You know, before we make any moves?'

Symbols nodded. 'Of course. Anything you tell me is in the strictest confidence. My job is to help you – not get you deeper in trouble. But Mr Box, do think carefully about this. And remember that the sooner you do get your affairs sorted out, the better. The longer you leave it, the deeper you are in debt.'

'Ten grand,' Robby murmured, not asking a question.

'Give or take a few hundred,' Symbols agreed with gnomic good humour. 'I'd need to go into greater detail.'

'Yeah.' Robby stood up, swallowing hard. 'Thanks. I'll be in touch.'

Symbols went on smiling as he watched the door close. Robby wasn't: there were too many doors closing on him. Ten thousand pound doors.

He went home to find another problem, though in comparison it really wasn't anything, just the mess Vi's dusting had made of his chess board. He stared at it, then saw the taxi cab pamphlets beside the board. They seemed to mock him and he picked them up with a sorry shake of his head. Tore them to hopeless pieces.

'Another brilliant idea up the shooter then, son?'

Tommy stood at the open door, watching Robby with a concerned expression on his weather-beaten face.

'Looks like it, mate.' Robby let the pieces drift onto the disarranged chess board. 'Was a bit unrealistic when you weigh it all up.'

Tommy moved into the room, face framing a question. Robby shrugged and said, 'I just fronted up to something I've been running away from for far too long.' Then he smiled at Tommy's confused frown, changing the subject. 'You finally did it, then! Mum's well chuffed.'

'Yeah!' A smile replaced Tommy's worried look. 'What's the score with you an' Jan? Still a prospect?'

'Shouldn't wait on us, Tom.' Robby grinned ruefully. 'The way things are shaping, that could be fatal.'

Tommy decided that silence was the better part of friendship. If Robby had problems, he'd keep them to himself; if he wanted to talk, he'd let his friends know. Instead of speaking, Tommy studied Vi's rearrangement of the chessmen. Then he did speak. 'Bloomin' hell!'

The Railway Arms was crowded. Noisy with the sounds of celebration: despite his own problems, Robby was as good as his word, and the party to baptise the engagement was in full swing.

'There you go!' Robby poured champagne for Vi and Tommy. 'Get that down you!'

He filled his own glass and passed the bottle on, waiting until everyone was topped before shouting over the cheers of encouragement, 'Right! A toast! To my old mum and Tommy. Health, wealth, and all the happiness in the world! Go on, get sozzled – the pair of you.'

He smiled as the glasses were emptied and the toast echoed, then threw a wad of notes down on the bar. 'Let us know when you need some more.'

Gil and Juicy Joan broke away from the crowd studying Vi's ring. Gil asked, 'Where's your good lady, son?'

'Geordie's pickin' her up,' Robby answered.

'Don't worry, luv,' Joan winked suggestively, 'I'll be discreet, I promise.'

Robby laughed, then looked away as the door opened and Geordie escorted Jan and Debby into the room.

'Hallo, Princess. Debs. Come an' meet the gang.'

It was the first time Jan had encountered Robby's betting shop cronies. They seemed a friendly bunch and before very long she was feeling completely at home, drinking champagne and congratulating the engaged couple as Debby fussed over Ferret's greyhound.

'I should mind how you go with that mutt, Debs,' Kipper warned her. 'You're likely to catch something 'orrible.'

The dog looked at him lazily, then returned to luxuriating in the unusual attention.

'Do you race him, Ferret?' Debby asked, producing a hoot of derision from Kipper.

'Not yet, darlin'.' Ferret glared balefully at Kipper, then smiled at Debby. 'He's a bit young. But soon I'll start trainin' him.'

'Oh, my Gawd!' Kipper spluttered.

Over by the bar, Robby and Jan were talking to Joan and Gil. Gil was saying, 'Old Irish looks a bit rough.'

'Yeah.' Robby craned round to study the grey-faced man. 'Geordie said he was gonna take him home.'

'I'll give a hand,' Gil announced, moving away.

Vi called Joan over and Jan turned laughing to Robby, 'She's quite taken with you.'

'Leave off.' Robby put both arms round her, enjoying the feeling. 'What about you?'

'Mmm.' Jan raised her eyebrows archly. 'I can take you or leave you.' Then, more seriously, 'Robby, did you see the accountant?'

For an instant a cloud darkened Robby's face. He sighed as he said, 'Yeah, I saw him.'

Jan waited for something more, but all he said was, 'Later.'

'Robby,' she began, only to be interrupted by the barmaid.

'Burnt a hole in that lot I'm afraid, Rob.'

'Keep it coming, babe.' Robby extracted more notes and handed them to her, knowing that Jan was waiting for some kind of explanation and not wanting to spoil the party. Not really wanting to think about it. He grinned at her. 'Well, it ain't every day your mum gets proposed to, is it?'

Jan watched him move to help with Irish, knowing he was avoiding an explanation and that his very reluctance to talk about it meant bad news. *Oh, Robby,* she thought, *we have to talk about it. We have to face up to it. Together. If we just do it together I know I can help you. Please let me.*

'Oh, I'm exhausted!'

Jan collapsed onto her sofa, smiling at Robby and her daughter.

'Me, too,' agreed Debby. 'Had a good time, though.'

'You gonna be a bridesmaid then?' Robby smiled.

'It won't be a church wedding, will it?' Debby asked.

'No, it won't,' Jan said. 'And the plan is to marry in the spring. Now, young lady ...'

'I know.' Debby nodded dutifully. 'Bed.'

She kissed her mother, then Robby.

'Night.' She paused at the door, winking as she caught Jan's eye. 'Spring's a good time, I reckon.'

'Cheeky monkey,' smiled Jan, catching her daughter's drift. 'But bed sounds like a good idea.'

'Yeah.' Robby nodded, realizing that the time for explanations was rapidly approaching. 'I'll second that.'

He took his time in the bathroom, putting off the moment as he studied his face. Smeared toothpaste apart, it wasn't bad. Not considering what he had on his mind. Forty-one years old and not even existing officially. Living with his mother, who was soon going to be married again. Living off cards and horses and dogs, with the promise of a £10,000 bill if he did what Jan wanted and tried to go straight. He sighed as he wiped his mouth. Then grinned as he thought that in the bedroom there was a very pretty blonde waiting for him. Things couldn't be all that bad.

He joined her in bed and told her what Symbols had said.

'That's what the man estimates,' he told her. 'Could be less, but I doubt it, knowing my luck.'

Jan felt her plans crumble and snuggled tighter into the crook of his arm.

'Oh, Robby! What hope is there?'

'Hey, c'mon. It ain't as bad as all that.' Robby grinned despite his own doubts, not wanting to spoil the evening. 'With a little bit of old Lady Luck I can rake that up in no time.'

There was less confidence behind the words than he put into them, and Jan knew it. She eased away from him to prop herself up on a worried elbow.

'Robby, please! You're talking about ten thousand pounds. Maybe more!'

'I know what I'm talking about, Princess.' There was a decisive finality to his tone. 'And there's only one way I'm gonna get that sort of money.'

'Gambling,' Jan said; with a different kind of finality.

'That's all I know,' he murmured.

'I could sell this place ...'

'No!' Robby cut her short abruptly. 'No way!'

Loving him, wanting to help him, Jan began to protest, but he over-rode her.

'I said *no*, and I mean it! That ain't even in the frame.'

'Gambling's not the answer.' There were tears in Jan's eyes now.

'Well, what else do you suggest I do?' Robby found it hard to keep the bitterness from his voice. 'Rob a bank? Do a bit of skull?'

'No,' Jan snuffled. 'But if I sold this we could maybe go to Australia and start ...'

'No!' Again he cut her off, and this time Jan saw that she had to accept it. It was part of the independence she admired in him. An essential part of Robby Box. She heard him say, 'I don't wanna hear that any more. OK?' And closed her eyes in hopeless resignation, fighting the tears that threatened to spill over the pillow.

Robby pulled her close, speaking into her hair.

'To the average guy, ten grand's a lifetime's work. I've gone through that sort of dough in weeks.'

'That's just the problem,' she whispered.

'I can do it,' he said fiercely. 'I can do it my way. Have a bit of faith.'

'Robby,' she said, 'I don't have any option.'

He looked into her eyes and saw the love there. *Can't be all bad*. He drew her closer and kissed her full on the lips.

'Listen. I've got nearly two grand in my sky, so we're off to a flyin' start.'

'Have you?' Jan was surprised.

'Put to work in the right quarter over the next few days …'

Jan leant on her elbow again, clutching at the straw of hope. 'Why don't you put some – say half of it – in a bank? Or a Building Society?'

'I don't have a bank,' he retorted. 'Or a Building Society.'

'You could start an account.' She was enthusiastic now. 'I'll do it for you.'

'Nah.' Robby shook his head. 'I need it where I can get me hands on it. I've got to make it work for me.'

'But it will be working for you, love,' she protested.

'Let me do it my way, Princess,' he asked. 'Trust me.'

Robby was gone early in the morning and Jan busied herself getting Debby ready for school.

'Come on, young lady!' she warned. 'You'll be late again.'

'It's all right.' Debby answered the admonishment with a yawn. 'Pauline Harvey's gate monitor.'

'And what's that got to do with the price of coal?' Jan asked.

'She won't put my name in the book,' Debby explained.

'Oh, what it is to have friends in high places,' chuckled Jan. 'C'mon, move your bum!'

Reluctantly, Debby climbed to her feet, remembering at the last moment to hand Jan a small package.

'Oh, yes. Robby left this.'

Intrigued, Jan murmured goodbye as her daughter left the house, and tore the wrapping. Inside was a rectangular box. In the box was the gold necklace.

Despite everything, Jan began to laugh.

CHAPTER SEVEN

Robby had never been the kind of man who hoards his money. So far as he could see, the point of making the stuff was to enjoy spending it: it was easy come, easy go, and no point crying over the losses. Mostly, he managed to stay far enough ahead of the game that he usually had at least a few pound notes in his pocket, and when he found himself short there was always a way to organize a stake – using Jan's necklace, often as not. Now all that was changed: coming so close to losing Jan had taught him that there was more he wanted, and the only way to secure their future looked to be saving up like any regular punter. It wasn't easy for him, but he was determined to give it a go, and when Robby Box made up his mind about something he usually stuck with it to the bitter end. At Jan's suggestion, they had worked out an arrangement that he was doing his best to keep to.

'Two and a half,' he said, handing Jan notes. 'OK?'

'Two and a half it is, Mr Box,' she smiled. 'There's no need to be so grudging.'

'I'm not,' he replied; grudgingly.

Jan laughed as she walked across the bedroom to deposit the money in her dressing-table. 'Anyone would think you were giving it to me.'

'I am!' Robby protested.

'It's still your money, mate.' Jan slid the drawer closed.

Robby watched it like a man watching an old friend go out of his life. 'But it's not in my pocket, is it?' he said.

'It's the only way.' Jan smiled encouragingly.

'I know,' Robby allowed, reluctantly.

'Kept any for yourself?' Jan asked.

'No.' Robby shook his head.

'I don't believe you,' said Jan, smiling at him.

'Well.' Robby shrugged. 'A fiver for some fags.'

'And something for the two o'clock at Haydock?'

'Newbury,' he corrected automatically, grinning as he realized he had been tripped up.

'Say no more,' Jan chuckled.

Robby asked, 'How much you got now?'

And Jan answered, 'Never you mind.'

'Just need the big one, he said, thoughtfully.

'That must be the gambler's motto,' Jan murmured reprovingly.

'I've done it before,' he told her. 'There've been times when I've walked out of a spieler with three grand in my sky.'

'And times,' Jan countered, 'when you've walked out potless.'

'I'll do it, you know.' There was determination in Robby's voice.

Jan nodded. '*We'll* do it.'

Robby put his arms around her waist and kissed her. Jan responded, then pulled away as he sought to manoeuvre her to the bed, protesting that she had a job to go to. It was one of the difficulties of their affair: Robby's way of life kept him up most of the night and by the time he got to her place, Jan was usually getting ready for work. It was one thing that would be resolved by the regularization of his life.

'The office calls.' Jan slipped free of his grip, smiling. 'Get yourself a cup of tea and a cold shower. I'll see you later.'

Robby looked disappointed as she quit the room, then wandered into the kitchen where Debby was finishing her breakfast. The teenager grinned at him.

'How was your night at the office, dear?'

'Murder.' Robby joined in the game as he investigated the teapot. 'Stocks rising, shares dropping. I don't know if I can go on much longer.'

'You'll have to cut down on the staff,' Debby laughed.

'I have,' said Robby solemnly. 'Had three of them shot at midnight.'

Debby spluttered toast crumbs. 'You're a hard man, Mr Box.'

'It's either that or go under.' He poured tea and joined the girl at the table. 'Competition is cut-throat in the City. One of our competitors threw himself off the NatWest tower this morning. Strawberry jam all over Threadneedle Street.'

'You'd think they'd be more considerate,' Debby managed before dissolving into helpless giggles.

Robby sipped tea, then caught sight of the time, his face getting serious. 'You'd better get a move on.'

Debby pouted. 'I don't fancy it today.'

'You don't fancy it any day,' Robby countered.

'It's all right for you,' Debby said, serious herself now.

'What's that supposed to mean?' Robby was confused by her abrupt change of mood.

'Well,' she replied, 'when did you leave school?'

'You haven't got that long.' Robby frowned as he studied her pretty face. 'Just hold on, that's all.'

'What's the point?' Debby stared at him. 'It's not going to make any difference how many exams I pass. We're all going to be equal on the dole queue. You need to have been at Cambridge these days to get a job sweeping the streets.'

There wasn't any answer he could think of, so he said, 'Just stick it out, that's all.'

'I'll end up getting married like the rest of them.'

Debby's tone was flat, cynical. Robby protested, 'Don't be silly.'

'It's true,' Debby told him. 'Do you know that sixty per cent of last year's class are pregnant now?'

'Debby,' he began, not sure what he was going to say next and almost grateful that she interrupted him.

'It's all right for you. Your generation had it easy.'

'You think so?' Suddenly he was feeling uncomfortable, unable to find any countering arguments other than the usual patronizing platitudes.

'I know so,' she told him definitely. 'You had a choice. We haven't.'

'Look, I know it's difficult,' he attempted. 'But it's not impossible.'

'That's just chat, Robby Box.' Debby stared at him with something like hostility in her eyes. 'You sound like one of my teachers.'

'Do I?' He felt hurt.

'It's not even worth going in.' Dully now.

'You've not been skiving, have you?' Alarmed.

'No.' Debby shook her head, staring morosely at the dregs of her tea. Robby studied her blonde hair, wanting to reassure her, wanting to help her. Not knowing how.

'Let's drop it, shall we?' he suggested.

'Oh, yeah.' She looked up, lips curling in contempt. 'Avoid the issue. Change the subject.'

'You're gonna be late,' he warned again.

Debby looked at him for a long moment, her youthful face very serious. 'It's all very well playing the substitute dad,' she said at last. 'But when it comes to the nitty gritty, you don't want to know, do you?'

That hurt, and Robby didn't know what to say. Finally he decided on, 'Well, I better be going.'

He put his cup in the sink and moved towards the door, halting as Debby said, 'Why don't you just marry Mum and get it over with?'

'Eh?' He was taken aback.

'Nothing.' Grumpily. Then, mood changing abruptly as it had begun, 'Come on. You can walk me down the road.'

'That's a oner, OK?' Robby handed money to Vi. 'Keep a score for yourself and put the rest by for me.'

'What you givin' it to me for?' Vi asked.

'I'm trying to save, aren't I?' he explained.

Vi frowned. 'Why can't you do it yourself?'

'How long've you known me?' Robby grinned.

'Well.' Vi assumed a serious expression. 'According to the medical reports, I was the first person you met.'

'Exactly,' Robby nodded as though that explained

everything. 'Shove it under the mattress 'til I need it?'

Vi shrugged, folding the notes into a pocket of her apron, 'Why don't you give it to Jan?'

Robby's face stayed straight as he said, 'Don't be soppy.'

'She'd be much better than me,' Vi protested.

'You're my mum, aren't you, Doll?'

'What's that mean?'

'Blood's thicker, ain't it?'

'Eh?' Confused.

'She could always do a runner, couldn't she?' Blandly.

'Not Jan.' Vi was definite on that point.

'No,' Robby agreed. 'But you know what I mean.'

Vi shrugged and poured him tea. 'Are you two going to settle down, or what?'

'I'm thinking, ain't I?' Robby left it vague.

'Yeah.' It was beginning to feel like Robby's day for lectures. 'Well, start thinkin' sense. Sort yourself out before it's too late.'

'Leave off, will you?' He wondered why he was getting so much aggravation now that he was making a genuine effort to do exactly that. 'You sound like the Doomsday Book.'

'She's smashing,' said Vi, positively.

'I know.' Robby grinned his agreement.

'Too good for you.'

'Leave it out, will you?' he asked. 'I'm knackered.'

'Well,' said Vi, 'why don't you start living the day the right way round?'

'I will,' he agreed wearily.

'Havin' breakfast before you go to bed.' He might not have spoken. 'It ain't natural. You should get yourself a job in Regent's Park.'

'Eh?' Robby wondered what she was talking about.

'Nocturnal House,' came the explanation. 'Where'd you get this anyway?'

Robby grinned as she patted the wad of notes. 'A pair of queens. Give us a shout at twelve?'

Vi sighed as her son left the kitchen. It was well past time he settled down and, so far as she was concerned, Jan was the one he should settle down with. At his age, he should be sleeping nights and working days, not sitting in smoky spielers all night long and getting home at an hour when working folk were just starting their business, only to get up in time for the betting shop, never knowing whether he'd have money at the end of the day or nothing in his pocket. She patted the notes he had given her: at least that was a start in the right direction.

Robby went into his room, where Tommy was sitting studying his threatened bishop. The prospective bridegroom looked up as Robby tossed his sheepskin on the bed and remarked, 'I've met three women this mornin' and they've all had a go at me.'

'That's wimmen, ain't it,' Tommy philosophized.

'Is it?' asked Robby.

'No,' was the answer. 'You've just got one o' them faces.'

'Thanks, mate,' Robby grinned.

'How'd you get on last night?' asked Tommy.

'You know me,' Robby said. 'A good gambler never drinks when he's playing, and never shows his cards unless you pay for it.'

Tommy shrugged. 'Just curious, that's all.' He indicated the chess board. 'You been lookin' at them books again?'

'Got you, have I?' The grin on Robby's face got broader.

'That'll be the day,' said Tommy indignantly.

Robby threw himself on the bed alongside the coat and announced that he was worried about Debby. Tommy turned from his threatened chessman.

'Are you?'

'There's somethin' going on in her head,' Robby nodded. 'And I can't get to it.'

'How d'you mean?' asked Tommy.

'That's what I'm sayin'.' Robby frowned. 'I don't know.'

'She's growing up,' Tommy suggested by way of explanation.

'Yeah,' Robby sighed. 'I suppose so. Sometimes she's twelve and the next minute she's forty. Know what I mean?'

'I've never tried to understand women,' said Tommy

placidly. 'I've just gone through life bein' constantly amazed.'

'Yeah.' Robby sounded thoughtful as he sat up and began to remove his shirt, yawning prodigiously. 'Right! That's me then.'

'I'll leave you to it.' Tommy rose to go, pausing at the door to indicate the chess board again. 'Let's go to one some day.'

'Eh?' Robby was confused. It was getting to be a habit.

'Chess match,' said Tommy. 'I've always fancied that. They put it on a screen, just like the pictures. We could go an' have a look.'

'Why not?' Robby agreed sleepily, and began to peel off his trousers.

When he woke again, Robby left the house and made his way to the market. There was a stall there run by a West Indian called Aaron who sold records: he had promised to locate some Mantovani for Robby. En route, however, Robby wanted a word with Albert, an old friend who manned a fruit and vegetable barrow and whose sense of humour was usually guaranteed to cheer him up. Right now, he felt, he needed some cheering. He was making an honest effort to put enough money by to get himself sorted out, but it felt like all the women in his life were getting at him for one reason or another. Albert might just lift him out of the mood.

He spotted the ruddy face under an ancient flat cap as Albert finished dumping five pounds of King Edwards into a green plastic shopping bag held by a woman who looked as if she had green plastic hair to match.

'How's it going?' he asked.

'Terrible,' answered Albert, sincerely. 'The arse 'as gone out of it, son. Ever since people went microbionic.'

'You what?' It was time to feel confused again.

'You know,' Albert explained. 'Brown rice an' all that horse manure.'

'I put it on me rhubarb,' said Robby.

'That's funny.' Albert said it with a straight face. 'I put custard on mine.'

They laughed together, his friend's irrepressible good humour working its effect on Robby.

'So what's occurring?' he asked.

Albert shrugged. 'George got a two-year suspended for kiteing, and the cat's dead.'

'Two years?' Robby felt his new-found good humour slipping. 'That's a result, ain't it? That's his second time around.'

'No room.' Albert grinned like he was delivering the punch line of a joke. 'Her Majesty's runnin' out of dossin' space.'

'Nice one.' Robby chuckled, feeling good again.

'Mind you,' Albert warned, 'he's got to sign on twice a day.'

'Better than filin' at an iron bar,' Robby commented.

Albert nodded, then, 'As it 'appens, you've crossed my path at a perfect time.'

'Tell us,' urged Robby.

'I tell.' Albert held up a paper folded to the sports pages. 'It's all here in black and white − Stroller. Eight-thirty at Windsor. Can't lose.'

'Don't tell me,' Robby said. 'It's the horse's mouth?'

'More'n that,' Albert said. 'The trainer of the horse's mouth!'

'Oh, yeah?' Robby was dubious.

Albert was earnest. 'Straight up! It's come in from Ireland. Just for the one off.'

'How'd it get here?' demanded Robby. 'Swim?'

'It's racin' against two donkeys,' said Albert. 'If it 'ad its legs tied together it couldn't lose.'

Robby remained wary and Albert continued, 'The brother-in-law of the trainer's sister gets her weekend cauliflower from yours truly. She's only blown in me ear once before, an' it laughed all the way to the winning post.'

'Was it runnin' on its own?' Robby queried.

'Listen.' Albert shook his head in mock exasperation. 'Do yourself a favour.'

'I will,' Robby agreed, deciding Stroller was too good an opportunity to risk turning down.

'She says get on the course,' Albert warned.

'Why's that?' Robby wanted to know.

'You won't get the odds in the shop.'

That piece of news confirmed it. Robby asked, 'She's that serious?'

'I'm tellin' you,' said Albert, solemnly.

'What sort of price you talkin' about?'

'Let's put it this way.' Albert winked. 'It's not goin' in as the favourite.'

'Ta, mate.' Robby ignored Albert's protest as he bit into an apple. 'I'll have some of that.'

'You can buy me a drink on the winnings,' Albert shouted as his friend wandered off in the direction of Aaron's stall.

Aaron was tall and skinny, the multi-coloured knitted beret that hid his dreadlocks making him resemble a psychedelic mushroom. Bob Marley blasted at close to full volume from the speaker cans rigged on his barrow and Aaron was fingerpopping to the reggae rhythms.

'Got any Mantovani in?' Robby asked.

'Not this week, man,' Aaron grinned. 'But I'm looking. I've still got your list.'

'Cheers,' Robby said, moving to go.

Aaron called him back, beckoning him to the rear of the stall, where he lowered his voice as he put his mouth close to Robby's ear so that he could be heard over the sound of the Wailers.

'Fancy a game tonight?'

'Where?' Robby always fancied a game.

'Same as last time.'

'You playing?'

'Can't afford it.' Aaron shook his beret ruefully. 'They won't let you sit down without two and a half showing.'

'What time?'

'Midnight.'

'Sounds good.'

Robby grinned, feeling the familiar tingle of anticipation as Aaron set out the requirements for taking part in what sounded like a biggish game. The kind that could help his stake along. When they had finished, Robby left the market and made his way to the betting shop. Apart from Ferret and Black George – and, of course, Ferret's dog – the place was empty.

'Where's Windsor?' Robby asked as he walked in.

'A few miles down the M4,' answered Ferret.

George laughed as Robby said, 'Don't be a turd,' impatiently.

'Here it is.' Ferret pointed out a newspaper. 'What do you want to know?'

'Stroller,' Robby explained. 'In the eight-thirty.'

Ferret and George joined him by the paper. Ferret said, 'Here we are. Stroller, eight-thirty. It's not been out before. Irish.'

'Five to one,' mused Robby.

'You know something?' asked Ferret.

'Maybe.' Robby was cautious.

'You gonna row us in, or what?' demanded the dog owner.

Robby grunted thoughtfully. Then he said, 'Come on. Let's have a swift half.'

'If you're payin',' said Ferret, urging the greyhound to its feet.

George just looked at the time and shook his head without saying anything. George seldom said anything: his system of communication consisted mainly of smiles, nods and shakes of the head. Robby shrugged and led the way out.

'So I need two and a half for tonight,' Robby explained as they propped up the bar of the Railway Arms. 'An' I ain't got it.'

'Well, don't look at me,' warned Ferret.

'There's no way Jan'll give me that much.' Robby spoke as much to himself as to his companion. 'A fifty at the most.'

'Well that's that, then,' Ferret said, turning to his beer.

'No.' Robby shook his head. 'If I can get a fifty, trot down to Windsor for the eight-thirty, get the best price I can, then I'll be back in time for the midnight special.'

'What happens if it loses?'

'It loses.' Robby was fatalistic. 'Listen, this lot are a bunch of wallies. I've played against them before. They're all flash and no brains. If they're all going in with two and a half, I could come out smiling.'

'Why can't you just have the bet in the shop?' Ferret wondered.

'Because, you berk,' Robby said, 'I wouldn't get paid out until tomorrow. By which time the little school will've flown. But if I get down to Windsor tonight, they'll pay me off on the course. And I'll be sitting in with Aaron's mates, smiling from here to breakfast.'

Ferret nodded his understanding and they finished their beers in contented silence. Matters were sorted out, well in hand: Robby was looking forward to increasing his 'straight' money.

A little way from the pub, Robby passed a chippy. A queue was lining the street outside and the man and woman behind the counter were working full time to keep their customers supplied. Robby halted, studying the place as he made a quick count of the heads.

'Two pound a head average,' he murmured as he walked on. 'That's got to be forty notes every ten minutes on a good night. And all for a bit of batter and chips.'

The early evening news was depressing viewers as the television in Jan's lounge lost Debby's attention.

'Why doesn't Robby move in here?' she called.

Jan spoke from the bedroom, where she was adjusting Carmen rollers, 'He likes his independence, and so do I.'

'Seems to me it would be more sensible.' Debby sounded thoughtful.

'Than what?' asked her mother.

'Than what we've got now.'

'Well,' Jan said, 'that's how I like it.'

'Do you think you'll ever get together?'

'In what way?'

'You know.' Debby shrugged. 'Marriage. Up the old two-handed aisle.'

'Not at the moment.' Jan paused to study her reflection. 'No.'

'You don't want to leave it too late,' Debby warned.

'What are you talking about?' Jan demanded.

'Well,' said her daughter. 'You're getting on, aren't you?'

'Getting on?' Jan was indignant. 'I'm in my prime, young lady.'

'If you say so.'

Jan sensed something more than casual chatter behind Debby's words. Forgetting her hair, she asked, 'What's all this about?'

'I was just curious, that's all. I mean, I don't think it's all that important. Marriage, that is. Not to my generation, at least. But when you get to your age living in sin's no longer romantic, is it? There's something a bit iffy about it.'

'I think we'd better stop this conversation,' Jan suggested.

Debby ignored the suggestion. 'Did you live with Dad before you married him?'

'We didn't have time,' said Jan, turning back to her hair.

'I think it's important,' said Debby.

'Do you?'

'Well, don't you?' Debby insisted. 'Perhaps if you and Dad had, things would have worked out differently.'

Jan didn't like the way the conversation was heading, so she asked, 'Haven't you any homework to do?'

'That's right, avoid the subject. Don't get involved.' Debby moved towards the door and her homework. 'I was just trying to help, that's all. I think he's fantastic.'

Jan returned to her coiffure, deciding that Debby was going through that difficult stage between childhood and becoming a young woman. A period made no easier by the absence of her natural father, or the irregular nature of Robby's life. She was, however, a resilient girl and Jan felt reasonably confident that she could handle the problem until Robby sorted out his affairs and they settled into some kind of more normal relationship. Until then they all just had to manage as best they could. Dismissing her fears, she rose from the dressing table and went, be-Carmened, into the lounge, settling in front of the television as she waited for her hair to dry. There was a programme she enjoyed showing, a funny-serious thing called *Give us A Break* that rather reminded her of Robby. She glanced up as she heard the front door open and he came into the room.

He kissed her on the neck and murmured, 'Hallo, Princess. I had a cold shower, but it doesn't seem to make any difference.'

Jan turned, responding to his caress, and he saw the rollers in her hair.

'I like the Easter.'

'I thought of wearing them to Ascot,' she giggled.

'You're on, girl.'

He sat down beside her and she saw that he was wearing a sweater and slacks under his old sheepskin. 'What have you come as?' she asked.

Robby was starting to feel that confusion was the order of the day.

'It's not a fancy dress, you know,' she frowned.

'Eh?' Robby frowned back. 'What are you talking about?'

'Well,' she said, 'you don't think you're going out like that do you?'

'Why not?' he shrugged.

'Not with me you're not.' She said it firmly.

And Robby replied innocently, 'I didn't know you wanted to come.'

'What?' It was Jan's turn to feel confused.

'Well,' Robby explained, 'how did I know you was going to Windsor Races?'

'Windsor Races?' Really confused now.

'Just the one.' Frowning: sensing something was wrong. 'I'll be down an' back. Can't lose.'

'Not you, my boy.' Jan shook her head. 'You're wining and dining. Dinner and dancing. It's the bosses' night out, remember?'

'Oh, no!' Robby struck the heel of his hand against his

forehead. 'I completely ...'

'Forgot,' completed Jan. 'Well, now you've remembered. Go on, get home. Put a suit on and get back here as soon as you can.'

'This horse can't lose.' Robby was hopeful.

His hope was soon dashed: Jan said, 'It just has.'

The closed sign was already hanging on the betting shop door when Robby caught Juicy Joan putting out empty milk bottles. She looked up smiling as he came panting towards her, then some more hopes got dashed as he pointed towards Gil's office and asked, 'Is he still here?'

'Yeah,' nodded Joan. 'Just finishing up.'

Robby went past her into the room where Gil Roach was tearing down the day's racing sheets. 'What's this?' the bookie grinned. 'Come to hold me up?'

'That'll be the day.' Robby smiled politely, wanting to get down to business. 'Listen, Gil. Can you do me a favour?'

'No,' was the prompt reply.

'Wait a minute,' protested Robby.

'No favours,' said Gil firmly.

'Look.' Robby pressed his point. 'There's one runnin' at Windsor tonight. I've got to have it.'

'I'm closed.' Gil had strict rules about his business.

'Just the one.'

'Business is done for the day.'

'Gil!' Robby came close to pleading. 'It's me you're talking to.'

'I know,' said Gil, indifferently.

'It can't lose,' said Robby.

Gil chuckled. 'All the more reason for me not to do it. What do you think I am?'

'A gambler like me,' said Robby.

'You tell me a horse can't lose and you expect me to take your bet.' It was, Robby had to admit, logical. Cruel, but still logical. 'What do you think this is? Charity week?'

'Stroller in the eight-thirty.' Robby knew he was appealing to a better nature that didn't exist, but he had to try it: short of offending Jan – which he wanted badly to avoid – he had little other choice. 'I was gonna go down there, but something's cropped up and I'm stymied.'

'Books are shut.' Gil folded the racing sheets and dropped them into a wastebin along with Robby's optimism. 'The accounts are done for the day. Good night.'

'Cheers, mate.' There was a hint of bitterness in Robby's tone. Sarcasm too as he said, 'You're hundred and one.'

He headed for the door, muttering, 'Nothing more depressing than an empty betting shop.'

'You're telling me,' agreed Gil, cheerfully.

He waited until Robby had gone, then went into his office and began to dial a number. When the phone was answered, he said, 'Frank, is that you? Gil here. Listen, could you do me a favour? Lovely. I want to put a oner on Stroller in the eight-thirty at Windsor.'

Robby checked his suit in the mirror above the chess board and slung a tie around his neck as Tommy listened patiently to his instructions.

'... So you get down the course an' get the best price you can find. As soon as it wins, phone the result through to Vi, here, and I'll give her a bell from the do and arrange to meet you before I go on to the spieler.' He handed Tommy money. 'Here. There's a score for you and a brown one for the petrol. I'll tell Vi to give you eighty.'

He began to knot his tie as he put his head around the kitchen door to interrupt his mother's ironing.

'Give Tommy that eighty I gave you this morning. And I'll give you a bell later, sexpot. See you.'

He went out in a hurry, feeling pleased with himself for arranging the bet without upsetting Jan. The annual dinner and dance he had promised her he would attend came close to the botom of his list of ways to spend an evening, especially as they were going as guests of Henry Diamond, but he had promised and he intended to stick to his word. Anyway, so long as Tommy got down to Windsor and came back with the money there shouldn't be any problems. A oner at course odds would supply the readies for Aaron's game, and come morning he should have a tidy bundle to add to the money already stashed with Jan. It was just as well he had had the foresight to cache some where he could lay hands on it without having to explain: Jan wouldn't approve.

So when Jan asked him if he minded missing the race, he could reply honestly, 'Princess, for you – anything. It was only a soppy old gee-gee race. There's plenty more where they came from.'

Jan smiled and moved closer to him on the seat of the mini-cab: this was definite improvement.

They reached the banqueting rooms and Robby suggested Jan go ahead while he settled up with their driver. He counted notes as she entered the hall, then leant close to the open window.

'Listen, mate, come back in an hour. I might need you.'

The driver nodded and Robby smiled happily as he followed Jan in to the dinner and dance.

Inside, a band was playing and couples were dancing as others ate at the tables surrounding the floor. Henry Diamond had a table close to the rostrum, his wife, Alison, Geordie and his wife with him. Robby caught up with Jan as she approached the group, noticing the admiring look Diamond gave her and the less approving glance of the builder's wife. Alison Diamond was a slim, dark-haired woman with a haughty look and a lot of jewellery. She was older than Jan, the years fought of with the aid of cosmetics and aerobics, and she appeared determined to slight her husband. Robby saw that she had been drinking more than was good for her, and that Diamond wasn't happy about it. The man's discomfort amused him. Introductions were effected and Alison dragged Robby onto the dance floor as Diamond seized his opportunity to get close to Jan. Neither dissatisfied partner had much of a chance.

'It's not the policemen who are getting younger,' Alison informed him during the course of a quickstep, 'it's the mothers. I saw one today who must have been all of fifteen. She had one in the pram and one in the hand. Two before

98

you can vote! What kind of a life is that?'

'A lot of people start young so they can get on with their lives afterwards,' Robby argued, trying to hold her farther away.

'Don't you believe it.' Alison did her best to get closer. 'They start young through ignorance.'

Robby thought about Debby as he said, 'You got any kids?'

'Of course.' Alison's laugh was brittle. 'We're the perfect couple, aren't we? Two cars, two kids, two houses. Too much.'

Abruptly, she stopped dancing. 'Come on. Let's have a drink.'

Robby escorted her back to the table, where Diamond and Jan joined them. Alison immediately demanded another bottle of wine and informed the table at large that the meal had been disgusting. That didn't please her husband – he had planned the dinner. Then she caught Robby glancing at his watch and asked him, 'Are you in a hurry, Robby?'

'Sorry,' he smiled. 'I promised to phone my mother.'

Alison roared with drunken laughter, ignoring Diamond's pained expression.

'She's not too well, that's all,' Robby explained, bringing a surprised stare from Jan. 'She had a bit of a turn earlier, and I said I'd ring just to check.'

'What's the matter with her?' Jan asked.

'I don't know.' Robby shook his head, assuming what he hoped was the right expression of concern.

'Isn't Tommy there?' Jan sounded doubtful.

'He had to go out,' said Robby, quickly.

Alison began to annoy Diamond by telling him she had ordered a local building firm to construct a patio, and Robby seized the chance to slip away. Ostensibly to phone his poor, sick mother.

'Vi, it's me,' he said when she answered the insistent ringing. 'What's the SP?'

'You've had a result,' came the answer.

'Terrific,' he said.

'He got there too late,' Vi said.

'What kind of a result's that?' Robby grimaced.

'It lost,' said Vi.

'It couldn't,' said Robby.

'It did,' said Vi.

Robby grunted and put the phone down.

'Listen,' he said back at the table, smiling an apology. 'I've got to shoot for about quarter of an hour. She needs something from the chemist.'

'Chemist?' Jan sounded less than convinced.

'There's a late night one down the road.' Robby was moving before anyone could object. 'Won't be long.'

The mini-cab was waiting outside. Robby jumped in.

Robby opened the door of Jan's house and entered the dark hall. Not bothering to switch on the lights, in fact feeling guilty, he went into the bedroom and slid open the drawer in which he had seen Jan deposit the money. It wasn't there, so he went through the other drawers. And drew blanks. Confused yet again, he flicked the light switch.

And came close to leaving his skin as Debby and a teenaged boy with the memories of pimples still on his face leapt guiltily from the bed.

'What's occurring?' he gasped as his heart began the slow descent from his throat.

'Nothing,' said Debby warily.

'Nothin'?' Robby glared at the boy. 'Out!'

The youth left the room like a greyhound coming out of the trap. Robby had enough time to see that he wasn't undressed; and that a second terrified teenager joined him from the lounge, the pair of them hitting the front door at speed and disappearing into the night.

'What the hell's goin' on?' he demanded of Debby.

'I told you,' she answered defiantly. 'Nothing.'

'Listen you.' Shock made Robby angry: an outraged adult. 'You tell your mum you're going to the pictures – I come back and find you on her bed with some geezer. An' another one running down the hallway. An' you tell me nothin's going on?'

'The other one was with Mau.' Debby was close to tears. 'My mate in the kitchen.'

'What is this?' Robby snapped. 'A bleedin' brothel?'

Anger came through Debby's tears. 'Who do you think you are?'

'Eh?' Robby was taken aback by her vehemence.

'Who the hell do you think you are? Anyone would think this was your place.'

'Just a minute ...' The truth of the statement got Robby confused. Yet again.

'This isn't yours and I'm not yours!' Debby was almost shouting. '*I* live here. She's *my* mum! Coming in here acting as though we're related. Well, we're not! You are not my father! You're my mother's lover, and that's a big difference!'

There was no argument he could muster in the face of that logic. All he could say was, 'Debby.'

She ignored him. 'What makes you think you've got the right to come screaming in here chucking people out? Eh? What makes you think you've got the right? Anyway, I wasn't doing anything wrong. And if I was, it's no different to what you and Mum do.'

'Yeah, but we're ...'

He knew it was feeble even before she cut in, 'Grown up? Don't make me laugh.'

'Yeah.'

Robby accepted defeat and turned towards the door.

'Anyway,' Debby demanded, 'what were you doing here?'

He was caught. There was no answer he could give except, 'Nothing. Same as you.'

The regulation raffle was taking place as Robby got back to the celebrations. As he crossed the floor, he heard the band leader announce, 'And the lucky number is ninety-five, blue.'

Automatically, he took his ticket stub from his pocket. Then halted, grinning in disgusted disbelief as he shook his

101

head and murmured, 'I don't believe it.'

The enormous teddy bear sat between them as the mini-cab brought them back to Jan's place. With no alternatives left, Robby had told Jan about the spieler. She was telling him why he couldn't have the sit-in money.

'I'd love to,' she was saying. 'After all, it's your money. But I can't.'

'Can't?' Robby was getting tired of confusion.

'Well, you don't think I left it in the drawer, do you?'

'Didn't you?' He hadn't explained everything.

'I mean, you're a gambling man,' Jan said. 'Why don't you just go there and win it?'

'There's an entrance fee,' he explained.

'I've got a tenner.'

'Forget it.' He shook his head, not certain whether he felt angry or amused. He knew he felt curious. 'Where is it?'

'What?' Jan stroked the teddy bear's nylon fur.

'The future.'

'Oh.' Jan opened her purse. 'There.'

Robby took the flat blue book she handed him, streetlights showing him the name of the Building Society; Jan's name printed on the first page.

'It's in your name.'

'That's right,' she smiled.

'Why?' he asked, still confused.

'You don't exist.'

He couldn't help grinning. Then Jan began to laugh, leaning across the bulk of the teddy bear to kiss him. He forgot about the spieler.

CHAPTER EIGHT

'You look shagged out, mun.'

Geordie glanced at Robby as the old van slowed for a red light.

'Was a heavy night, mate,' Robby grinned. 'Worth it, though, had a nice result.'

'I've heard that before.' Geordie sounded sceptical. 'Don't forget it's snooker night tonight.'

'Sorry mate.' Robby shook his head. 'I just can't make it.'

'Why not?' Geordie negotiated a corner with an ominous clatter from his gearbox.

'I forgot about the do at Henry Diamond's gaff,' Robby explained. 'It's tonight.'

'What's that got to do with anything?' Geordie protested.

'He's asked Jan to go along because its business,' Robby elaborated. 'Jan said she would only go if I got an invite.'

'And he agreed?' Geordie sounded surprised. 'I don't believe it. I mean, you ain't exactly very popular in that neck of the woods. What's the catch?'

'Trustin' little soul, ain't you?' grinned Robby. 'No catch — just that some of his business buddies are into a hand or three of poker after the dinner bit.'

'Oh, I knew there had to be a reason for you to accept,' chuckled Geordie. 'I should mind how you go, though, Rob. From what I hear, they don't exactly play for pin money.'

'That, my old mate,' Robby said, 'is why I'm going.'

He leaned forward to switch on the radio, noticing that it was considerably younger than the rest of the vehicle.

'Hold tight! What's with all this? Flash new radio?'

'Aye. Right good buy.' Geordie looked pleased with himself. 'A score of notes to Joan's new boyfriend. Terrific, eh?'

'Yeah.' It was Robby's turn to sound sceptical. 'An' for that sort of dough, bent as well.'

'He guaranteed it's legit.' Geordie shrugged. 'He's in the business, or something. Gil got a tannoy system off him. An' a video machine.'

'They have dents?' asked Robby, doubtfully. 'From fallin' off the lorry?'

'Cynic,' Geordie retorted. 'Ask no questions an' you don't get told no lies. Right?'

'Tell that to the Old Bill,' shrugged Robby.

'Thanks for popping in, James.'

Henry Diamond motioned for his accountant to take a seat.

'So what was so important it couldn't wait until tonight?' asked Cook.

'Well, it's about tonight that I wanted to talk to you,' said Diamond.

'Don't tell me there's been a hitch.' Cook shook his head as Diamond offered him a drink. 'You need that contract.'

'Yes, and I've got it.' Diamond sounded confident. 'James, Alison won't be there tonight.'

Cook said, 'Oh,' in a vague way, knowing about Alison's penchant for liquor and not wanting to be involved in his client's personal problems.

'It's all right, James.' Diamond smiled. 'You needn't look so surprised – I think you understand why I've sent her to her parents for a few days.'

'Well,' allowed Cook. 'Under the circumstances, perhaps it's for the best.'

'Too bloody right!' Diamond was fierce. 'The last thing I need tonight is my wife getting pissed out of her tiny mind in front of Dempster and his wife.'

'You're being a little harsh, Henry,' suggested the accountant.

'I know what I'm doing.' Diamond's voice was hard. 'Besides, even when she's sober, Alison hates this kind of evening. She finds it extremely dull. So Jan – my PA – has kindly agreed to stand in. She's far better qualified for the job.'

Cook shrugged. Just as he knew about Alison's drinking problem, so he knew that Diamond had designs on Jan. He did not approve.

'And you needn't look like that, James.' Diamond smiled and sipped whisky. 'This is strictly business. Besides, she'll have the obnoxious boyfriend with her.'

'Oh,' murmured Cook. 'The gambler chappie I was supposed to meet?'

'Yes, the very same.' Diamond's smile got ugly. 'The situation presents a wonderful opportunity, James. Wonderful!'

'I don't follow, Henry.' Cook wasn't sure he wanted to, but he maintained an expression of polite interest.

'We are going to play a few hands of poker after dinner,' said Diamond. Then laughed out loud. 'And I intend to send this waster of a man home penniless. It's high time my lovely PA was made to realize the man's a loser.'

'I thought this was all to be strictly business.' Cook was dubious.

'And so it is, James. So it is,' nodded Diamond pompously. 'But then you know me – never one to miss an opportunity to kill two birds with one stone, eh?'

'Henry, the man may not be the loser you think he is,' warned the accountant. 'You could end up with egg on your face.'

'Oh, come now.' Diamond shook his head. 'James, you of all people know me better than that. When I play, I play to win. And win I shall!'

'You sound confident,' said Cook. 'I'll give you that.'

Diamond nodded conspiratorially. 'Suffice to say, James, that like all good businessmen, I'm not without insurance.'

Diamond raised his glass in a toast to himself. 'Cheers!'

Gil Roach looked up from the centrefold of his *Playboy* as

Tommy knocked on his office door.

'Any luck on that little item I ordered, Gil?'

The bookie stood up and came around his desk, whisking the cover from a new video recorder like a magician climaxing some intricate feat of prestidigitation.

'When I say I can get something, Tommy, I'm as good as my word. It's a cracker, eh?'

'Gor blimey, mate.' Tommy stroked the machine admiringly. 'That really looks the business. Vi'll love it. She always wanted one o' these.'

'She certainly will.' Gil smiled smugly. 'An' at two hundred an' eighty sovs it's a real bargain.'

He ommitted to mention that he had bought the machine from Joan's new boyfriend for only one hundred — a small profit was fair on any deal.

Diamond lounged back in his massive executive chair, toying with a large glass of scotch as he studied the smartly-dressed man sitting across the desk. He was smiling like a cat that has just found a nest of baby mice.

'Albert at the club tells me you're one of the best, Larry,' he remarked.

'I try, Mr Diamond.' Larry shrugged modestly. 'I try.'

'Modest, too,' Diamond chuckled. 'I like that. Show me a sample of Albert's faith.'

He took his feet off the desk long enough to extract a pack of cards from the topmost drawer and pass it to the middle-aged man. Larry took the cards with a faint smile, breaking the seal and executing an eye-dazzling shuffle.

'Would you be so kind?' He motioned for Diamond to cut the deck, then dealt two hands. Diamond lifted his to find four kings and the jack of Diamonds.

'Now that's a nice hand,' Larry,' he said.

'Yes,' agreed the card player. 'But this one's better.'

He spread four aces and the queen of Diamonds on the desk. Henry came close to choking on his drink.

Tommy frowned at the repair shop manager, indicating the new video machine.

'The red light comes on an' it makes a noise an' that's it. Can't get nothing else out of the blooming thing.'

'Have you tuned it in to your TV set, mate?' The repairman had the long-suffering patience of someone used to dealing with idiots. 'If you ain't done that ...'

'Tuned it in?' Tommy stared at the man with incomprehension written large on his face.

'Yeah, it's got to be tuned in,' said the man patiently. 'Look, what kind of set have you got?'

'Like that one over there.' Tommy pointed at one of the televisions shelved along the wall. 'Same as that.'

'All right, leave it with us old son.' The repairman tore a ticket in two, handing one half to Tommy. 'I'll see what I can do. It sounds like all it needs is re-tuning. Call back in half an hour, OK?'

'Right you are.' Tommy smiled his gratitude. 'Thanks, son.'

The manager watched him go out of the shop, then lifted the video recorder to study the serial numbers stamped on the base with a thoughtful frown.

Robby and Jan had had lunch together and Robby had seen her back to the office, arriving just in time to see Larry leaving. Robby stood aside to let the man through the door as Diamond called cheerfully, 'Thanks for your time, Larry. See you tonight.' Then, with the same cheerful expression, 'And how's Robby?'

'So, so, Henry.' Robby was not accustomed to such bonhomie. 'Yourself?'

'Fine! I'm fine,' said Diamond. 'See you tonight?'

'Looking forward to it, Henry.'

'Yes, so am I,' smiled Diamond, going back into his office.

'Who was the face that just left, Princess?' Robby asked. 'D'you know?'

'I've no idea,' Jan said. 'There wasn't anything in the appointment book. Why, love?'

'Oh, nothing,' frowned Robby. 'He looked familiar, that's all.'

They were about to kiss, but Diamond opened the door, interrupting them to ask Jan to call the caterers and warn them there would be an extra guest.

'Yes, Henry,' she agreed dutifully, turning to Robby as the door closed to say, 'This is turning into the last supper.'

'Yeah.' Robby was thoughtful. 'That bloke that just left? Henry did say, see you tonight, didn't he?'

Tommy returned to the repair shop to find the manager looking worried. In answer to Tommy's enquiry, the man said, 'Just a moment, mate,' and ducked through a door at the rear. Tommy waited for him to re-emerge with the tuned video machine, but instead two men in dark suits came out, one of them carrying the recorder in a clear plastic bag. They both had short-cut hair and serious expressions. The larger of the pair asked, 'This item belongs to you does it, sir?' And showed Tommy a CID warrant card. 'Would you mind stepping down to the station to answer a few questions?'

It wasn't really a request.

Debby came home from school to find an envelope on the mat by the door. Typed on it was the word 'urgent' and 'Mr Robert Box'. Debby studied the envelope curiously, then decided that she had better take it round to Robby straight away.

Vi opened the door and smiled. Debby said, 'This was round home,' waving the envelope. 'It's addressed to Robby.'

'He's in his room,' said Vi. 'Come in.'

She led the way to Robby's room, where he lay in bed, sound asleep.

'Cor, just look at it, would you?' murmured Vi. 'He don't sleep – he goes into a semi-coma.'

'Does he always sleep with his mouth open?' wondered Debby. 'Looks horrible, doesn't it?'

'I dunno if I should wake him,' said Vi.

'It does say "urgent", Vi.' Debby shrugged, intrigued by the mysterious letter. 'That's why I brought it round.'

They looked at one another and began to giggle.

'I'm dying to know what's in it,' Vi remarked.

'Yeah,' said Debby. 'Me, too.'

'Well.' Vi took a step into the curtained room. 'Let's see if I can bring him back from the dead.'

'Where was he last night?' asked Debby as the older woman shook her son.

'Where d'you think?' Vi had to lean across the bed as Robby grunted in his sleep and rolled over. 'A spieler. Like always. Up all night, then sleeps the day away. I hope your mum can mend his ways for him – I've just about given up.'

She went on shaking Robby as she spoke and after a few turns, he opened his eyes and peered blearily over the covers.

'Gordon Bennett! What's up? The house on fire, or something?'

'Debby's got a letter for you,' said Vi.

'It's marked "urgent",' said Debby. 'I found it when I got home.'

'Eh?' Robby sat up, rubbing at his eyes. 'Home?'

'My place,' said Debby. 'Addressed to you. All very formal.'

'Give it here then,' Robby yawned.

Debby handed him the envelope and he tore it open, unfolding the single sheet of notepaper inside as the two females watched him, fascinated.

'Well, well, well,' he murmured, grinning. 'Thanks for bringing it round, Debs. You'd better get off home now.'

He folded the note back into the envelope and tucked it under his pillow. Then he settled down again, dragging the covers up to his chin.

Curiosity frustrated, they stared at him in disappointment.

'Ain't you going to tell us what it says, Robby?' asked Debby.

'Is it important?' asked Vi.

Robby peered at them from under the covers. 'Look, d'you mind? I'm dead tired.'

Vi and Debby stared at the bed, then at one another. In the hall, the phone began to ring. Robby groaned.

'You sleep with your mouth open,' Debby observed. 'Did you know that?'

'No.' Robby sat up again, reluctantly. 'No, I didn't know that. Now, if you don't mind?'

He began to settle back to sleep, but Vi came in with a panic-stricken expression.

'Robby! Robby, it's Tommy! He's been arrested and he wants you to go down the nick!'

'Tommy?' All thought of sleep left Robby. 'Arrested?'

'Why won't they let us see him, Robby?'

Vi paced anxiously up and down the station room as her son sat trying hard to stay awake.

'They will, don't worry.' Robby yawned. 'Do you know who he bought this video recorder from?'

'I don't know a thing about it.' Vi came close to tears, starting nervously as a youthful Detective Constable entered the waiting room.

'Right,' he said. 'Sorry to have kept you. If you'd like to go through to the second door on the left, madam?'

'I can see him?' The way Vi said it, made it sound like a visit to Alcatraz.

'Five minutes, OK?' nodded the DC.

Vi went in a hurry. Robby moved to follow her, but the officer halted him. 'My guvnor would like a quick word. D'you mind?'

'Oh, yeah?' Robby felt an instinctive wariness around the law. 'What about?'

'Just a quick word.' The DC smiled politely, ushering Robby out.

They went down the corridor to the office of the Detective Superintendent. Robby was waved to a chair across from a bluff, grey-haired man with a littered desk and nicotine-stained fingers. He began to explain the situation, outlining an operation in thievery they had been watching for some time.

'It's very simple, Mr Box. The Spanish half of the team

110

suss out potential targets – they normally get a young woman to get friendly with a couple they've selected. And then, if they think they're right, they set them up for a mugging. Lift their keys long enough to get copies made so the home team can walk into a place they know is empty and take their time clearing it. They got it all worked out – it's a real tidy operation.'

'An' you think Tommy's involved in something like that?' Robby forgot his weariness as he glared at the DS. 'You're off your rocker, chief.'

'Listen, son.' The detective sounded careworn, accustomed to aggravation and hostility. 'I know your future dad-in-law ain't involved. Look, all we want from Tommy is the name of the person he purchased that machine from. If he gives us that, he can be released inside ten minutes.'

'You can't hold him for much longer even if he stays schtumm,' said Robby.

'I can hold him for ever, old son.' Irritation came into the policeman's voice. 'Now you listen and listen good. I'm trying to help. Now, in less than an hour from now two very heavyweight coppers are gonna come through that door. And when that happens, the whole thing'll be out of my hands.'

Robby's confidence left him fast. He stared at the officer. 'What? Over one poxy little video recorder?'

'Yeah,' agreed the DS. 'Over one poxy little video machine.' He paused for emphasis, staring intently at Robby. 'Over thirty-six flats and houses have been turned over by this little firm. One of the heavyweight coppers coming down is from the Yard's Serious Crimes squad. And the other is even heavier. The Anti-Terrorist boys, no less.'

'For Christ's sake!' Robby felt a sudden coldness in the pit of his belly. The whole thing was deeper and nastier than he suspected. 'What's occurring here?'

The DS sat back, pleased with the effect. 'It is believed that some of the profits from the sale of stolen goods is being channelled back to the Basque terrorist movement in Spain.'

111

The coldness expanded to fill Robby's belly. He said, 'Oh, shite!' softly.

'Yeah, a killer, ain't it?' said the detective. 'Now perhaps you can see why Tommy's got to tell us who he purchased the video from. If he won't tell us, how about you?'

'Have you told him what you've just told me?' Robby asked.

'No, not yet.' The DS shook his head, looking sympathetic and worried at the same time. 'Tommy's an old man, son. I didn't want to lay that one on him until I had to. We're not the heartless bastards we're made out to be. My old chap's about the same age.'

'What if he won't tell me?' asked Robby, genuinely worried now. 'What happens then?'

'He'll be detained for sure.' The DS leaned forwards, face serious. 'Talk to him, son. Tell him he'll not drop anyone in it who doesn't deserve it.'

Robby stared at the policeman for a long time, then nodded slowly, almost reluctantly.

'All right, I'll have a go. But I hafta warn you — Tom's an old trooper. You know? No names, no pack drill. He won't grass on a mate.'

'Tell him what I just told you,' suggested the detective. 'A mate wouldn't drop him in it like that, would he?'

'No.' Robby shook his head. 'Not a mate. OK. Where is he?'

The same DC who had brought him in took him to the bleak room where Tommy sat. There was nothing in it except a table and a chair and a single ashtray with stubs overflowing. Tommy looked frightened and defiant, and pleased to see Robby.

'All right,' said the younger man when they were alone, 'you better listen to me. An' listen good. We got problems.'

Tommy nodded, losing colour fast as Robby explained the situation.

'Blimey!' he murmured when Robby was finished. 'I never thought Gil'd be mixed up in anything like that.'

'Gil?' Robby gaped. 'You got it from Gil?'

'That's why I can't say nothin', son.' Tommy shook his

112

head, looking desperate. 'I can't drop Gil in the cart, can I?'

'Well, he don't seem to have done too bad with you, mate,' Robby countered. 'Listen, Tommy. You've got no choice – you could be in dead lumber here.'

'What can they do to me, eh?' Tommy sailed a small smile of faint hope. 'I bought it in good faith. I'm old. I never been in any bovver.'

'They can. And will.' Robby said. 'Keep you banged up here for the night.'

'So what?' Tommy grinned ruefully: bravado. 'I ain't never spent a night in jail before.'

'Tommy, that ain't funny, mate.'

'I know, son, I know.' Tommy shook his head. 'Look, go an' see Gil for us, will you? Explain the score, an' if he's got no come-back on him, I'll tell 'em what they want to know.'

'Tell 'em anyway,' urged Robby.

'Would you?' asked Tommy.

Robby opened his mouth to say yes, then stopped as he realized it would be a lie. Instead, he said, 'That's not the point. And besides, I'm younger and I've spent the odd night or three in a peter.'

'You think I can't handle it?' Tommy sounded affronted. 'Is that it?'

'Oh, for Gawdssakes, mate!' Robby was exasperated.

'Robby,' Tommy said firmly, 'go an' make sure Gil's in the clear. Then I'll tell 'em. Not before.'

Robby was about to protest, but the expression on Tommy's face told him it would be useless. So he nodded.

'All right, mate. We'll try it your way.'

By the time he reached the betting shop Gil had closed up for the day, looking surprised and wary when Robby's pounding brought him to the door.

Robby wasted no time. 'I don't wanna fall out with you, Gil, but you've got ten seconds to get your coat on an' come with me.'

Gil stared at him in bafflement. Robby looked angry and worried at the same time. And he hadn't mentioned a bet.

'Coat?' Gil flustered. 'Why, Robby? What's up?'

'You flogged Tommy a video earlier,' Robby snapped. 'Right?'

'Oh, that.' Gil wondered what the hard man act was about: it wasn't Robby's style. 'What's up? Gone wrong? Don't worry about it – get it fixed up an' I'll square the costs.'

'Where did it come from, Gil?'

Robby glowered at the betting shop owner like a detective in a television series grilling a suspect. The intensity of his expression eroded Gil's confidence and he spluttered, confused, 'Why? Robby, son, what's up?'

'Tommy's been lifted by the Old Bill,' rasped Robby. 'That machine's so bleedin' hot the tapes'd melt. Now where'd you get it?'

Gil's mouth fell open and he shook his head in bewildered disbelief.

'Oh, Robby! I didn't know, son. Straight up!'

'If you didn't know, you got nothin' to worry about.' Robby's tone softened slightly. 'You do two things – first, you tell me who you got it from; second, you get straight down the nick an' get Tommy clear.'

Gil was not without his own share of instinctive reluctance where the law was concerned: he began to prevaricate. Then stopped as Robby grabbed the front of his jacket and snarled, 'I mean it, Gil! That old man won't tell the Bill nothin' until you've had a chance to get clear.'

'All right! All right! Don't get stroppy.' Gil plucked at Robby's wrists in an effort to break free. 'I got it off Joan's new boyfriend. Steve Charter.'

'The same guy who sold you this new speaker system?'

'Yeah. And Geordie a radio.' Gil couldn't break the grip. 'Now will you let me go?'

'Well, I tell you, Gil, that's one right bad egg.' Robby let go the lapels. 'Stay clear of him or anything he's flogging. Now let's go an' get Tommy out.'

'Yeah, all right.' Gil nodded reluctantly. 'I'll get me coat. How bad an egg is he, Rob?'

'I don't know the full SP on him,' murmured Robby,

'but the firm he's with are a bunch of political nutters. Money for shooters.'

'Oh!' The colour left Gil's face. 'What about Joan?'

'Joan?' Realization dawned on Robby and his expression matched Gil's. 'Oh no! She ain't with him now, is she?'

'Yeah.' Panic lifted Gil's voice up the scale. 'They went about five minutes ago. Went for a drink.'

Both men left the betting shop in a hurry, pausing just long enough for Gil to lock up before crashing into the Railway Arms like two favourites leaving the gates at White City. The pub was quiet at this hour, just the regulars up at the bar, Geordie looking up in surprise at the dramatic entrance.

'Joan?' Robby yelled. 'She been in?'

'Joan?' Geordie was confused by the urgency. 'What, from the shop?'

'Yeah,' Robby barked. 'Our Joan.'

'Cor, dear,' offered Kipper. 'You've just missed 'em by two minutes.'

'Did she leave with the new boyfriend?' Gil demanded.

'Aye,' nodded Geordie. 'Just now.'

'Any idea where they went?' Robby asked.

'No.' Geordie felt the urgency. 'Why? What's up?'

'He's bad news, that's why.'

Robby's lips pursed in frustration as he wondered what to do next. Gil could safely square off the law and get Tommy out of the nick, but that still left Joan in the company of a possible terrorist, heading for an unknown destination.

Ferret came to the rescue. 'When he was out in the bog at the same time as me, he asked where the nearest garage was. Said he needed petrol right bad.'

'What motor does he drive?' Robby asked Gil.

The betting shop owner thought for a moment. Then he said, 'White sports job. Dunno what make.'

'Looked like an MG if it were the one parked outside when I came in,' supplied Geordie, lifting his pint.

'Sorry, son.' Robby's hand halted the mug halfway to Geordie's mouth. 'You're driving. C'mon, we'll try the nearest garage.' He was already hauling the protesting Geordie towards the door as he told Gil, 'Get down the nick an' get Tommy clear.'

Gil nodded in the direction of the closing door as Robby and Geordie ran for the old Thames. They didn't see the unmarked car holding the sympathetic Detective Superintendent and the young Detective Constable slide into the early evening traffic behind them. But they did see a white MG pull out as they approached the garage.

'There!' Robby yelled, triumphantly. 'Follow 'em!'

'In this?' Geordie protested. 'You're off your head, mun.'

Grumbling, he thrashed gears as he struggled to keep the sports car in sight.

The two policeman had an easier time. Geordie's van was bulky enough to stick out from the traffic, and all they needed to do was keep it in sight, the DS having guessed that Robby would lead him to the villain of the piece. They hung back so that they wouldn't be spotted by any of the involved parties and tailed the van until it coughed to a halt a little way behind the MG, which was parked neatly outside an expensive-looking detached house in Fulham.

'Which one'd they go in?' Robby panted. 'I didn't see.'

'I dunno, mun.' Geordie was more concerned with his empty petrol tank and empty pocket. 'Nor did I.'

Robby glanced at the white sports car, then at the house fronts, pacing up and down the pavement as he tried to determine which door Charter and Joan had used.

A neighbour made it easy for him.

'Well, I must say that was quick.'

It was said in tones of admiration. Robby said, 'Eh?' in a bewildered voice.

'I only phoned a few moments ago,' explained the neighbour. 'You are the police, aren't you?'

Robby caught on fast. 'What's the problem, sir?'

'Didn't your officer explain the situation?'

'Oh, er.' Robby nodded in an authoritative way. 'Well,

we were in the area, you see. All we got was to report to this address on the quick.'

'Ah, yes.' The man's doubts were mollified. 'Well, the situation is my next-door neighbours are away on holiday, you see …'

Robby put two and two together fast and came up with, 'Spain, I understand, sir.'

'Why, yes. That's right.' The citizen was impressed with such efficiency. 'Anyway, I have the only set of spare keys.'

'Ah, you keep your eye on the place, right?' Robby did his best to sound like a policeman.

'Yes, that's right,' nodded the neighbour. 'Anyway, earlier today this young fellow …'

'Which house is it, please sir?' Robby cut in. 'This one?'

'Yes. And I'll be damned if a man and a woman haven't just this moment gone in.'

'Right, sir. Leave it to us. Back-up's on its way.' Robby had been around enough policemen he could sound like a detective. 'Could I have your spare set of keys, please?'

Leaving the baffled Geordie to keep the excited man company, Robby went up to the front door and quietly inserted the key in the mortice lock. He opened the door and went inside fast, halting in the hall to listen for sounds of activity as he guessed that Charter must have lined up the house for a raid and brought Joan there for something else. He went on tip-toe down the hall and heard what he expected from the partially-open door of the sitting room. Easing the door open, his eyes confirmed what his ears had told him: Joan and Charter were locked in a heavy duty clinch on the sofa, too engrossed to hear him come in.

At least until he said, 'Sorry to barge in.'

Joan emitted a muffled scream. Charter jumped to his feet. Which gave Robby a perfect opportunity to swing a right-handed uppercut from around his knees to the point of Charter's chin. It was a punch Frank Bruno would have applauded. Charter's mouth closed as his eyes crossed. He took a few paces backwards and hit the sofa as Joan stood up, leaving him room to topple full length as his conquest gaped and Robby shook his hurting hand.

'Sorry, sweetheart, no time to explain.' Robby grabbed Joan's arm, steering her towards the door. 'Out! Quickly! gotta get out double fast.'

'But why?' Joan was wondering just what was going on. The evening was turning out somewhat different from her expectations. 'Why did you belt Steve?'

'I'll explain later.' Robby hauled her away from her examination of the supine form on the sofa. 'Just get your arse out the door before the law gets here.'

'The law?' The word succeeded in catching Joan's attention. 'But ...'

'Get a bloody move on!' Robby was shouting now, dragging Joan down the hall to the front door.

Geordie was standing by the gate with the neighbour, trying hard to look like a policeman. He started to say, 'What's up, Rob?' But Robby shushed him.

'Get her along the street on the quick.' Then louder, for the neighbour's benefit. 'Right, Sergeant, take this one in.' He handed the thoroughly bewildered Joan to a confused Geordie and turned to face the baffled neighbour. 'Right, sir. I've handcuffed the villain to the staircase. He'll not be going anywhere.'

The neighbour started to speak as Robby handed back the keys, but Robby cut him officiously short. 'The rest of the squad should be here any moment. It's vital that I get this woman down to HQ. Thanks for your co-operation, sir.'

Before the man could say anything more, Robby hurried after Joan and Geordie. Just in time to meet the two coppers climbing out of the plainclothes car.

'Just a moment, Mr Box,' said the DS. 'I think you and me better have a little chat.'

Robby's assumed authority evaporated like a folding flush in the face of the real thing.

CHAPTER NINE

Jan looked at the clock on the mantel shelf. It was a quartz mechanism, guaranteed accurate to thirty seconds a year, so it was probably showing the correct time. Nonetheless, she checked her watch, too. That showed the same time because she had set it against the radio that morning. They both showed Robby was late. She did her best to stifle her irritation, but it was difficult: she was all dressed up for Diamond's dinner party, and before long she'd have to go. With or without Robby.

'I knew it!' she muttered at the end of one circuit of the living room. 'I knew he'd be late! Why doesn't he ring, or something?'

From the sofa, Debby asked, 'What did Vi say when you rang?'

Worry joined the irritation on Jan's pretty face. 'The police have released Tommy, and Robby and Geordie went rushing off after Joan and her boyfriend.'

'Joan?' enquired Debby.

'Yes, Joan.' Frustration made Jan impatient. 'You know, the lady that works at the betting shop.'

'Oh, yeah.' Debby nodded sagely and unhelpfully, 'She's the one who's got the hots for Robby.'

The remark didn't help much and Jan was about to make a comment when the door bell saved her daughter.

'Oh, God! That's the hire car. Look, I'll have to go, love. If that toad arrives or rings, Henry's address is on the shelf. OK?'

'OK.' Debby remained unperturbed. 'Have a nice time.'

Jan doubted that she would, but didn't have much

choice. There was something fishy about the whole affair: Diamond's wife was sent tidily away, leaving Henry with a perfect excuse for asking Jan to stand in – after all, it was a business dinner, wasn't it? The whole point was to smooth Dempster and thus secure a handy new contract for the firm, so Jan hadn't been able to refuse. What she had succeeded in doing, however, was convincing Henry that Robby had to be there, too. That way there was no chance of Henry attempting any extra-mural propositions of a non-business nature. And – to her considerable surprise – he had raised few objections to Robby's presence once she had made it clear it was no Robby, no Jan. Indeed, he had seemed almost too agreeable. Something was going on, but she didn't know what it was; and she didn't like that. And she didn't like Robby letting her down after their heart-to-heart about the future. It did not bode well.

So she was not in the best of moods as she pulled on her coat and went out to the waiting car.

At Diamond's place, she put on her best business face, smiling politely and joining in the dinner-table talk as she wondered where Robby had got to. Henry played the perfect host, the meal layed on by a catering company and a selection of drinks to appeal to the most esoteric tastes. Fortunately for Jan, he spent most of his time talking with the Dempsters, while James Cook got into a conversation with the mystery man, Larry Hindes. Which left Jan to fend off the attentions of the twenty-five-year-old Nigel Dempster, whose first name should, in her opinion, have been Henry, with a hurrah in front of it. Nigel was delighted that her boyfriend had failed to show up and Jan had to use her role as official hostess to the full to avoid his pursuit. She was escaping from him with the excuse that drinks needed freshening when she heard James Cook ask, 'Well then, Henry, are we still going to play a few hands of poker?'

For some reason Diamond appeared reluctant to play without Robby present, and Jan heard him say, 'Well, with the other guest not arriving, I wonder if it's worth it.'

'Well, why not, Henry?' asked Dempster enthusiastically. 'Four is a nice number. And I must say I was rather looking forward to taking a few bob off you.'

Diamond chuckled politely, but Jan could tell his heart was not in it. 'Well, fine,' he agreed with almost palpable reluctance. 'As long as the ladies don't mind?'

As she was there only – officially – as an extension of her daily duties, Jan was hardly likely to object. Which only left Mrs Dempster to smile her agreement and tell the men they were welcome to play. Her husband and son were enthusiastic, and Larry Hindes seemed to be taking his cues from Diamond, while James Cook looked rather like a man nursing a secret joke as he added his vote to those in favour of a game. Diamond had no choice but to break out the cards.

'This real nice of you, chief.'

Robby grinned at the Detective Superintendent as the unmarked car ferried them towards Diamond's home in the suburbs.

'No problem, old son,' assured the officer expansively. 'It's on my way home.' He glanced sideways at Robby's face, looking the worse for wear now. 'If you don't mind me saying so, you look as though you should be gettin' some kip instead of goin' off to some dinner party.'

'Yeah, well. It's been one of those days.' Robby grinned ruefully, then frowned as a thought crossed his mind. 'How long you been on the manor, then?'

'Too long!' chuckled the DS. 'Why'd you ask?'

Still frowning, Robby tugged the urgent letter from his coat pocket and read the message typed there.

'Ever come across a face name of Larry Hindes?' Curiously.

'Larry the deck?' The policeman nodded. 'Card mechanic works down at the Nix club?'

'Yeah.' Thoughtfully. 'The very same.'

'Oh, yeah. Me an' Larry go back a long way. Nicked him a few times in the past.' It was the detective's turn to look thoughtful. 'Don't tell me he's gonna be at this little party of yours?'

'So I've been informed,' said Robby. 'He any good?'

'Cor, not half, old son!' confirmed the copper. 'Can deal you up any hand you like, when you like.'

'Interesting,' murmured Robby.

'Well, if he is there, tell him DS Freddie Phillips sends his regards,' chortled the officer. 'That'll make his bottle twitch a bit. You see.'

Robby nodded, leaning back in the seat as they approached Diamond's home. The detective pulled up where wrought iron gates fronted a gravel drive with carefully tended flowerbeds either side and Robby climbed out, leaning over to speak through the open window.

'Ta very much, chief. You've done us proud.'

Pleased with his collar, the Detective Superintendent was in expansive mood. 'Night, old son,' he said. 'Listen, if you really want to see Larry Hindes' bottle twitch, rib him about the night he tried it on with Frank Aldino.'

'Aldino?' Robby was surprised. 'Does he know Aldino?'

'He sure does.' DS Phillips nodded vigorously. 'He's on a good behaviour bond with our Frank. He wouldn't dare risk trying it on with anyone he thinks is a friend of that animal.'

'Ta,' said Robby, thoughtful again. 'Ta, chief.'

He waved as Phillips pulled away, then went through the fancy gates up to the fancy door.

Jan answered the chiming bell, staring at him as though she expected to see the cat that dragged him in.

'Hallo, Princess,' he smiled. 'Sorry I'm late. Missed the nosh, I suppose?'

'Yes.' Jan sighed in exasperation as she closed the door, studying the battered old sheepskin and the sweater beneath. 'You've missed the nosh.'

'I'm sorry, Princess,' he repeated. 'Cor! The aggravation I've had today.'

Jan shook her head. There was no point in asking for an explanation. Not yet. She pointed to the sitting room.

'Sorry for bein' so late, Henry,' he apologized as Diamond rose to greet him. 'A bit of business cropped up.'

'Not to worry, Robby.' Diamond seemed torn between distaste at Robby's dishevelled appearance and genuine pleasure at seeing him there. It was out of character. 'Er, you've missed dinner, I'm afraid. Drink? You're just in time for poker.'

'Well, that's all right then, isn't it?' Robby was cheerful as he removed his coat and handed it to the nonplussed Diamond. 'A Jack Daniels if you've got it, ta.'

Diamond stood holding the coat as though afraid it might soil his hands. Jan took it from him with a look that said, *Is this what he calls dressing for dinner?* Robby went on smiling, waiting for his host to effect introductions.

'Right, Robby.' Diamond indicated the men seated at the round table. 'Meet Peter, James, Nigel and Larry.'

'Evenin' all. Sorry about being late.' Robby moved towards a vacant chair. 'Anywhere, Hen'?'

He knew that Diamond hated the shortening of his name, but there wasn't anything the builder could do, so he just nodded as Robby sat down and took his own place at the table.

'OK, we'll start again. First jack gets the deal. Straightforward five card stud, Robby.'

Robby nodded as Jan returned from hanging his coat to thud a glass down by his elbow. He winked at her, and got a glare in return as the jack went to Nigel Dempster and the young man raked in the cards to shuffle and start the deal. As usual, the betting was opened by the owner of the highest card showing, and that was Larry Hindes. Robby noticed the tight, anticipatory smile on Diamond's mouth and the quick glance Hindes gave him as he opened modestly with a pound.

Everyone followed suit, and the third round left the cardsharp with a pair of aces showing.

'Nice cards, Larry,' said Dempster. 'You'll no doubt make us pay to stay the course?'

Hindes smiled as he agreed. 'Yes. Two pounds the bet now, Peter.'

Dempster studied the cards showing before him: the four and five of Clubs. He nodded. 'Yes, I'll keep you guessing.'

James Cook looked at his jack and two of Hearts and folded. Robby said, 'Called,' on the strength of a king and an ace. Diamond looked around the table and followed Cook out of the game. Nigel Dempster took a look at his hole card and shook his head, 'No, not for me.' He folded his hand and dealt the final cards. Hindes got a six of Clubs; Dempster, the nine of Hearts. Robby picked up another king.

Hindes said, 'Well now, the aces will bet a fiver.'

Dempster said, 'No. Fold. Too rich for me, as they say in the westerns.'

Robby said, 'Called and raise. Your five and up five.'

Cook said, 'Looks interesting.'

Diamond glanced surreptitiously at Robby, whose face remained the classic deadpan as Hindes tossed a fiver in the pot and said, 'I'm there.'

Nigel dealt the final card, face down. Hindes' eyes made a quick circuit of the table.

'Well, now,' he murmured, lifting three blue five pound notes. 'My pair of aces are still looking good. Fifteen pounds the bet.'

'Called and raised,' said Robby, without hesitation. 'Up another fiver.'

'Aces against kings,' said Diamond.

'Bet called,' said Hindes, smiling at Robby. 'You have …?'

Robby turned his cards, exposing two pairs: aces over kings. The cardsharp looked surprised. Diamond looked disappointed. Hindes nodded and murmured, 'Nice cards.'

Robby grinned as he raked in the pot, enjoying the dissatisfied expression on Diamond's face. James Cook studied him with a small smile tugging at the corners of his thoughtful mouth.

'Like I said,' said Diamond, 'the night is young. Your deal, I believe, Larry.'

'Nice play, young man,' applauded Dempster. 'Nice play.'

'The cards were kind,' Robby said modestly.

'They can, of course, be cruel at the drop of a hat,' Diamond warned ominously.

'Or a change of dealer,' countered Robby, turning to

look at Hindes. 'Funny old game is poker. Ain't that right, Larry?'

Hindes darted a look at Diamond before he replied, 'Cards are like life – what will be, will be.'

Nigel Dempster glanced longingly at Jan, then at Robby as he murmured dramatically, 'Life can be very cruel at times. Very cruel.'

Hindes dealt the hole cards and the first of the show cards. Dempster received a two of Diamonds face up; Cook got a ten of Clubs; Robby got another ace of Spades; Diamond, a king; and Nigel got a nine of Clubs; Hindes, an eight.

'Your ace to bet, Robby,' announced the dealer.

'Pound note on the bullet,' Robby said.

The others went with him and Hindes dealt more cards: a queen to Dempster; a five to Cook; a second ace to Robby, prompting surprise and admiration around the table; Diamond, a second king; Nigel, a nine.

'Well, well, well,' smiled Diamond. 'Three pairs out. This is interesting.'

Hindes dealt himself a six of Spades and said, 'You again, Robby.'

Robby said, 'A fiver on the bullets.'

'Five and up five.' Diamond smiled at Robby as he put the notes down.

'I must go with it,' announced Nigel. 'Called.'

'Not here.' Hindes shook his head.

Dempster said, 'No.' And Cook added, 'Nor I.'

'I'm there,' said Robby, and put another fiver in.

'Just three runners,' said Hindes as he dealt the last face cards.

This time Robby got a third ace, prompting a reaction that attracted the attention of the two women, who moved closer to watch the hand.

'Three aces!' Dempster chuckled. 'That's sure to cost you, Henry.'

Diamond remained unperturbed although his three kings lacked the clout of Robby's aces.

'Good God!' Nigel stared disconsolately at his queen. 'I've no chance.'

Robby glanced at Jan, then at Diamond, a smile on his lips as he said, 'A friendly school. A score the bet.'

Two ten pound notes went into the pot. Attention focused on Diamond, who smiled tigerishly and said, 'Well, let's make it interesting, shall we? Three aces are a hard hand to beat. How much have you got on you, Robby?'

'That's a silly bet, Hen'.' Robby's smile gave nothing away.

'I thought you were a gambling man,' Diamond sneered. Then to the room at large, 'A professional gambler, I'm told.'

Jan saw the hostility between the two men and stepped forward, not certain what was going on, but knowing something unpleasant was building towards a climax.

'Robby, please? This is silly, Henry.'

'Stay out of it, Princess,' Robby warned gently, his tone hardening as he asked Diamond, 'What you trying to prove, Hen'?'

'Prove, Robby?' Diamond's face was a poorly painted picture of innocence. 'I'm trying to prove nothing. I thought you were a gambling man, that's all. So I'm wrong.'

'I've got about three hundred pounds on me,' Robby said evenly.

'Oh, is that all?' Diamond sounded disappointed. 'Oh well, that will have to do. Three hundred pounds the bet.'

Dempster's mouth hung slack in amazement. 'Good Lord, Henry! I thought this was a friendly school.'

Jan said, 'Don't Robby! Please don't!'

Robby's face was impassive as he looked away from Diamond's triumphant face to Hindes.

'Well, as me old friend Frank Aldino always says: it ain't an arm or a leg, is it? It's only money.'

Hindes' mouth dropped open as his sallow complexion went several shades paler. Diamond missed it in his gloating anticipation of victory guaranteed. Robby asked, 'You really want that bet, Hen'?'

'Why yes,' Diamond responded. 'Perhaps you'd care to raise the stakes?'

He glanced at Jan as he said it, and Robby caught the look and understood its meaning, so that when he spoke again, his voice was hard.

'You're well out of order, Henry. Bet called.'

The non-participants gasped in shocked amazement. James Cook closed his eyes in despair. Larry Hindes looked worried for different reasons.

'By the way, Larry me old china,' Robby continued. 'Freddie Phillips said to say hallo to you. Says he might be seein' you real soon.'

The calmly-spoken words reduced Hindes' pallor a few more shades. He swallowed hard as beads of sweat moistened his forehead.

'I ... er ... F ... Freddie ... Ph ... Phillips?'

'You two already know each other?'

Diamond's voice had lost its confident sneer in direct proportion to Hindes' discomfort.

'In a manner of speaking, Hen',' Robby acknowledged. 'We know some of the same people, you might say. Deal 'em up, Larry.'

Hindes' hands had lost their dexterity as he dealt the final cards. Diamond picked up his three kings, regaining a little of his composure. Then lost it as he turned his hole cards to show a ten of Clubs, and instead of the fourth king he expected, the jack of Diamonds. Bewildered and very angry, he glared at the hapless Hindes.

Robby flipped his hole cards: a pair of sevens, joining his three kings to give him a full house.

'Must be my lucky night,' he murmured.

Diamond's rage tautened the tendons along his neck, his lower lip trembling as he dropped his cards, climbing jerkily to his feet to stalk from the room. His guests watched him in baffled surprise. Robby hauled in the big pot as Jan stood behind his chair trying to guess what had happened. Robby's face was almost deadpan, but even he found it difficult to suppress the little smile of pleasure as the door banged shut behind Henry Diamond.

'Thanks very much for the lift, James. It was very kind of

you.' Jan smiled her gratitude. 'More coffee?'

'No thanks, my dear. And it was my pleasure.' Cook stood up, smiling back. 'I'd best be making tracks.'

'Nice to have met you, Jimmy.' Robby shook hands with the accountant. 'And thanks very much for the lift.'

'Think nothing of it, Robby,' said Cook. 'And don't forget what I said — when you're ready to tackle your income tax problems, give me a call.'

'I will,' Robby agreed. 'And thanks again.'

Jan leant forwards to kiss Cook on the cheek. She wasn't sure exactly what had happened, but she knew that Cook had something to do with Robby coming out a winner despite Henry Diamond's carefully-laid plans.

'Remember what I said,' she told him. 'You're welcome round any time.'

'If I were twenty years younger ...' Cook winked at Robby. 'Who was it said, lucky at cards, unlucky in love?'

'Dunno,' Robby chuckled. 'I'll see you to the door.'

The accountant said his goodnights and followed Robby into the hallway of Jan's house. Robby opened the door with a big, genuine smile on his face.

'And thanks for the note tippin' me about Larry Hindes, Jimmy. You saved me from a right stitch-up.'

Cook's eyebrows lifted in mock astonishment. 'Don't know what you're on about, my boy.'

'No, of course not.' Robby smiled back at the older man. 'Night, Jimmy.'

Cook chuckled, then halted at the door.

'Forewarned is forearmed, as they say, Robby. But how in God's name you managed to turn it all about intrigues me.'

'All's fair in love and poker, Jimmy.' Robby winked. 'Know what I mean?'

Cook chuckled as he walked away. By the time he reached his car he was laughing out loud. Robby waited until the car started, then shut the door, leaning back as he began to laugh himself. All in all, the day had turned out nicely: Tommy was cleared, Joan was safe, he was ahead a few hundred, and Henry Diamond's scheme had backfired beautifully. Best of all, he had put things to rights with Jan.

He was still laughing as he headed for the living room, where she was waiting.

CHAPTER TEN

You meet all kinds of people at a spieler, and often as not the only thing they have in common is a fondness for cards. They'll have money, of course. They wouldn't get in without it and the general aim is to come away with more. But it's usually accepted that you win some and you lose some, so you don't cry into the early morning milk when you wander home bleary-eyed and broke potless: that's part of the game. And outside the really big money operations, the sums changing hands aren't vast – big, but not the kind of money devout muslim oil sheiks lay out. Mostly it comes from honest graft of one kind or another and the players are ordinary working folk who just enjoy a spice of excitement to go with the Friday night chips, though – given the illegal nature of the spieler – there's often a criminal element involved. Players don't ask questions: they're there for the game, not This Is Your Life, and so long as the participants can front their sit-down money and take their cards with good grace, no one is much interested in what his neighbour did to make it. Where a professional like Robby Box is concerned, he'll generally know at least one person there, and if the game is taking place in his home manor he'll probably recognize a few more faces. The result of all this is that unspoken rules are observed: a backstreet spieler is strictly a cash only operation and there's no cheating – the gaming fraternity is too close-knit and justice comes short, sharp and immediate – so usually it's safe to sit down to a game, knowing all you can lose is money.

Robby wasn't. He was ahead of the game and pleased

with the spieler Andy had organized in the back room of the mini-cab office. Three of the faces around the table were vaguely familiar to him, and the fourth – a man called Max – was vouched for by Andy. Max hadn't been doing too well and by the time he matched Robby's fifty and raised it, he was close to cleaned out and more than a litle impatient for Robby to make his next move. The thing was, Max felt he was on to a winning hand at last and Robby's leisurely response was fraying his nerves. Which was maybe exactly what Robby wanted. At any rate, he took his time rolling a smoke as he studied the pot on the table.

'Come on, will you?' Max urged.

'This isn't a game of chance, mate, this is a game of skill. Or hadn't you noticed?' Robby put the cigarette in his mouth and lit up, enjoying the tension. 'Just like the pictures, ain't it?'

'All you gotta do is jack it in,' Max retorted, sounding like he was spitting razor blades.

Robby allowed a ribbon of smoke to escape from the corner of his mouth as he lifted notes from his wad and studied Max's tense expression. The man was close to played out, wide open to a blow-out raise. Robby added a few more notes and tossed them into the pot.

'And up a hundred.'

The other remaining player folded and attention focused back on Max, who looked as though the sight of Robby's blood would not displease him. He looked at the pot, which he couldn't match, and at Robby's face, which remained implacably impassive, and asked foolishly, 'Will you take a kite?'

Robby looked at the cheque book and said, 'You jest.'

Max said, 'You won't have to cash it.'

Robby asked, 'What are you? Some sort of comedian?'

Max said, 'I mean I'm gonna win, ain't I?'

'The only way you can win is by havin' a better hand than I've got,' said Robby. 'And the only way you can prove that is by paying to see the pictures. No money, no peepshow.'

Max could have cracked nuts between his teeth. His eyes

narowed and he turned to Andy, 'Could you do me one?'

Andy's craggy face stayed blank. 'This ain't a bank.'

'Come on,' pleaded Max. 'I've done me cobblers.'

'Sorry.' Andy shrugged.

'This is a stitch up,' Max muttered morosely.

'Listen mate,' said Robby. 'If you can't swim, don't get in the water.'

'I know I've got you beat,' said Max.

'Prove it,' said Robby, evenly.

'Just give me some credit.'

'Try the Woolwich.'

Max looked to the other players for support and found none.

'That it then?' Robby enquired. 'Game, set and match.'

He leant forwards, reaching for the pot.

And Max said, 'You bastard!' as he lurched to his feet with a switchblade flicking steel in his right hand.

'Hold up!' Robby managed as the blade thudded into the table too close to his hand. 'You been watching too much telly.'

'So have you.' Max tugged the knife loose and pointed it at Robby as the onlookers moved out of harm's way.

It was an unreal situation. A scene from a movie. Knives didn't get flashed in a spieler in the backroom of a north London mini-cab firm. Robby observed it with a curious lack of passion, as though it were happening to someone else. 'What's your game, son?' he asked mildly. 'You want a row, go pick on someone your own size.'

'You stitched me up!'

Robby stared unbelievingly at Max's furious face. A tic was pulsing on the man's left temple and the words were spat from snarling teeth. The knifeblade was a sliver of light held towards Robby. He said, 'Look mate, the one thing I don't do is cheat, and the other thing I don't do is have punch-ups with strangers. That way you don't get hurt. Know what I mean?'

The words came out calmly, which wasn't how Robby felt. Watching Max's contorted features, he decided he was looking at some kind of maniac without knowing just how

133

far Max was prepared to take it. He became aware of pain and raised his hand to stare at the blood oozing from a deep cut on his right-hand forefinger.

'That's my dealing finger, you wally,' he complained.

Max said, 'Show us your hand.'

Robby held up his hand.

Max said, 'Your cards, pratt!'

Robby said, 'You what?'

'Show us your cards.'

'There's no need to get carried away over a soppy little game of snap.'

It was said almost gently. It had no effect on Max, who kept the knife pointed at Robby as he demanded, 'Show us!'

'You serious?' The question was unnecessary: Max's face gave the answer. 'You want to see my cards, pay for it. Rules of the game.'

'Stop muckin' about, you pratt, and show!'

'What do you think, chaps? Bit unorthodox, ain't it?'

Neither the attempt at humour nor the appeal for help were any use. The others were backed off, anxious to stay out of trouble and unwilling to go to Robby's aid. Nor was Max prepared to listen to reason. He said, 'Show!' moving the knife a little closer to Robby's face.

'Well, what can I say?' Robby began to feel angry as the initial shock wore off. 'You've asked me so politely.'

He picked up a card and flicked it across the table. Followed it with the other four. Max turned them over, his snarl turning to a sneer.

'You had rubbish!' He sounded outraged. 'You had a pile of garbage!'

'So?' Robby asked.

'I knew I had you beat.' Max sounded pleased with himself.

'That's not the point, is it?' Robby countered. 'That's not the game.'

'You blanked me out of it.'

'This isn't kindergarten, mate,' retorted Robby.

'An' it's not charity week either.'

Max leant forwards across the table to collect Robby's winnings. Robby said, 'You can't do that.'

Max said, 'Watch me.'

As he said it, he was scooping the money towards his side of the table, his eyes leaving Robby's face for a moment. It was the moment Robby needed. A mug of tea stood beside his bleeding hand, steaming. He lifted it and threw it, the contents splashing full into Max's face. Max yelled, dropping the knife as he lifted his hands to his scalded features. Then yelled again as Robby came across the table with both hands fastening on his lapels to drag the man's head down into the butt that cracked solidly against his nose.

There is nothing romantic about streetfighting. Nor anything very exciting. The sole objective is to down your opponent and inflict as much damage as possible in as short a time as possible. Such fights are brief and brutal, a matter of knees and elbows and head butts: the only rule, to win. Robby was not by nature an aggressive man, but in his chosen profession he had learned to look after himself. And Max's knife had frightened him, which made him angry. Max went down to the floor with blood on his face and his hands cupped over his genitals. Robby kicked him. Then kicked him again.

He was drawing his foot back a third time when Andy stepped in.

'That's enough! You want to kill him?'

'That's what he'd've done to me.' Robby was breathless. 'Who is he, Andy?'

'I don't know.' The big man shrugged, studying Max's groaning form. 'Someone sent him. OK?'

'Well, you'd better send him back, hadn't you?' Robby grunted, collecting his money. 'Thanks for the game, gentlemen.'

He walked out into the morning, the early air cool on his skin as he felt the aftermath of the fight take hold. Abruptly, he ducked into an alley and emptied his stomach.

Andy finished settling a plaster over Max's cut nose and

stepped back to admire his handiwork. Max climbed to his feet holding his ribs and studied his reflection with a grimace.

'So where's this geezer's place?'

'I've got his address in the office,' said Andy. 'How long are you down for?'

'As long as it takes,' Max grunted. 'Should get back tomorrow.'

'What's it like living in Birmingham?' Andy asked.

'London with a different accent.' Max stroked his ribs gingerly.

'Don't you miss the Smoke?'

Max shrugged. 'Plenty of it up there.'

Robby walked into Jan's place with a plaster on his cut finger as Debby was walking out with a hangdog expression.

'Hallo, Babe,' he grinned.

'Hallo,' came the morose reply.

She moved to pass him, but Robby blocked her way, pressing for an explanation of her black mood until she told him, 'We're having a disco at school and I'm sort of in charge.'

'All come on top, has it?' he sympathized.

'Run out of bread, that's all.' Debby shrugged. 'And there's still a lot of things I've got to get.'

'And Mum won't come across, eh?'

'Yeah.'

Robby studied her pretty face for a moment, then fetched a ten pound note from his pocket and put it in her hand.

'Not a word, OK?' he warned.

Debby kissed him as she nodded. 'OK.'

He was grinning again as he watched her run off, the slump gone from her shoulders. Jan wouldn't approve, but what Jan didn't know wouldn't hurt her. He found her in the bathroom, putting the final touches to her make-up.

He asked, 'Have you seen the papers?' after a perfunctory kiss.

'What's the matter?' Jan looked up curiously, hearing urgency in his voice.

'The morning paper,' he said. 'Have you seen it?'

'It's in the kitchen.' Jan frowned, wondering what the problem was. 'Why?'

She followed him into the kitchen, where he snatched the newspaper to stab a plastered finger at the headline announcing a cut in mortgage rates.

'Oh, that.' Jan smiled. 'Good, isn't it? Pity we don't have a mortgage.'

'It might be good for them,' Robby grumbled, 'but what about us?'

'What about us?' Jan was confused.

'The wedge we've been investing?' Robby's tone said this was simultaneously a question and an explanation.

'What's the problem?' Jan glanced at the headline, not sure why it was upsetting him.

'Well, won't this affect it?' he demanded.

'Probably.' Jan shrugged, more concerned with preparing for the day's work.

'So we're going to lose.' Grimly.

'For a money man you're as naïve as a newborn babe sometimes,' Jan smiled.

'What's that supposed to mean?' queried Robby as she made for the door.

'It means it's good all round.'

'You sure?' Anxious, he trailed her back to the bathroom.

'I'm sure.'

'I mean, you're certain we've got it in the right place?'

'Robby, you're behaving like a two year old.'

'A lot of graft's gone into collecting that pot.' Warily.

'This isn't your grandmother you're talking to.' Jan settled back in front of the mirror.

'You know what I mean, Princess.'

Robby frowned from the hallway, not yet satisfied. He would have asked for further explanation, but the letterbox rattled as two envelopes came through, interrupting him. He collected them, carrying them into the bedroom as Jan finished dressing.

137

'One electricity bill,' he announced.

'Is it red?' she asked.

'No.'

'Good.'

'And one boomerang from the Kangas. They've been writing a lot lately.'

'They miss me.' Jan took the letter from her parents and dropped it in her handbag. 'I'll read it at the office.'

'They still goin' on about you goin' over?' Robby asked.

'Yeah.' There was a wistful note in Jan's voice.

'You still fancy it?'

'We could do worse,' she replied.

'Sounds like my school reports,' Robby smiled.

'They love it,' said Jan.

And Robby chuckled as he said, 'So do the kangaroos.'

Jan glanced at him, her eyes speculative. Then she pursed her lips as though biting off a question and returned to brushing her hair.

'Aint'cha gonna ask me how I got on last night?' Australia was dismissed from Robby's mind.

'How did you get on last night?' Jan asked dutifully.

'Thought you'd never ask.' Robby grinned as he layed his winnings on her dressing table.

'What have you done to your finger?' Jan demanded.

'Cut it on a cardsharp, didn't I?' Robby was more interested in the money they could add to their stake.

Jan looked at the notes. Then looked closer. Then picked one up to study at close range. 'What have you been up to?'

'Eh?' Robby was thrown by her tone.

'Look,' she ordered, holding a note close to his face.

'What?' he asked helplessly.

'Where are your glasses?' Exasperation sounded in her voice.

'What's the problem?' Robby wondered what was going on.

'Your eyes have gone, mate,' she told him. 'Where are your glasses?'

'In the drawer.'

'Well,' Jan said firmly, 'I think you'd better start wearing them.'

'Don't be soppy,' Robby protested.

'Go and get them.'

This time there was no doubting her tone. Robby located the spectacles and settled them on his nose. Jan passed him the note she was holding and he saw what was troubling her. The forgery wasn't all that bad, but nor was it good enough to pass close inspection. He said, 'Oh, Jesus!' softly and began to sort through the pile of money.

'I don't see how you didn't spot it.' Jan moved to help him.

'It was dark in there,' he complained, 'wasn't it?'

'Dark?' Jan sounded scornful. 'You must have been playing by braille. How come the others didn't see it?'

'You don't expect it.' Robby sounded outraged. 'It's an unwritten law. It ain't done.'

'Sounds like a card school for geriatrics,' remarked Jan.

'Leave off.' Robby was hurt. Mostly by embarrassment. 'How much is dodgy?'

'Two hundred.' Jan separated the piled notes.

Robby said, 'The bastard!'

'Who?' asked Jan.

'The geezer who accounted for this lot.' Robby stabbed his cut finger at the counterfeit notes. 'An' my bleedin' hand.'

'You should have worn your glasses.' Jan shook her head. 'You're getting too old for this game. Anyway, what are we going to do with it?'

'I'll burn the monopoly money,' Robby said, 'and you bank the rest. All right?'

As he picked up the forgeries a memory surfaced and he said, 'Jesus! Debby!'

'What?' Jan was alarmed by the worry in his voice.

'I gave her a tenner,' he explained.

'You did what?'

'She was going out as I was coming in.' Robby shrugged, feeling guilty. 'You know how it is.'

'No.' Anger put an edge on Jan's voice. 'I don't know how it is.'

139

'She was a bit down,' he explained, 'so I thought ...'

Jan cut in, 'So you thought you'd undermine my authority.'

'Now you know I wouldn't do that,' he protested, knowing he was in the wrong.

'I say *no* and you say *yes*.' There was real anger now. 'She's my daughter, for God's sake!'

'Look, Jan, I didn't mean ...'

'Didn't mean? Of course you meant!' Her eyes blazed with the rage of a mother. 'How can she ever have any sense of values if every time I say *no*, you say *yes*?'

Robby shuffled his feet, shamefaced. 'It wasn't like that, Princess,' he muttered, realizing how weak it sounded.

'Then how was it?' snapped Jan.

Robby accepted defeat and looked for an escape.

'I better go and capture her before she spends it.'

'Do you realize what's going to happen if she gets caught?' Jan asked.

Robby nodded, swallowing hard as he made good his escape and hurried through the front door. Jan heard it slam shut and slumped on the bed. Robby was getting old for the kind of life he led, but it was the only one he knew, and the only way he could ever hope to collect a stake big enough to escape it. If he really wanted to. She picked up the good money and dropped it in her handbag, the action revealing the red and blue markings of the airmail envelope. She took it out and stared at the familiar handwriting. It had been years since her parents emigrated, years since she had seen them. They corresponded regularly and each letter contained an invitation to visit. If not permanently, then for a holiday for whch they would be more than happy to pay. She wondered what blandishments this letter would contain.

And found out as she tore the envelope open to extract the letter and saw two Quantas tickets flutter to the bed. She picked them up, staring at them, seeing they were the open-ended kind. For her and Debby, the letter explained, any time she chose to come out. She'd like Australia, and it was a fine place for a girl to grow up. Why not come take a look? It needn't be for ever, just a month, or two – to get the feel of the country. So she could see what she was missing. There was nothing new about it, except the tickets. They had never sent her tickets before.

Not sure what to do with them, she carried them into the kitchen, where she stood bemused, unsure of her own feelings.

After a while she lifted the bread bin and slid the tickets underneath. Then she left for work with a thoughtful expression on her pretty face.

CHAPTER ELEVEN

Henry Diamond was not usually the first in to work, but on this particular morning he was at his desk early, the surface littered with files and accounts ledgers as his office door opened and a man enquired, 'Henry Diamond?'

Diamond confirmed it as the man came in, studying the nondescript dark suit and equally forgettable face, its only real distinguishing feature the strip of sticking plaster across the bridge of the nose. Max said, 'Andy sent me.'

Diamond nodded, motioning for him to close the door and sit down as he flipped the ledgers shut and glanced over his shoulder at the empty yard like a man with something to hide. Max took a chair and waited for the builder to start talking.

When Diamond was finished Max said, 'I'll have a twoer now and the other three when the job's done.' Then shook his head as a cheque book was produced and murmured, 'Cash.'

'The cheque's fine,' Diamond protested.

'Cash,' Max repeated.

'You don't think I'd stop the cheque, do you?' Diamond's tone was one of not-quite-aggrieved innocence.

'I don't think anything.' Max's face was blank. 'I operate in cash, that's all.'

Diamond shrugged. 'You'll have to wait 'til the banks are open.'

'You must have something floating around.' Max shook his head minimally, as though dismissing a patently foolish idea. 'Haven't you? I mean, it's not all credit cards and plastic notes, is it?'

Diamond sighed and put his hand into his jacket, bringing out a pigskin wallet from which he counted notes.

'One hundred and sixty. That's it.' He passed the notes across the desk, watching as they disappeared into Max's pocket, waiting for the man to rise and go, then suggesting nervously, 'Look, I don't think it's good that you should be seen around here.'

'We're forty short,' said Max, making no move to leave.

'I'll give it to you later.' There was a note of panic in Diamond's voice.

Max ignored it as he said, 'Now.'

Frowning, Diamond said, 'Hang on,' and rose from his desk. He went into the outer office and took a petty cash box from Jan's desk, extracting the notes and leaving the change.

'Fifteen,' he told Max. 'That's all I can do.'

'I can see why you need me.' Max's voice was cynical.

Diamond said, 'Take this and I'll give you the rest tonight.'

'We are in a mess, aren't we?' Patronizing.

'Do me a favour.' Diamond resented it.

Max said succinctly, 'I am.'

'I just don't think you should be seen here,' Diamond complained. 'Do you?'

'OK.' Max took the offered notes and stood up. 'Meet me in the Plough eleven o'clock tonight. Just down the road from the mini-cab office.'

'Right.' Diamond was anxious to see the back of the man.

'And be there,' Max warned.

'Of course,' said Diamond.

'You try and go the other way on me and I'll have your ears off.' Max stood staring ominously at the builder. 'I mean it. Three-two-five in cash. And maybe the train fare, for the delay.'

'Train fare?' Diamond frowned.

'I've come down from Birmingham,' Max elaborated.

'I didn't know.'

'Makes it easier, doesn't it?' Max allowed a small smile

144

to crease his mouth. 'Job done, I slip away — nobody knows any better. You forget me, I forget you. Right?'

'Right,' Diamond agreed.

'Now remember what I told you,' Max added. 'Make sure you're somewhere else tonight. And not at home.'

'What's wrong with being at home?' asked Diamond, confused.

'The wife's evidence is useless,' Max explainèd patiently. 'Best thing to do is take out a bird.'

'Why?' Diamond asked.

And Max sighed, adopting the attitude of someone explaining the obvious to a recalcitrant child. 'If it all comes on top and your alibi is that you were doing the dirty on the missus, they'll believe you. See what I mean?'

'Yes,' Diamond acknowledged.

'Right.' Max moved towards the door. 'See you tonight, then.'

Diamond nodded with a mixture of relief and apprehension, watching the door close before opening a filing cabinet to extract a botle of scotch and a glass. He poured himself a big measure and swallowed it in one, then took the bottle to his desk and sat down before filling the glass a second time. He took it a little slower this time, pausing as his door opened and Jan's bright face showed in the opening with a cheery, 'Morning.'

'Hallo, Jan,' he responded, less cheerfully.

'Sorry I'm late,' she explained. 'Got caught up with domestic bliss.'

'Fine.' Diamond sounded like he didn't care.

'You're on an early shift, aren't you?' she remarked.

'Sorry?' Diamond frowned, distracted.

'Who was that I've just seen leaving?'

'What?' Absently.

'Just now.'

'Oh, him. Sorry.' Diamond shook his head as though clearing cobwebs. 'Out of town client.'

'Didn't have him in the book.' Jan sounded doubtful.

'Passing through,' Diamond shrugged. 'Phoned me last night. From Birmingham.'

Jan nodded, not sure what was wrong with her boss, but sensing something was amiss. She gestured at the whisky. 'Bit early for that, isn't it?'

'Toothache.' Diamond's response was automatic. Jan shrugged and decided to leave it.

She went back to her desk and sat down, preparing to open the morning's mail when she noticed the half-open drawer. Frowning, she took out the petty cash box and checked the contents. Her frown grew deeper as she saw only loose change where fifteen pound notes should have been. Then she turned as Diamond came into the room.

'Could you take this down to the bank and cash it for me, Jan?' He held a cheque towards her.

'Henry?' She ignored the cheque. 'How long's Alf been here?'

Alf was the nightwatchman. It was Diamond's turn to frown.

'I was asking him the same question myself this morning. Why? What's wrong?'

Jan indicated the petty cash box. 'There was fifteen pounds in here.'

'Oh, I see.' Diamond remained abstracted. 'I took it.'

'What for?' Jan seemed surprised.

'Taxi.'

'You came in the car.'

'For a client.'

'What?'

'He didn't have any change.'

Diamond left her with the cheque and the unsatisfactory explanation.

Andy was issuing instructions over the radio when Robby burst in to the office with an angry expression marring his good-humoured features.

'Where's that wally from last night?' he demanded.

'I don't know.' Andy's battered face remained impassive.

'Well, who put him on to you?' Robby asked.

'You know the rules, Robby,' the big man admonished.

'I want to know,' Robby insisted.

146

'Can't be done,' said Andy.

'Listen, dickhead.' Robby leant across the radio console. 'That little turd has done us over for two hundred sovs.'

'You what?' Surprise worked its way to the surface of Andy's visage.

'I don't know about the others, but that's my account,' Robby grated. 'And I want him. OK?'

'Two hundred?' said Andy.

'You deaf or something?' snapped Robby. 'Where is he?'

'He was only passing through,' Andy said. 'He was catching a train this morning. Only the one night, that's all.'

'Shit!' said Robby, with feeling.

'I'm sorry, mate,' Andy offered.

'Thanks a million.' Robby's tone was bitter.

'I'll put the word about,' Andy said. 'OK?'

'You do that.'

Robby left the office and walked morosely down the street, heading for Debby's school. The playground was deserted as he approached, but a lollipop man was waiting for customers by the pedestrian crossing outside, and he told Robby that the midday break started at half past twelve. Robby thanked him and walked off.

In the mini-cab office Andy tossed a set of car keys to Max and said, 'It's round the back.'

Max caught the keys and nodded his thanks.

'But I want it back tonight,' warned Andy. 'OK?'

'No problem,' Max agreed.

'In one piece,' said Andy.

Max grinned and said, 'Leave off, will you?'

'They won't cash it.'

Jan put Diamond's cheque on his desk.

'What's that?'

Diamond looked up, surprised.

'They won't.'

'There must be some mistake.'

'I don't think so, Henry.' Jan shook her head. 'They were pretty adamant.'

'This is ridiculous.' Diamond sounded petulant.

'That's what I said,' Jan agreed.

'I'll go down and see them.'

'They asked if you would.'

'Lunchtime,' Diamond murmured thoughtfully. 'I'll go down at lunchtime.'

Jan could see there was something on his mind, but before she could ask what the problem was the phone rang. Dutifully, she lifted the receiver.

'Oh, hallo Mrs Diamond. Yes, he's here.'

She passed the receiver to her boss, who put his hand over the mouthpiece and said, 'Thanks, Jan. I'll sort that out later.'

She took the hint and left his office, closing the door behind her so that she could not hear his end of the conversation.

'What's that? You been drinking?' There was an edge of unmasked irritation in his voice that was abruptly replaced by a note of panic as he responded to the babble in the earpiece. 'Two men in bowler hats? You didn't accept it? The piece of paper. Oh. Yes. Never mind. What? I don't know. I'll speak to you later.'

Robby couldn't see Debby amongst the stream of youngsters emerging from the schoolyard, but he recognised her friend, Maureen.

'Where's Debs?' he asked.

'She went out earlier,' Maureen told him.

'What?' Robby felt his hopes sink.

'Oh, it's all right.' Maureen misinterpreted his concern. 'It's all legit.'

'What are you talking about?' Robby felt panic threatening.

'She got let out,' Maureen explained.

'What for?' Robby demanded.

'She's doing the disco, isn't she?' Maureen elaborated.

'Where did she go?'

'Went to buy one or two things.'

'Where?' Robby felt the last vestiges of hope slipping away fast.

'I dunno,' Maureen shrugged. Then unwittingly threw him a straw. 'I'm gonna meet her now if you want her.'

Robby clutched at it. 'Where?'

'Down the chippy.'

Robby lead the way down the street at a brisk stride, the bemused Maureen breaking into a trot alongside.

They found Debby close to the head of the queue winding up to the serving counter, confused as Robby demanded urgently, 'That money. What did you do with that money?'

'The tenner?' Debby was more concerned with getting her lunch. 'I've spent it. Well, not all of it. Some.'

'Where?' Robby asked.

'Eh?' Debby was taken aback by his vehemence.

'Where did you cash it?'

'Oh.' Debby shuffled a place closer to the counter. 'The newsagent's. Harry's.'

Robby let out a sigh of relief that made Debby's confusion total: Harry was a friend: there would be no trouble with Harry.

Diamond came out of his office as the shadows lengthened across the yard. He paused, surveying the site like a man taking stock of his domain. Or a man looking for a witness. He saw Alf tidying sand into a neat pile near the office building and went over to the old man.

'Night then, Alf.'

Alf was taken by surprise: this was a distinct change from the boss's normal routine, which excluded such familiarity with so lowly an employee. He said, 'Night, Mr Diamond,' in a puzzled voice.

'I'm off,' Diamond said needlessly.

'Have a nice evening,' Alf responded.

'I think I will.' Diamond winked conspiratorially. 'A little bit of dinner with a friend.'

Alf stared at him, wondering what was going on: he had known Diamond's father, known Henry from childhood, but until today Diamond had scarcely acknowledged his existence. Now he was suddenly effusive, winking like the comedian in a pantomime.

'Not a word to a soul, mind,' Diamond admonished, leaving Alf to wonder just who he might tell as Diamond climbed into his car and wound down the window to call, 'Just between ourselves and the office walls. Right?'

'Yes, Mr Diamond,' Alf agreed, nodding dumbly as the Jaguar purred into life.

Across the street, Max sat in a battered Ford Cortina, watching Diamond leave.

'Why couldn't you talk in the office?' Robby asked irritably as he watched Jan tidy her hair. 'I mean, you're there all day with him. Why spend the night with him as well?'

'I'm going out for a couple of hours, that's all.' Jan ignored her lover's aggrieved tone: after all, the situation was usually the other way around.

'Yeah,' said Robby sarcastically. 'Magic!'

'Listen.' Jan suppressed her own irritation, making her voice reasonable. 'He wants to talk. I think he's in a bit of a mess. If he's having problems, my job's on the line as well. And the last thing I want at the moment is to be out of work. All right?'

'What kind of problems?' Robby queried.

'I'm not sure,' she replied honestly.

'Well, you must have some idea,' he pursued.

'We'll talk later,' she told him.

'Thanks.' Robby's voice was scornful. 'Perhaps you'd like to pin it up on the notice board and I'll read it in the morning.'

'I don't want to jump to conclusions, that's all.'

Robby refused to be mollified. 'It's a wind-up. He'll invent anything to get you out to dinner.'

There was, Jan had to admit — but only to herself — some truth in that. She smiled as she said, 'Well, there's life in the old dog yet.'

'What's that supposed to mean?' Robby pounced, dog-like himself.

'Your'e jealous,' Jan chuckled, not entirely displeased.

'Your'e joking.' Robby recognized the truth and changed the subject. 'Did you keep some back this morning?'

'What?' Jan was thrown off balance.

'The wedge,' he explained.

'It's all there.' Jan nodded. 'I didn't have time to go to the Building Society.'

'Where?' Robby asked.

'In the book in my handbag.'

'Can I have some?'

'Please yourself.'

Jan felt irritation grow again as Robby continued to worry at the matter.

'Since you're going out to dinner.'

'Oh, Robby.' She turned from the mirror to face him square-on. 'That's beneath you. Since when did you need an excuse?'

'I fancied a bit of a dinner meself,' he countered petulantly.

'Well, you can take me tomorrow,' she suggested, trying to defuse the situation.

'It's Saturday,' he countered. 'It'll be crowded.'

'What will?' she asked.

'The chuck up.' He sounded defensive even to himself.

'There are other places, you know,' she protested.

'Are there?' Like a child refusing to be reasonable.

Jan gave up and said, 'Help yourself.'

Robby stood up and crossed to where the handbag lay open on a shelf. He looked inside and frowned, his irritation forgotten now.

'It's not here, Princess.'

'It must be,' she said.

'It's not.' He carried the bag to her, holding it open so that she could see he was right.

'Office,' she said after a moment's thought. 'It's in the office.'

'You what?'

'I took it out to check the figures,' Jan explained. 'Then I had to go down to the bank, so I put it in the desk drawer.

I'll get it in the morning.'

'It's the weekend,' Robby told her, impatiently.

'It's all right.' Jan dismissed the argument. 'I've got keys.'

'Well, give them here an' I'll go round tonight.' Robby thrust out his hand.

'You don't want to do that,' Jan said.

'Got nothing else to do.' Hurt.

'It's not going to disappear, you know.' Jan tried to appease him. Uselessly, because he grunted and repeated, 'I'll go tonight.'

Jan shrugged, giving up, and passed him the keys as her doorbell rang. 'Don't mention the keys in front of him, will you?' she warned.

'Doesn't he trust me?' Robby remained determined to be unreasonable.

'Give him a drink,' Jan urged, 'and try not to act as though you've just come out of the trees.'

Robby grunted again as he pocketed the keys, leaving the bedroom to open the door for Diamond. With ill grace, he led the man into Jan's lounge and poured whisky for them both. 'She won't be long,' he promised. 'How's things?'

'Never better,' Diamond announced bluffly. 'You?'

Neither man was interested: the words merely filled the awkward silence between them. Robby said, 'Nearly there, Henry. Nearly there.'

'Good,' Diamond nodded. 'Good.' Then sipped his drink before asking, 'I hope you don't mind about tonight?'

'Tonight?' Robby was deliberately dense.

'Taking Jan out,' Diamond said.

'She's a free agent.' Said in a way that let Diamond know Robby did object.

'Just some bits and pieces that need tidying up.' Diamond smiled weakly. 'Easier over dinner.'

'Of course,' agreed Robby, insincerely.

Diamond sipped his drink some more, then cleared his throat, seeming almost furtive as he asked, 'You're a cash man aren't you, Robby?'

'What do you mean?'

'You carry,' Diamond said.

Robby refused to make it easy for the other man. He frowned, aping incomprehension. 'You make me sound like some disease.'

'What I mean is,' Diamond faltered, not enjoying the conversation. 'In your line you carry cash.'

'If I'm ahead,' Robby allowed reluctantly. 'Yes.'

'It's just that I need some and the nearest night cash is twenty minutes away.'

'What do you want?' Robby asked.

'Fifty?' Diamond took out his cheque book. 'I'll give you a cheque, of course.'

Robby thought for a moment, then his stern expression yielded a fraction to be replaced with a small, secret smile. 'No problem.'

'Thanks.' Diamond sounded relieved.

'You better make it out to Jan,' Robby said as Diamond started to make out the cheque. 'Listen. Do you want more?'

'More?' Diamond paused with the sheet not yet completed.

'Well,' Robby smiled, 'I had a bit of a turn-up last night and I haven't put it away. It's only going to be hanging around here all weekend.'

Diamond's apologetic smile turned into one of genuine pleasure. 'Well,' he said, 'it's always handy.'

'How much?' asked Robby affably.

'What can you spare?' asked Diamond eagerly.

Robby pulled the counterfeit notes from his pocket with his own smile getting wider by the second.

Max waited until Alf had finished tidying the yard and padlocked the gates. He hunched down in the seat of the old Cortina until the caretaker had disappeared up the road, then waited some more until he was confident the darkening street was empty before climbing out of the car to cross the road and check the gates. The lock held firm under his shaking and he went back to the ford to open the

153

boot. He checked the street again, then lifted out a petrol can and a bundle of rags that he carried swiftly over to the gates. He made a final check of the deserted street and tossed his burden over into Diamond's yard. Then shinned rapidly over himself.

Inside, the yard was dark and secluded, the high walls cutting off unwelcome observation as Max picked up the can and the rags and walked leisurely over to the office building. He was humming softly as he wadded the cloths into several bundles that he doused with petrol.

After Jan had gone Robby poured himself another drink and wondered what to do with the evening. There was no sign of Debby and he felt lonely in the empty rooms, so he pulled on his coat and decided to go looking for some action in time to find Tommy about to ring the doorbell.

'Just passing,' said the grey-haired man. 'Thought you might fancy a pint.'

'Lovely.' The suggestion cheered Robby. 'Got the car?'

'Yeah,' Tommy nodded.

'Take me down Diamond's first, will you?' Robby asked. 'Got to pick up something for Jan.'

'Sure.' Tommy led the way to the car and settled behind the wheel. Robby climbed into the passenger seat, cinching the safety belt tight in anticipation of Tommy's usual hair-raising driving style. He was not disappointed, though – as usual – Tommy remained oblivious of the terror he caused.

'Young Stan said that if I was to bump into you, he knows of a spieler on for tonight,' he remarked as a tyre-squealing manoeuvre left rubber burns on the road. 'An' that you'd be welcome if you fancied it.'

'*Young* Stan?' Robby braced himself against the dashboard. 'He's sixty, mate.'

'That's right.' Tommy took a few years off Robby's life as he took his eyes off the road to turn and smile. 'Never got on the footplate though, did he?'

Robby made an inarticulate reply, his own gaze fastened firmly on the traffic ahead, waiting for the moment of impact he felt certain must come soon.

'Where's Jan?' Tommy asked after a while.

'Gone out with the boss,' Robby told him.

'That's nice.' Tommy was deliberately noncommittal.

'I dunno, Tommy,' Robby remarked as they hit a clear patch and he felt his stomach settle for a while. 'Trying to get back into the system's like doing twenty rounds of the Grand National. Except every time you turn a corner, there's another brick wall. Maybe she's right. Maybe Australia is the answer.'

Tommy shook his head. 'You've left it too late for that, Robby.'

'What are you talking about?' Robby protested. 'Her mum an' dad didn't go there 'til they were fifty.'

'Your roots are too strong, mate.' Tommy was definite, as though the possibility of Robby emigrating was as likely as him taking a space shuttle to the moon. 'They go down as far as the Central Line.'

'I'm adaptable,' Robby argued; not sure he meant it.

'You're about as adaptable as Nelson's Column.' Tommy chuckled, dismissing the impossible.

Robby didn't reply this time, concentrating on surviving the ride.

They reached Diamond's yard and Tommy brought the car to a shuddering halt inches from a battered Cortina. 'Hang on here, Tommo.' Robby unfastened his seat belt and opened the door. 'Won't take a minute.'

He climbed out and crossed the road, taking Jan's keys from his pocket and trying a couple before he found the one that opened the padlock. He dragged the big wooden gates open and went inside, squinting across the shadowy yard. Building materials bulked out of the darkness and he picked his way amongst the stacks as he headed for the office. He had to try more keys before he found the correct one, and as he fumbled with the lock he sniffed the air, aware of an unusual smell. It was like petrol, but it was mingled with the odours of timber and cement and creosote, and he dismissed it as the door opened.

As he went inside the timber-frame building Max came

out of the shadows and sprinkled the last of the petrol liberally around the entrance. The office was raised a few feet from the ground on breeze block pillars and the petrol-doused rags were wadded at intervals beneath the floor. Max eased one strip of cloth loose from its bundle and struck a match, holding it to the rag. Flame shone blue in the night, then became yellow as the petrol ignited and ran swiftly down the length of cloth to take hold of the bundles beneath the building. Max dropped the match and ran for the open gates.

Tommy saw the dark figure emerge and wondered why Robby was in such a hurry. Then he realized it wasn't Robby. And saw yellow flame sparkle behind the man. He jumped from the car, ignoring the running figure as he raced for the yard, shouting Robby's name.

Max was good at his work: the office building was wreathed in flame now, the inflammable bundles taking hold on the woodwork so that fire tongued the entire frontage. Inside, Robby heard Tommy yelling and quickly stuffed the Building Society book and the money into his trouser pocket, turning for the door in time to see a wall of fire.

'What are you playin' at?' he shouted through the crackling. 'Guy bleedin' Fawkes?'

Not waiting for a reply, he dragged his coat off and tugged the sheepskin over his head, taking a run at the door that brought him leaping with the agility of desperation through the flames.

'C'mon!' Tommy shouted urgently. 'Let's get out of here.'

'You're joking!' Robby threw his coat aside, staring at the fire that was threatening to consume the office. 'Come on!'

He saw a pile of sand close by and snatched up a shovel as Tommy stared dumbfounded and gasped, 'You what?'

'Nobody's gonna burn down my girl's work!' Robby began to spade sand furiously. 'Get a shovel, you!'

'I'm a pensioner,' Tommy protested.

'You'll be a nicely cooked one if you don't hurry,' Robby yelled.

Tommy muttered, 'Oh, shite!' But he picked up a second shovel and joined Robby in the fire-fighting.

'So that's really all I can tell you.' Henry Diamond toyed with his coffee cup, lines of worry etching his face as he stared at Jan. 'It's been building up over the past few months. I've tried just about everything.' He shrugged, smiling wanly. 'Too many creditors and not enough to go round.'

'I see.' Jan's voice was sympathetic, breaking off as a waiter presented the bill for their meal. 'Let me do that.'

'You're joking.' Diamond still had some pride. And the cash Robby had given him. He settled the bill and helped Jan into her coat.

'Thanks, Henry,' she murmured.

'I'll work something out,' he told her confidently. 'You'll see.'

'What you reckon, eh?'

Robby wiped sweat from his face, staring at the blackened frontage of the office. There were panels that would need replacing, but the fire was out and the yard saved. Jan's job, too. He felt tired and dirty and pleased with himself.

'You can join my fire brigade any time,' Tommy panted.

Robby nodded, grinning as he planted the shovel in the sand.

'Come on. Let's get cleaned up.'

Max drained his glass as the landlord of the Plough shouted time, and glanced at his watch. He was about to leave when Diamond walked in.

'Evening.' There was a question in Diamond's eyes as he handed Max an envelope. 'That's my side of the bargain.'

Max smiled slightly as he took the money and said, 'Mine's done.'

Diamond nodded and walked out. Max's smile got a

157

little broader as he thumbed the envelope open and slid the contents into his hand. All nice, used notes. Impersonal and untraceable.

And familiar.

He barely heard the landlord say, 'That's your lot, sir. Well after time.' He was too busy staring at the forgeries he had passed off the night before. The smile was no longer on his face.

Henry Diamond was feeling pleased with himself. Things were nicely sorted out. The insurance policies would cover his debts with sufficient left over to get another business started. A bit smaller, perhaps, but with careful handling he could build it up, and with his debts wiped out he could look forward to a prosperous future.

It was a pleasant, comfortable feeling, and he decided to reinforce it by taking a pass by the yard.

Apprehension began when he saw the street was deserted: no crowd; no fire engines; no police. No nothing. Just the empty street with the yard gates standing open.

He drove inside with the only ashes around forming in his mouth. He stopped the car and turned off the ignition. Got out. Looked at what he didn't want to see: the yard intact, the office still standing, scorch marks marring the frontage and the piled sand evidence of impromptu fire-fighting. Bile soured his mouth and he swallowed hard as he saw the future looming large and ugly before him. Slowly, feet leaden, he went into the office and closed the door behind him.

Robby and Tommy sat in Jan's kitchen freshly washed and drinking tea. Robby hadn't told her about the fire and she assumed they were merely killing time. She found Diamond's cheque where Robby had left it in the living room and took it through to the kitchen.

'What's this?' she asked before realization dawned. Then, 'You didn't?'

Robby nodded with mock solemnity. Jan stared at him with an expression dangerously close to contempt.

'Well, I've got news for you, Mr Box. This isn't worth the paper it's written on!'

The grin that had been shaping on Robby's face faded as the events of the night fell abruptly into place. His mouth dropped open as Jan added, 'He'll be bankrupt in the morning.'

'Shit!' was all he could think of to say.

Experience is an excellent teacher, so Robby was wearing his glasses as Tommy drove him to the spieler, their route taking them past Diamond's yard. Robby was still smarting from the lecture Jan had given him and the sight of Diamond's Jaguar inside the still-open gates prompted him to say, 'Hold up, Tommo! He's there. Pull over, will you? I'm gonna have a few words with Flash. Blow a few facts down his ear.'

'We've got to be there by twelve,' protested Tommy.

Grimly, Robby repeated, 'Pull over. I won't be a minute.'

'That's what you said last time,' Tommy complained. But he stamped on the brake.

Robby climbed out and walked purposefully across the street towards the yard. A light was showing from the inner office as Robby entered, his face set in determined lines. He knocked on the door.

There was no answer, so he knocked again.

There was still no answer, so he pushed the door open.

An empty bottle of whisky stood on Diamond's desk beside an empty glass. They threw shadows across the ledgers spread there. Against the wall there was a longer shadow that trembled slightly, swaying gently. It came from the body of Henry Diamond. That was dangling from the ceiling, held there by the rope around Diamond's neck. The bulging eyes stared sightlessly at Robby, the protruding tongue mocking him.

This time all he could think of saying was, 'Jesus!'

CHAPTER TWELVE

High above the cemetery a sparrow-hawk circled the blue,
sky attracting Robby's attention as the vicar droned through
the burial service for a man who had never set foot in his
church. Beside Robby, Debby noticed his upturned face
and followed his gaze to where the predatory bird
quartered the air in search of prey. Unlike her mother, who
stood weeping as the coffin was lowered into the grave, the
girl had few tears to spare for Henry Diamond: the bird
was of more interest than the service, which now ended
with a loud 'Amen' from the vicar. Across the grave, Alison
Diamond was supported by Jeremy Cook as she stooped to
take a handful of soil. She looked worn out by grief and too
much gin, the shadows beneath her eyes matching the
sombre colour of her clothes, her face pale save for the
shadows and the twin spots of bright colour on her cheeks.
She clutched the dirt, compressing it as her hand tightened
spasmodically, making no move to commence the closing
act of the ceremony so that another of the mourners, seeing
that she was verging on breakdown, stepped forward to
deposit a spill of earth on the coffin. The others followed
suit as the widow began to tremble, filing past with
downturned eyes and mumbled condolences until only Jan,
Debby, Robby and Geordie remained. Then Alison broke
from Cook's grasp and hurled the balled dirt against the
coffin, the ferocity of the movement pitching her to her
knees.

'You coward! You cheat!' Her voice was strident with
grief and rage and fear, tears coursing freely down her wan
cheeks. 'You bastard, Henry!'

Cook reached to help her up, but she waved him angrily

back, head lashing from side to side in a gesture of mute denial. Abruptly, she wailed and tumbled forward into the grave, landing on the earth-splattered coffin to beat her fists against the polished wood. Robby and Geordie stepped forward to help Jeremy Cook lift her from the grave, not knowing what to say.

'I'll take her home,' Cook murmured as Jan brushed dirt from the distraught woman's clothes.

Robby took Jan's arm, knowing that Diamond's suicide had hit her hard. Jan leant against him, her own eyes red as he steered her towards Geordie's old van. Above them the sparrow-hawk swooped away in search of more profitable hunting, leaving the sky blue and clear and empty. He settled her in the passenger seat beside Geordie while he and Debby climbed into the back of the Thames.

'She was right, you know,' Debby remarked as the van eased noisily into the traffic flow.

'Mmm?' Robby was lost in his own thoughts. 'Who, babe?'

'Mrs Diamond,' said the girl. 'I know it's sad and all that, but she was right when she called him a coward. I know you shouldn't speak ill of the dead, but topping yourself is just like running away, isn't it? It's the easy way out.'

'I dunno about easy, babe.' Robby stared at her soberly. 'I mean, thinkin' about it is one thing. To actually do it … Can't be easy. No way.'

'It's her I feel sorry for, though,' Debby continued with the implacable logic of youth. 'She won't get no insurance or anything. I mean, she's got nothing now, has she? Not even a home.'

'She's got family,' Robby murmured. 'Friends. She'll manage.'

'Yeah, no thanks to him.' Debby shook her head slightly, as though dismissing in advance any pleas on Diamond's behalf. 'I still think it was a shitbag thing to do.'

'Don't let your mum hear you talking like that,' Robby admonished. 'She was close to Henry. Thought a lot of him.'

'Yeah, I know.' Debby craned her head round to peer in through the window of the cab. 'All she's done for the past few days is cry.'

'Don't I know it!' Robby sighed. 'She'll be all right, though. Don't worry.'

Debby turned from her observation of Jan to stare at Robby. 'God knows how she'd be if something were ever to happen to you. Or me, even.'

The way she said it told Robby it was something that had been on her mind. 'Now don't start goin' all morbid on me,' he said. 'Nothing's gonna happen to you. An' as for me – well, I ain't the suicidal type, am I?'

'No.' Debby was not entirely reassured by the statement. 'But then I didn't think Henry Diamond was, either.'

'True,' Robby allowed, 'but I'm different. I can't think of anything that'd get to me that bad. Nothing.'

In the betting shop Kipper and Ferret were discussing the likely – and unlikely – runners in the 3.45 at Goodwood. Ferret's greyhound was demolishing a rubber bone in one corner and the most exciting event of the afternoon was the arrival of Black George with a newspaper full of fish and chips. Uninvited, both men helped themselves to George's dinner. The dog looked up optimistically, then growled as the door banged open and Denny More strode in like an accident looking for somewhere to happen.

'Robby Box been in?' he demanded.

'Might've been,' Kipper grunted through a mouthful of chips. 'Then again ...'

He broke off as Ferret, recognizing More as Frank Aldino's minder, nudged him in the ribs.

More glared at him. 'Look pal, don't get leary. Right? Just answer yes or no.'

Kipper took exception to the thug's attitude and said defiantly, 'On yer bike!'

It was a mistake: Denny More's expression did not change as one polished shoe slammed viciously into Kipper's ankle. Kipper yelped, leaning forwards and down as pain exploded up his shin. More pivoted, snatching Black George's fish and chips to grind the package against Kipper's descending face.

163

'Want any more, son?' One meaty fist locked on Kipper's collar, pushing the smaller man back against a pillar. 'Well?'

'What the hell's going on?' Joan came out from behind the window as Ferret's greyhound pounced on the spilled food with a speed that matched Denny More's.

'No trouble, luv,' said the minder, grinning nastily at Kipper's soiled face. 'Right pal?'

'No.' Kipper shook his head, dislodging pieces of potato. 'No.'

More became almost affable. 'If Robby Box comes in, just tell him Frank Aldino wants a word. OK? Good.' He let go of Kipper. 'Now that weren't so hard, was it?'

'You berk!' Ferret turned to Kipper as More exited. 'That was Denny More. One of Frank Aldino's mob.'

Kipper grunted through compressed lips, bending down to rub vigorously at his bruised shin. Joan asked, 'You all right, Kip?'

'Yeah,' winced Kipper, blinking tears. 'The slag! Me leg hurts.'

'Never mind about your leg.' Black George stared woefully at the greyhound. 'What about me dinner?'

'I still can't believe it.' Geordie slumped in one of Jan's armchairs, holding a can of beer. 'Henry Diamond! It don't make sense.'

'What you gonna do now?' Robby asked.

'What, for work you mean?' Geordie frowned at his friend. 'Don't know, mun. I managed before. Something'll turn up.'

His face was drawn, the shock of Diamond's abrupt exodus robbing him of his usual cheeriness. Both men turned as Debby entered the room.

'She's having a lie-down.' The girl explained Jan's absence. 'Any more beer, anyone?'

'Yeah, I'll have another,' Robby said. 'Geordie?'

'No, ta.' The Newcastle man climbed wearily to his feet, sighing. 'I'm gonna get along home. Be a long time before I forget today.' He shook his head, his eyes moist. 'That poor woman. An' I liked Henry, y'know. We had our run-ins, but I liked him.'

He sniffed noisily as Robby stood up and said, 'Yeah, I know you did, mate. Go home. Go put your arms around that lady of yourn.'

'Aye.' Geordie nodded slowly, swallowing.

Robby could see he was close to weeping. 'An' Geordie? Don't worry. You'll make out. You can always come into business with me, mate.' He winked, trying to comfort his friend. 'Another few days an' I'm legit for the first time.'

'Aye, an' I'm pleased for you, mun.' Geordie smiled. 'For you an' Jan. See you. Bye, Debs.'

'Be lucky,' Robby said.

'Thanks for the lift,' Debby added.

Geordie nodded and went out. Robby took the can of beer Debby offered him, ignoring the second she had brought for herself.

'Nice bloke, he is.' Debby settled on the vacated armchair.

'Yeah.' Robby started to says 'a diamond', but caught himself in time and changed it to, 'Nice bloke. Cheers.'

'Cheers.' Debby took a swig of her beer, young face thoughtful. 'Rob? Has Mum talked to you about going out to visit her mum and dad lately?'

'She's always talkin' about it,' Robby shrugged. 'Why?'

'She was talking about it again yesterday, that's all.'

'What? Goin' out to Aussie?' Robby chuckled softly, dismissing the idea. 'Like I said, babe – she's always talkin' about it. Besides, it ain't that easy, is it?'

'Why not?' asked Debby.

'Well, it ain't as simple as jumping on an airplane no more. You need visas an' all that crap now.'

'Oh, we've got them.' Debby saw the surprise on Robby's face. 'Didn't you know? Yeah, Mum went down to Aussie House a few months ago. You know, during that period you and her were rucking.' She chuckled at the memory. 'She was so sure she could keep away from you then.'

Robby laughed softly at the fantasy: unimportant now.

'What about you, babe? Would you fancy it?'

'You know, it's funny.' Debby frowned, her face serious as she thought about it. 'Three months ago I'd have said no straight off.'

'An' now?' Robby asked as she shrugged pensively.

'Now I think I'd like to go and see,' Debby told him. 'Could be good. All that sunshine; all those big, bronze fellas.'

'Ugh!' Robby shook his head, laughing at the thought. 'I'll pop in and see how she is.'

'Rob?' Debby's voice halted him. 'Were you being straight with Geordie just now? I mean, are you nearly all sussed out? Legit?'

'Yep.' Robby grinned as he nodded: pleased with himself. 'I got nearly nine grand tucked away now. Should just about get me back in the system. Gonna break my heart to part with it — still, gotta be done, ain't it?'

'Is that what you want, Rob?' Face and voice were both serious now. 'To be back in the system?'

'It's what me and your mum want, babe.' Robby stared at her, wondering what was going on behind that clear-eyed gaze. 'Why?'

'I know it's what Mum wants.' Debby shrugged. 'I ain't so sure about you, though.'

'I can't carry on the way I am, can I?' He grinned. 'An' as you've often pointed out yourself, I ain't getting no younger. Gotta think of me pension.'

'Yeah, I suppose so.' Debby didn't sound entirely convinced. 'Remember that hawk we was watching at the cemetery?'

'What about it?' he asked.

'That's how I see you,' she explained. 'Flying free. A wanderer. Doing what you like, when you like. Can't imagine you any other way.'

For a long moment Robby stood in the doorway, staring at the girl with nothing showing on his face. Then he said, 'I'd best go see Jan.'

Frank Aldino used a 7 iron to wing the ball down the

fairway to the short par 3 hole. Beside him, standing an inch or two taller, with expensively-cut grey hair and the lean figure of a man who likes to keep in shape despite his age, an American called Hal Brookman nodded admiringly.

'Sonofabitch! That's one fine golf shot, Frank.'

'I'm happy with it,' Aldino allowed modestly.

Brookman teed his own ball, checking the fairway. 'Pity about the Frenchman dropping out.'

'Yeah.' Aldino stood back as the American prepared to drive off. 'But like I said, I'm working on getting his place filled.'

'Won't be easy, Frank. Not at such short notice. Good poker players with that kind of bread are not thick on the ground. Side bet?'

'I know. But I've got a player in mind. He's good. The bread might be a problem. We'll see. How much?'

'Nothing too heavy.' Brookman displayed expensive dentistry. 'Fifty bucks says my ball lands closer to the pin.'

'You got a bet, Hal,' Aldino agreed.

Brookman went on smiling as he positioned his feet and brought the club round to send the ball arcing after Aldino's. While it was still in flight he picked up his bag and started towards the green.

'Fifty bucks coming my way, I reckon. Who's the guy you're trying to pull in, Frank?'

'You won't know him.' Aldino fell into step beside the taller man. 'Guy name of Robby Box. If he can come up with the dough he'll have some of it. He won't be able to say no. He's a compulsive.'

Brookman laughed. 'A good loser, I hope?'

'Dunno,' Aldino said. 'Never seen him lose.'

'You will.'

'That's what I like about you, Hal,' Aldino chuckled. 'You're such a cocky bastard.'

Laughing amiably, both men trudged towards the green.

'What about the Dutchman, Van Kessel?' asked Brookman. 'He'll show?'

'Flyin' in day after tomorrow,' confirmed Aldino. 'So's

the Finn.' They reached the green and the smile on the Englishman's face got wider. 'You owe me fifty bucks, mate.'

Brookman's smile faded, anger flushing his tan as his lips curled in something close to a snarl. It was the expression of a man who hates to lose. At anything.

'I just don't understand why, Robby.' Jan's voice was confused and sad and tired. 'I thought I knew Henry so well.'

'Not a lot to understand really, Princess. The man had got himself into such a mess financially ...' Robby turned from the window to face Jan where she lay curled on the bed. 'Some people just can't handle it when the pressure's on. Henry was a desperate man, and desperate men do desperate things. I know – I've seen enough of 'em across a poker table.'

'I knew he was in trouble financially.' There was a hopeless note in her voice, a tone of bewilderment. 'But to do that! To ... To ...'

She could not bring herself to say the words, as though uttering them would unleash the tears misting her hazel eyes. Robby came across the room to settle on the side of the bed, gently stroking away a tear.

'Look, Princess, the man topped himself. It's sad and it's a waste, but it happens. What you've got to realize is it was his choice. He played the wrong hands at the wrong time, and lost.'

'I know,' Jan admitted, softly, tremulously.

'He lost an' couldn't live with it.' Robby spoke firmly, seeking to assuage her grief with positive words. 'Blokes like that get used to winning all the time. Get so used to it they get cocky, get over-confident. So when they do finally lose, they lose hard. They fall to earth like a stone.'

The feeling in his voice drew her eyes to his face. She said, 'You sound as though you've been down that road yourself, Robby.'

'Not me, Princess.' A smile, half-cynical, half-defiant, creased Robby's mouth. 'You see, I learned how to lose a long, long time ago. I learned how to take a fall. You have to in my line of work. Know what I mean? Like the song says: Pick yourself up, dust yourself down, and start all over again.' He touched her face tenderly, feeling moisture on his fingertips. 'That's what you've got to do now, Princess.'

Slowly, Jan smiled. She took his hand and brought it to her mouth, kissing the palm.

'Yes, you're right. That's one of the things that most attracted me to you when we first met.' She kissed his hand again, lifting her face to look into his questioning eyes. 'Your weaknesses are, in fact, your strength.'

'Now that,' said Robby, 'sounds Irish.'

'Yes, but it's true.' Jan sat up, kissing his lips now, speaking against his chest as he put his arms around her and held her comfortingly close. 'I love you, Robby Box. Lend me some of your strength.'

His lips moved against her hair as he replied. 'You got enough of your own, Princess. Listen, I know you can't just forget about Henry and what's happened, but ...'

She put a finger to his lips.

'I know, Robby. I've got to think about the future. *Our* future.'

'Right! *Our* future.' He cradled her head in his hands, triumph in his voice. 'We've cracked it now! I'm almost home and dry. Legit! Another grand an' I can give the accountant the nod. In fact, I'll maybe go and see him tomorrow morning an' get the ball rolling. It's gonna hurt me to part with all that dough, but there you go.'

Jan looked at him with a rainbow of emotions brightening her face. Not long ago she had doubted he would – *could* – ever quit gambling; had doubted he could ever raise the capital he needed to break free of the treadmill. But he had told her he would, and he had done it. He had been true to his word. The love she felt for him had grown in the process, and was tempered now with new-won respect. 'Yes,' she said softly, 'you've done it, Robby. And I ... I ... Robby, I'm sorry for having been such a nag. And for doubting ...'

Now it was Robby's turn to place a gentle finger on her lips.

'Shush. Don't say no more. If it hadn't been for your nagging I'd never have got my act together. An' remember – I didn't exactly do it on my own, did I? I had a lot of help along the way. Now you get some kip. OK?'

He kissed her lightly, pushing her down onto the pillows. 'Where are you going?' she asked.

'To work,' he responded. 'To work.'

He smiled as he closed the door, thinking that Jan made it all worthwhile. Worth all the hustling to raise that much money only to give it away to the Inland Revenue and all the other featureless departments that regulate the lives of regular citizens. That if Jan hadn't been there he'd have continued his life the way he had always lived it, not even existing officially, running from spieler to spieler, betting shop to race track, always anticipating the big win and shrugging off his losses as the years grew longer and the knocks harder to take. Well, he'd pulled off the big one now: Jan. Close on nine thousand in the Building Society and only a little more than one grand needed to make the ten that would start him off as a respectable citizen. He couldn't have done it without Jan. Without her there wouldn't have been any point: she was the point. He began to whistle as he left the house and hailed a cab.

When he got home it was to the sight of Tommy wearing his best suit as he burrowed under the bonnet of his old Ford while Vi sat indecorously on the garden wall, watching with impatience.

'Problems?' he asked helpfully.

'Nah.' Tommy took his head from under the bonnet with an exasperated expression on his face. 'I like messin' about in the engine in me best bib an' tucker.'

'How'd it go, son?' Vi asked. 'All right?'

'What can I say?' Robby shrugged. 'They buried him. That's it.'

'Jan all right?'

'Still upset,' Robby answered. 'She'll get over it. Where you off to? Anywhere nice?'

Tommy slammed the bonnet down and replied in Vi's place. 'We was gonna go to the Stow for the evenin' meet. Probably end up watchin' the box now.'

'Oh, no we aint,' said Vi firmly. 'If we can't go to the dogs, you can buy me a drink over the Railway.'

'Yeah, all right,' Tommy agreed, turning to Robby to ask, 'Comin'?'

'I'll be over in a bit,' Robby nodded. 'I'm meetin' Dick Mayor there anyway. We got a game to go to.'

'Your dinner's in the oven, luv.' Vi eased herself from the wall, brushing at her dress. 'Oh, yes. A bloke came round for you earlier.'

'A bloke?' Robby frowned.

'Yes,' Vi told him. 'Said would you give Frank a ring as soon as you got home.'

'Frank?' Robby was none the wiser. 'Frank who?'

'Dunno. Didn't say.' Vi shrugged. 'Said you'd know. Big Frank, or something like that.'

'Big Frank?' Robby made one guess at the surname and came up with an answer he didn't like. 'Oh, yeah. Yeah, I think I know who he means. I'll see you across at the boozer in half an hour. If Dick Mayor's there, tell him I'm on my way.'

He went indoors and opened the oven door, staring at the food with a thoughtful expression. Then he pushed the door shut and stood up, going out of the kitchen into the hall. At the door of his room, he paused to stare at the telephone, then crossed the hall, pulling a small, well-thumbed notebook from his pocket. Opening the book to the third page, he checked Frank Aldino's number and lifted the phone from its cradle. He had the dial turned halfway round to the first digit before he thought better of it and shook his head, letting the receiver drop.

'No,' he murmured. 'Bound to be aggro. Sorry, Frankie-boy. Not this time.'

CHAPTER THIRTEEN

The Railway Arms was crowded with the usual mob of regulars. Kipper and Ferret were leaning on the bar discussing Kipper's injured ankle; Vi and Tommy were seated at a table, talking with Gil; Juicy Joan was deep in conversation with Dick Mayor. She was saying, 'He'll never change. Never.'

'That's what I thought in the beginning, luv. But now?' Mayor's bearded face got thoughtful. 'He's a reformed man. Well, almost.'

'I've known Robby for a long time, Dick.' Joan matched her companion in seriousness. 'Betting, cards, coming an' going as and when he likes, that's his scene. He might think he likes the idea of being back in the fold, but ... Tell you what. I'll give him a month – top whack – then he'll be at it again. He won't be able to stay away. You'll see.'

'Dunno.' Dick stared at his beer. 'Jan'll keep a tight hold on him.'

'Huh! You gotta be kidding.' Joan snorted scornfully, revealing a twinge of resentment. 'Listen, Lady Jan doesn't realize.'

'She's all right, that one. I tell you, good as gold, she is.' Dick broke off as he saw Robby making his way up to the bar. 'Wotcha, Rob. All right?'

'Yeah. Tasty.' Robby nodded. 'Evenin', Joan.'

Joan gave him a smile as Dick called for a drink. Robby asked who was as good as gold. Dick glanced warily at Joan and said, 'Don't matter.' Then changed the subject. 'I had a word with Geordie before he left. Bad news, that Henry geezer.'

'Yeah, a sickener,' agreed Robby. 'He tell you about the mum fallin' down into the grave?'

'Yeah. Real sad.' Mayor shook his head sympathetically. 'Poor cow.'

'Have you spoken to Kipper yet?' Joan asked.

'Kipper?' Robby glanced along the bar. 'No, ain't seen him yet. Why?'

'He's limping around with a big lump on his shin thanks to one of your pals,' Joan told him. 'When you see him, tell him from me he's banned from the shop, the no-good bastard.'

'What you goin' on about?' Robby was taken aback by her vehemence.

'Your pal.' Joan turned to call down the bar. 'Oi, Kip! Show Robby your shin.'

'Hallo, Rob.' Kipper limped up. 'Didn't see you come in.'

'Show him your leg,' urged Joan. 'Go on.'

'Oh, leave off, will you?' Kipper was embarrassed.

'What's up?' Robby was confused.

'I'll show you what's up.' Joan was not to be deterred. Kipper grinned as she put her drink down and stooped to drag at his trouser-leg.

'Might've been worth it. Ouch! Mind what you're doin', Joan!'

'Bragging again, Kipper?' Ferret chuckled as he joined them. 'Big boy, he is, Joan.'

'I don't happen to think it's funny.' Joan lifted the trouser, exposing a blue-purple swelling with an ugly redness at the centre. 'Look at it! That's what your pal did.'

'Jesus!' Robby winced in sympathy. 'That looks bad, Kip. Who'd you say did it?'

'A bloke was askin' where you were,' Kipper began.

'It was Denny More, Robby,' Ferret supplied. 'That Frank Aldino's mate.'

Robby's face got serious. 'Why'd he do that?'

''Cause Kipper wouldn't say where you was.' Black George entered the conversation, round features indignant.

174

'An' he threw my bloomin' dinner in his face an' all.'

'Leave off, George,' protested the object of their discussion. 'I'm tryin' to forget that bit. Know what I mean?'

'Like I said,' snapped Joan, 'Nice friends you've got.'

'Listen, that weren't no friend of mine. Right?' Robby's face was grim as he turned to the landlord. 'Roy, give us some tens for the phone, would you? Might be better if you shoot along to the game, Dick. I'll meet you down there later.'

'What's the SP then, mate?' asked Dick. 'I can hang about it you like.'

'I dunno.' Robby turned to Kipper. 'What did he want? He say?'

'For you to ring Frank, that's all.' Joan spoke before Kipper could open his mouth.

'What are you? His brief, or what?' Robby demanded irritably. To Dick Mayor, 'I'll catch you up later, mate.'

Dick nodded as Robby tossed a fifty pence piece onto the bar and picked up five tens. All eyes watched him as he pushed across to the phone.

Frank Aldino's taste in women matched his taste in furnishings: like his home, the two girls being served drinks by Denny More were smooth, glamorous, and expensive. Aldino was paying them no attention; he was more interested in his American guest.

'I heard whispers you an' a few others had a big spieler goin' on in the White House,' he was saying. 'That right?'

'That's right, Frank. We sure enough did.' Brookman advertized his dentist. 'Three senators and, would you believe? The then-Vice President of the US of A. All around a table playing stud poker. A lot of money changed hands that night, I kid you not.'

'Yeah, I can imagine.' Aldino glanced away as Denny More answered the ringing phone. 'Who is it, Denny?'

'It's that Robby Box geezer,' More explained. Then, into the mouthpiece, 'What's up with you, pal?'

On the other end of the phone, Robby said, 'You heard

175

me the first time, you thick bastard. You want to see me, fine. But don't touch my friends. Now, what d'you want? I'm in a hurry.'

More's features flushed as he said, 'Simple enough – just tell your mug friends to have a little respect, that's all.'

'What's the going rate on respect for pig shit?' asked Robby.

More fed a stream of obscenities into the phone before Aldino, directing an apologetic smile at Hal Brookman, took the receiver from him. 'Bobby,' he said, 'that ain't nice, son.'

'Oh, sorry, Frank. I was talkin' to that animal of yours a moment ago.'

'We'll sort that out later,' said Aldino. 'Right now I've got a proposition for you.'

'Yeah. Well.' Robby sounded dubious. 'Thanks all the same, Frank, but I remember the last time I enjoyed your company.'

'This is a straight game, Bobby.' Aldino was not to be put off. 'Big, but straight. Meet me at the Slipper in an hour. Be there.'

Without waiting for Robby's agreement, he put the phone down: a man accustomed to having his commands obeyed.

In the Slipper a three-piece band was playing watered-down Beatles numbers for the punters, most of whom had the appearance of well-heeled businessmen. And were, if their commercial ventures were not subjected to close scrutiny. Frank Aldino and his party were talking at a quiet table as a heavyweight in a generously-cut dinner suit ushered Robby up.

'Bobby, my son! Glad you could make it.' Aldino's affability did not quite hide the assumption that Robby would not have dared do anything else. 'Have a seat. Denny, take the ladies for a drink at the bar.'

Reluctantly, More did as his boss ordered, pausing irritably as Robby, grinning, said, 'Woof! Woof!'

'Denny!' Aldino snapped. 'Go on. Have a drink an' cool

off.' And to Robby, 'Don't push your luck in that quarter, Bobby-boy. Denny runs on a very short fuse.'

'Tell him not to hurt my friends,' Robby answered, then saw the ice in Aldino's eyes and added, 'There was no need, that's all I'm saying, Frank.'

Aldino stared at him for a long, tense moment, then nodded. 'OK Bobby, I'll have a word in his ear. Bobby? Meet Hal.'

Robby shook Brookman's hand, wondering why the face seemed familiar.

'Have we met before?'

'Nope.' Brookman shook his head. 'I never forget a face, Bobby. If we had, I'd remember.'

'This is Hal Brookman,' Aldino supplied.

'Brookman? Brookman?' Circuits linked in Robby's brain, supplying an answer. 'Hal Brookman the poker player?'

'The very same!' Brookman chuckled, flattered by the admiration he saw in Robby'e eyes. 'Hey! Fame at last. Terrific!'

'World Champion 1980, right?' Robby was impressed: this was one of the big time poker players. Very big time. 'Cleared up in Ireland two years ago. Flew back to the States with twenty-three grand in winnings after twenty-four hours of non-stop stud poker?'

'Well, not quite twenty-three grand, Bobby.' Brookman smiled modestly. 'But close enough. The man knows his poker, Frank.'

'I told you,' agreed Aldino, turning to Robby.

'Know a guy name of Van Kessel?'

'Henk Van Kessel?' Robby nodded. 'The Dutch poker player?'

'The very same.' Aldino smiled, pleased with his chosen protégé. 'He's flying in on Friday evening. so is a guy from Finland.'

'Lafe Hemmerson?' There was awe in Robby's voice now.

'Yep,' said Brookman easily. 'And a kraut named Dieter Bernhardt.'

'There was also supposed to be a Frenchman,' said Aldino.

'Raoul Lafitte?' Robby's voice was soft as realization dawned, wonderment shining in his eyes. 'You've got all the top spielers comin' to town. That can only mean one thing.'

'A twenty-four hour school comin' off,' Aldino confirmed. 'We start at midnight Friday night.'

Robby stared at the gangster. At Brookman. His customary deadpan expression was lost in his excitement: this had to be the annual international game. The biggest of the big time. The dream game. The one game every serious poker player was ready to mortgage his soul for.

'We do have one slight hitch, Bobby.' Brookman's tone was casual. 'We – or should I say Frank? – had the idea you might be able to help us out.'

'Me? Shu ... sure! Anything!' Robby made no attempt to hide his excitement: there was no way he could, it was too great. 'You want a dealer, right?'

'Bobby, the Frenchman has to drop out.'

Aldino left the sentence dangling like bait, studying robby with a small half-smile on his face. Brookman puffed on a giant cigar, exposing his dazzling teeth. Robby felt a lump form in his throat as his heart went into over-drive. They couldn't be getting at what he hardly dared think they were getting at. Could they? No! It wasn't possible. It couldn't be. Frank Aldino might be a godfather, but he wasn't a fairy godfather. They couldn't mean it. They couldn't be suggesting it. He scarcely dared ask. Found it hard to with his heart racing like the Derby winner. He forced the lump in his throat down, trying to keep his voice even.

'You ... mu ... mu ... mean?'

'That's right, Bobby,' said Aldino casually. 'If you can raise the sit-down, you can have the Frenchman's seat.'

If it had been a movie the background music would have swelled to a triumphant crescendo. The *Halleluja Chorus* or the *1812*. Something victorious that suited the realization of a dream; the fleshing of fantasy. Instead,

Robby had muted Beatles music and the dull drone of conversation. It didn't matter, because he couldn't hear it. All his attention was riveted on the two men smiling at him from across the table. Had Frank really invited him to sit in on the world's biggest poker game? Was Robby Box really invited to sit down with the finest poker players in the world? It was some kind of joke! It had to be. Didn't it?

Brookman broke the awe-struck silence. 'Well, what d'you say, Bobby? You in?'

The lump was harder to swallow. 'How much do I need to raise?'

'Ten grand.' Aldino said it like the figure was pocket money. 'The Dutchman, the Finn, the kraut, Hal, me, and you. Ten grand apiece. Sixty grand up on offer, Bobby. Nice pot, eh?'

'Not many!' Robby let a long, soft whistle escape his lips. 'When's deadline for makin' the frame?'

The question prompted Brookman to glance at Aldino with a question on his tanned face. Aldino asked, 'Have you got the dough, Bobby?'

'I can get it,' Robby answered quickly, seeing the doubt on Brookman's face and hurrying to reassure them. 'Look, I'm sitting on nine right now. I'll have the other long'un by mid-day tomorrow.

Aldino glanced at Brookman, who studied his cigar for a moment that felt like a lifetime to Robby before nodding. Aldino said, 'Fair enough, Bobby. The seat's yours until tomorrow lunchtime. If I ain't heard from you by then you're out of the frame. OK?'

'You'll hear from me!' Robby stood up and shook both their hands, more in gratitude than farewell. 'I'll be there. And thanks. Thanks very much.'

'Don't thank me, Bobby-boy,' Aldino smiled. 'You may end up potless.'

'So might you,' grinned Robby.

The two men watched him walk away, his step light. Brookman tapped ash from his cigar and said, 'He's out of his class, Frank.'

'He's a big boy.' Aldino shrugged. 'He might well shock

179

you, Hal. The guy knows his way round a deck of cards.'

The Oriental girl who met Robby at the entrance to the Chinese restaurant had long, glossy black hair and a deep slit in her cheong-sam that was the only loose part of the figure-hugging garment. Robby studied her appreciatively as she asked if she could help him.

'Is Lee about?'

A small smile decorated her inscrutable features as she nodded. 'Ah, please. You come round this way. I direct you to see Lee.'

Robby followed her towards a door at the rear of the restaurant, admiring the way her hips swayed so that he failed to spot Tony Cannon sitting in a booth with a pile of spare ribs in front of him and barbecue sauce smeared round his mouth. Until, that was, Cannon spoke.

'Well, well, well. If it ain't old granpappy himself.'

Robby halted, looking at the younger man.

'Don't you know it's rude to talk with your mouth full?'

'You don't need manners in a dive like this.' Cannon saw Robby's direction and sneered. 'New job? Just about your mark, washin' dishes.'

The arrogance broke through Robby's calm: Cannon had a way of rubbing him the wrong way. He took a step towards the man.

'I'll feed them spare ribs to you up the wrong end in a minute, son.'

Cannon saw that he was serious and took a step back. 'Now, now. Just windin' you up.'

Robby grunted and turned away to where the girl was waiting by the door, then paused, looking back at Cannon.

'You carryin', son?'

'Could be. Why?'

'Get shot of your fan club,' Robby indicated the two women and the man with Cannon, 'and there might be a vacant seat.'

'A spieler?' Interested.

'That's what I like about you son,' insultingly. 'You're so sharp.'

180

Cannon glared at Robby, then smiled, glancing at his friends; back at Robby.

'You're a mug for punishment, grandad.'

Robby shrugged, tapping on the door as Cannon came up behind him.

Beyond was a large room with a circular table at the centre and crates around the walls. Dick Mayor was sitting at the table with two Chinamen. Lee, small and smiling, opened the door, the smile becoming a frown as he caught sight of Cannon.

'Wotcha, Lee. How's your luck?' Robby beckoned Cannon inside. 'This is a ... He's all right, Lee. OK?'

'OK.' The oriental accepted Robby's word. 'Have a seat.'

He locked the door as Robby and Cannon sat down. Dick Mayor said, 'All right, Rob?'

'Tasty. Couldn't be better.' There was real enthusiasm in Robby's voice. 'Right! What's the opposition like?'

'Poker ain't their game, Rob,' Dick grinned. 'It's like takin' sweets from kids.'

'Great!' enthused Robby. 'They carryin' much, you reckon?'

'Ain't really sure,' shrugged Dick. 'Must have a fifty minimum each, I suppose.'

'Pity,' Robby murmured thoughtfully. Then brightened again. 'Never mind, Lee's always good for a oner or more. What you carryin'?'

'Bout two an' a half.' Dick frowned, perplexed. 'Why?'

Robby was making calculations in his head: fifty apiece from the two unknown Chinamen; say a oner – no, one and a half – from Lee; Dick's pot made it five hundred. He was holding £250. He dumped the notes ostentatiously on the table.

'Two an' a half! I feel lucky.'

Cannon rose to the bait. 'Three hundred!'

It was enough. Including his own pot, there would be five hundred over the thousand on the table. Take that and add it to the nine in the Building Society and he had enough for the big one. 'Bingo,' he murmured, smiling slyly. 'Bloody bingo!'

'What's up?' Dick didn't understand. 'You all right or what?'

'Like I said, mate: tasty. Just tasty.'

Dick frowned at his friend, wondering what Robby was up to. He had no chance to ask any further questions, though, because Lee sat down and announced ceremoniously, 'OK gentlemen, the game is seven card stud poker. Two face cards, five hole cards. First jack deals.'

Tony Cannon got the starter card and told the baffled Dick, 'I'll wipe that grin off his face, pal, don't worry.'

Robby just went on smiling, singing softly. 'I'm sitting on top of the world.'

Jan sat in the kitchen staring at the paying-in book. She found it hard to believe they were so close to their target, but the figures still added up to just under nine thousand, and if Robby continued to pay in as he had been doing, there would be ten thousand in no time. Ten thousand! She shook her head in delighted bewilderment and slid the air tickets from under the bread bin, grinning as she thought how easy it would be to take the money and run. She felt almost guilty when Debby came sleepy-eyed into the room and saw the tickets in her hand.

'What's all this, then? Going to do a runner on us?'

'Maybe,' she smiled.

'That's what I'd do if I was Robby,' Debby said, helping herself to orange juice. 'Grab my nine grand and go. Coo! Just think of all that money and a new start in a new country like Australia. Be smart!'

'Mmm, a nice thought,' Jan chuckled. 'I could sell this place. The chap next door keeps making me a good offer.'

'Yeah,' grinned Debby, 'I know what he's offering, all right.'

'Debby!' her mother scolded.

'Well, every time he sees me I can feel him undressing me with his eyes,' Debby stated. 'The randy old sod.'

'By offer, I meant financial,' said Jan. 'For this place. With Robby's cash and what I'd get on this place, we could have a wonderful start out there.'

'Yeah.' Debby picked up the tickets. 'Robby wouldn't go, though, would he?'

'Not at the moment.' Jan shrugged, her pretty face pensive. 'Once he's paid off his tax and got himself all straight, though. Maybe he would then.'

'What's he gonna do after?' Debby asked. 'You know, once he's legit?'

'For a living you mean?' Jan queried.

'Yeah,' nodded Debby. 'I mean, he's not exactly your nine-to-five type, is he? I just can't see him holding down a proper job.'

'Oh, I don't know.' Jan chose to ignore her daughter's doubtful expression. 'He's really determined this time. You think he'll drift back into gambling then?'

'To use one of Robby's own sayings,' said Debby, 'Has Pinochio got a wooden ...'

'Debby!' Jan interjected.

Robby, Lee, and Tony Cannon were the only players left in the hand. Lee had two pairs showing, tens and fives, his fifth open card was the two of Spades. He put £25 on the table. Robby was showing three Clubs and a pair of aces. He said, 'Yeah. Your pony and up a brown one,' as he added £35 to the Chinaman's bet. Cannon had the makings of a ragged run: the two of Clubs, the three in the same suit, the four of Diamonds, and the five of Hearts. His other face card was the nine of Hearts. He studied the cards and shook his head.

'No, not this time.'

'Just you an' me, Lee,' Robby said cheerfully. 'Thirty-five sovs down to you.'

'OK. I call,' said Lee. 'I no hit full house.'

'I knew that, mate.' Robby turned his cards. 'Flushin'. Ace on top.'

Lee groaned, his face easily read as Robby hauled in the pot. Cannon said, 'Cor! That's three flushes in a row you've pulled. Bleedin' unnatural.'

'When you're hot, you're hot,' grinned Robby, pleased with himself.

'I must've just come out of the bleedin' fridge then,' complained Dick. 'I can't even win an argument.'

'Way it goes,' said Robby. 'Sometimes you just get lucky.'

'Yeah.' Dick grinned ruefully. 'Trouble is, tonight the only luck I got is bad.'

The cards went round again. Robby went on winning, the pile of notes at his elbow growing steadily larger as the others diminished. Cannon was close to his limit, his temper not improving as he watched Robby take his money.

'Bastard hands!' he complained as Robby blew him out with a full house.

'Now, now,' Robby said. 'Win with style; lose with dignity. That's what my old Dad used to say.'

Seeing the last of his pot cross the table did nothing to improve Cannon's humour. His lip curled as he snarled, 'A pox on what your dad used to say.'

'Tut, tut, tut.' Robby shook his head; amused.

It was the last straw for Tony Cannon. Angry and humiliated, he sprang to his feet, face darkening as his fists clenched. Abruptly, Lee's chair toppled back as the Oriental came upright in the stance of his namesake, Bruce Lee. Cannon's mouth gaped as the small, dark man extended menacing fingers towards him.

'I'd be very careful, son,' Robby warned mildly. 'This man could break every bone in your body in seconds. He hates violence at his table.'

Cannon glowered at Robby, then – warily – at Lee. Impenetrable black eyes met his stare and he swallowed, fists unclenching. He snatched his jacket from the chair.

'Another time, Box. Another time.'

He headed for the door, halted by Robby's voice and the fiver that floated to the floor, just as he had once thrown a contemptuous hand-out to Robby.

'Get yourself a cab.'

'Get stuffed!'

The door slammed hard behind Cannon as Robby and Lee began to laugh, joined by the two otherwise silent Chinese.

'Great, but what's so funny?' said Dick Mayor, the

question producing fresh gales of laughter. 'Well, let us in on the joke then. What's so funny?'

'Tell him, Lee,' urged Robby. 'Go on, tell him.'

There was nothing in the least inscrutable about Lee as he chuckled, making chopping gestures in the air. 'Very simple for Chinese man to trick Englishman with this, yes? All English think we know Kung Fu or Karate.'

He collapsed in helpless laughter as Dick asked, 'You mean?'

'That's right, mate,' Robby confirmed, wiping humorous tears from his eyes. 'What Lee knows about the martial arts, you could get on the back of a postage stamp and still have room for your name and address.'

Dick gaped in amused disbelief as Lee began to prance around the room, faking lethal-looking hand and foot movements. It was a while before the laughter faded and they went back to the game.

'Fifty pounds.' Lee pushed the money to the centre of the table.

'I think I've got you beat.' Dick added notes. 'fifty and up a score.'

Robby, the only other player still in, said, 'Yeah. Your bet an' up another thirty. A oner to you, Lee.'

The Chinaman said, 'No,' and stacked his cards. Dick studied Robby's face cards: the king of Hearts, the queen of Hearts, the ace of Hearts, the three of Clubs, and the two of Diamonds. A potential run, even a running flush.

'Yeah.' Dick's tone was thoughtful, his face wary. 'A oner and up another score.'

Robby glanced at his friend's badly-depleted pot and asked, 'How much you got in front of you?'

Dick flicked notes. 'About a oner.'

Robby's face was deadpan, unsmiling as he said, 'Called.'

Dick smiled, assuming his friend was taking it easy on him. Then Robby added, 'And raise. Another oner.'

There was a sudden silence. Dick stared at Robby, trying to read something on the expressionless features. There was nothing.

'So what now, Rob? You know I can't even call. I've got a oner here. Stand me the other until tomorrow?'

Robby stared back. 'Sorry, mate. I can't.'

Amazement showed on Dick's face, washing hopelessly back from his friend's stony gaze. Dick saw that Robby was serious and anger took over from disbelief.

'Oh, cheers, pal! Thanks for sweet FA! I've stood you more times than I can remember. What's your game, eh?'

'Sorry, mate. Not tonight.' Robby's voice was flat, unyielding. 'I need a result.'

'Yeah, don't we all?' snapped Dick, turning to Lee. 'Lee? Stand me a oner? Mr Big here's turned monkey on me an' that can only mean one thing – he's bluffin'. Well?'

Lee looked from one man to the other, not sure what was going on, not sure why Robby was behaving in so uncharacteristic a manner. 'It's OK, Robby?' he asked.

'It's got fuck-all to do with him, Lee!' Dick's voice was harsh with anger. 'This is a private loan between me an' you. OK?'

'I'd rather you didn't, Lee.' From Robby; flat. Empty of emotion.

'No, of course you wouldn't!' snapped Dick. 'C'mon, Lee. I'll give back your oner plus ten per cent of what's in the pot. It'd be well worth it just to see this *pal* of mine get his.'

Reluctantly, Lee slid ten ten-pound notes to Dick.

'Cheers,' said the bearded man. And glared at Robby. 'Bet called. *Pal.*'

Robby sighed and turned his first hole card: the jack of Hearts. The second: the ten of Hearts. Dick's face paled as he saw the royal flush. His shoulders slumped in defeat and he climbed wearily to his feet.

'Lee, I'll square you up tomorrow. OK?' Lee nodded sadly and Dick said, 'Cheers.'

Without another word, he left the room. The two Chinese followed him, leaving Robby and Lee alone with the silence. Robby collected his winnings and fed them into his coat. Put the coat on. Moved towards the door.

Lee said, 'Robby, you always been very welcome to my

card schools. Always. We have many good nights, but no more you come here, please.'

'But, Lee.' Hurt.

'You come no more.' Lee eased Robby gently, but firmly, through the door. 'Please.'

Robby could feel the money slapping heavy against his leg as he walked through the deserted restaurant. Dawn light filtered grey and lonely through the windows as the silent Lee opened the outer door and stood back to let Robby through. Robby looked at the oriental, but now the face was truly inscrutable, the eyes as cold as when they had stared at Tony Cannon. Robby licked his lips, trying to find the words to explain. They didn't exist, so he went out through the door into the cold of the early morning. The door banged shut behind him. He turned, staring at Lee's face. An arm waved, dismissing him, and he shivered. Not from the cold. Despair turned to anger: he had had to do it. There was no other way to raise the extra grand fast enough. Nor any way to explain. He kicked the door.

'Stuff your pisspot games! You hear me? Stuff your games!'

There was no answer: feeling very lonely, he walked away.

187

CHAPTER FOURTEEN

Vi came into the kitchen anticipating a morning cuppa and found Robby sitting, unshaven and moody, at the table. His clothes were crumpled and he looked tired, but his mother recognized something else in his manner, some problem he was wrestling with. 'Want to talk about it?' she asked, setting the kettle to boil and emptying lukewarm tea from the pot.

'Eh?'

Robby frowned at her and Vi said, 'C'mon, Robby. I know something's worrying you. Is it Jan?'

'No. Well, not Jan. Just things.' Robby sighed, rubbing at his shadowed eyes. 'I got a problem. All my life ... Well, all my sort of workin' life ...'

Vi snorted. 'That's a joke! What would you know about work?'

'All right, you know what I mean.' He smiled ruefully. 'I've got the chance to fulfil a dream of mine.'

'I didn't know you had any,' said Vi.

'We've all got dreams, Mum. I ain't no exception.'

Vi saw that he was serious and sat down opposite him. 'All right, you've got this dream. So what's the problem?'

Robby sighed again. 'The problem is, if I go for the dream I gamble everything I care for.'

'You've been doin' that since you was twelve years old, boy,' Vi said mildly. 'You've always gambled.'

'Yeah, but this is different,' he frowned. 'This is the Big Deal. The stakes are high.'

'You've said what you'll lose if you lose,' Vi said. 'What do you gain if you win?'

'Well, that's the crunch, ain't it?' The frown got deeper

as he wrestled with the problem. 'I could come out with enough dough to pay up all me tax an' all that crap, an' have enough money to start a business. Buy a little shop, or whatever.'

'What does Jan think about it?' Her son's expression gave Vi the answer. 'Oh, I see. She doesn't know about it. Right?'

'Nope.' Robby shook his head. 'Thing is, it involves all me money, which she's got stashed away in a Building Society in her name.'

'So you can't try and pull it off behind her back, right?'

'Suppose not,' Robby shrugged.

'Well, good job an' all,' said Vi firmly. 'It's high time you had your wings clipped. You won't get no sympathy from this quarter on that one.'

'Don't I know it!' The rueful smile brightened. 'Be somethin' if I could pull it off, though. Eh? A right nice surprise.'

'I suppose so.' Vi rose to switch off the kettle. 'Where's the milk?'

'Mmm?' Robby was frowning again, lost in private thoughts. 'Oh, there's only tinned. Milky ain't been yet. Yeah. Wouldn't that be a surprise?'

The thoughts had coalesced into a decision: Robby got to his feet, heading for the kitchen door. Vi said, 'I've just poured you some tea. Where you goin'? Not out again?'

'A shower and a shave.' His voice was firm now. 'Got any clean shirts?'

Edward Symbols was surprised to find Robby waiting outside his office. Having explained the financial requirements of his entry to normal life, the accountant had not really expected to see Robby again.

'Why, Mr Box,' he smiled. 'How are you keeping?'

'Hallo, Mr Symbols,' Robby replied. 'Tasty, thanks. Yourself?'

'I'm well.' Symbols unlocked the door. 'I presume you've come to see me?'

'Yeah.' Robby followed the gnomic little man into the office. 'That's right.'

190

Symbols nodded and hung his coat on an ancient stand as Robby waited by his desk, eyes scanning the small room.

'Right then!' said the accountant. 'First things first. Some tea?'

'Er, no.' Robby shook his head, then changed his mind, smiling. 'Yeah! Yeah, sounds good.'

'Always my first job of the day.' Symbols took an electric kettle from a cluttered side desk. 'Excuse me a moment. Won't be a jiffy. Make yourself at home.'

He bustled out of the office, footsteps retreating along the corridor. Robby heard a door open. A tap begin to run. He stepped swiftly around the central desk and began to rummage through the drawers, one eye on the door. 'Bingo!' he murmured as he saw blank sheets with Symbols' letterheading printed across the top. He pulled a sheaf loose and folded them into his pocket. As the accountant's footsteps echoed in the corridor, he pushed the drawer shut and came back around the desk.

'Now then, just get this plugged in,' Symbols said genially, 'and I'll be with you.'

'Oh, I've just remembered something.' Robby grinned apologetically. 'Sorry. Can I come back and see you a bit later on?'

'Why, yes.' Symbols stared perplexed at his client's retreating back. 'A very strange man. Oh, well.'

'We're closed,' said Gil as Robby came in to the empty betting shop.

'Full of the joys of spring, are we?' Robby asked.

'If you had to put up with the naggin' I have,' remarked Gil, sourly. 'Oh, don't matter. What brings you in here at this ungodly hour? I thought this time of day turned you to dust.'

'You've got a typewriter out back, ain't you?'

'Yeah, of course I have,' Gil acknowledged. 'Why?'

'Can I use it for half an hour?'

'Help yourself.' Gil shrugged. 'Better get Joan to show you how it works – you need a bleedin' pilot's licence to operate that thing.'

Robby grinned his thanks and hurried to the inner office. Fifteen minutes later, Joan was bored with watching him peck one-fingered at the keys and offered to take over.

'This what you want?' She indicated his scribbled notes and Symbols' letterheading.

'Well, words to that effect.' Robby glanced round furtively, as though afraid Gil might come in. 'And, er, I'd very much appreciate a bit of schtum. Know what I mean?'

'Fine.' Joan favoured him with a suggestive smile. 'But that will really cost you, lover boy.'

'I thought it might,' sighed Robby.

'How come every time I drive past Gil's betting shop I get captured by you?' Geordie complained as he braked the ancient van in front of Jan's house. 'I'm nothing better'n a taxi for you, chum.'

'It's all in a good cause, mate.' Robby winked as he climbed out. 'Won't be long.'

He was true to his word, emerging only minutes later with a confused Jan in tow. She was clutching a letter, ostensibly from Edward Symbols, Chartered Accountant, that she read over and over as Geordie put the old Thames in gear and pulled away.

'This is all a bit sudden, Robby.'

She sounded doubtful. Robby hurried to reassure her.

'Yeah, I know. But like the letter says – if I can pay the tax people the nine grand by today, I'll save myself almost a grand in penalties.' He shrugged innocently. 'Gotta be worth it, Princess.'

'Well, yes. I suppose so.' Jan read the letter again, still frowning. 'But why cash? Surely the tax office will take a cheque? Or a bank draft, or whatever.'

'Princess, like the letter from Mr Symbols explains,' Robby said, 'if they suss out I've had money in somebody else's name … Well, it could mean aggro.'

'Oh, aye!' Geordie agreed. 'They don't like anything like that. Mind you, nine grand in cash. You sure you can trust this Symbols character, Rob?'

'Yes,' Jan nodded. 'That's a point, Robby.'

'Listen!' Robby's tone verged on the irritable. 'The man's a diamond. Oh! Sorry, I mean the man's as good as gold. Twenty-two carats. C'mon Geordie, mate, boot it a bit for us.'

'I'm going as fast as I can, mun.' Geordie wondered what all the rush was about. 'Bloody hell! You've got some front, you know.'

'Are you sure the Building Society will allow us to withdraw this amount at such short notice, Robby?' Jan was still dubious. 'I mean, I'm not really sure ...'

'I've already checked it out, Princess,' Robby cut in. 'They don't like it, but when I explained what the situation was, they were very co-operative. Besides, it is my money, ain't it?'

'Yes, it's your money,' Jan agreed.

'Well then!' Robby said quickly. All aggrieved innocence. 'Just be happy I'm gettin' meself sorted out. It's you that's been pushin' me to do it. An' now that I am, you're givin' me all the twenty questions.' He snatched the letter away. 'For two pins I'd forget the whole bloody thing and keep me nine grand.'

'I'm sorry, Robby.' Guilt showed on Jan's pretty face and she leaned across the seat to kiss his cheek. 'You're right. I should be happy you're actually getting yourself clear. Sorry, love.'

'Yeah, well.' Mollified. 'I mean.'

Geordie dropped them at the Building Society office and they went inside. Robby checked the clock against his watch as they waited for the manager to peruse the letter. Aldino's noonday deadline was approaching fast and Robby was unable to prevent himself from pacing the office as they waited.

Finally, they were summoned to the counter, where the manager passed various forms across.

'Very well, madam. If you would be good enough to sign these for me. Here, and here. Thank you.' He took the forms as Robby fidgeted, watching the second hand of the clock sweep round. The chief cashier came up with two thick wads of plastic-swathed notes. 'Would madam care to count it?'

'No! That's OK.' Robby snatched the money and deposited the twin bundles in his coat. 'We trust you.'

He spun round, almost running for the door. Jan hurried to keep up.

'Robby, what's all the rush?'

'I'm sorry, luv,' he grinned. 'I'm just nervous, that's all. Big day for me, y'know.'

'Yes.' A half-smile decorated Jan's generous mouth. 'Robby Box can now exist.'

'Yeah, that's it.' Robby nodded enthusiastically. 'Right. You go back home with Geordie an' I'll meet you there in an hour or so.'

'But, Robby.' The smile left Jan's mouth, replaced with an expression of puzzlement. 'I'll come with you to see Mr Symbols.'

'No! No ... I.' Jan's frown grew deeper as he shuffled from foot to foot. 'Look, Princess, this is something I've got to do on my own. OK?'

'OK, Robby.'

She was puzzled. He put an arm around her shoulders. 'Trust me. I need to do it for myself. Can you understand that?'

'Well, yes,' she allowed. 'Yes and no.' Then, smiling her trust, 'OK, gambling man, play it your way. I'll see you back home.'

Geordie sounded his horn from across the road, warily eyeing an approaching traffic warden. Robby kissed Jan and propelled her towards the van, anxious to make his phone call. Anxious to avoid any more difficult questions. Before Geordie had the Thames started, he was striding away, looking for a phone booth.

He found one still in working order and dialled Frank Aldino's number.

'Listen, Frank, I'm in – I've got the ten grand.'

'Terrific. The seat's yours. Just a little word of warnin', son – once you're in, you're committed. OK?'

'Hey! I know the rules.'

'Good. Just thought I'd point it out. No harm done – welcome to the big one. I'll send Denny to pick you up at eleven on Friday night. We start on the stroke of midnight. OK?'

'I'll be waiting. See you.' Robby wiped sweat from his forehead as he dropped the receiver on its cradle and slumped against the glass. He was in now. Win or lose, he was committed. He sighed. 'Welcome to the Big Deal.'

'Cheer up, luv.' Geordie wondered why Jan seemed so worried. 'You should be pleased for him. For the both of you. I am.'

'Yes, I know.' Jan smiled at him. 'I am really, Geordie. It's just that things have happened so fast. What with Henry and all that.'

'Aye.' Geordie nodded thoughtfully. 'Was a crying shame, that. Knew his old man, you know. Worked for him first.'

The memory of Diamond's suicide threw them both into a pensive silence, gloom threatening what should have been a joyous occasion. After a while, Geordie said, 'Hey, c'mon. This isn't going to do us any good, is it? Tell you what – let's go to the Railway and have a few beers.'

Jan glanced at Geordie's weather-beaten face and saw pain. Diamond's death had hit him harder than he let on. 'I told Robby I'd meet him back home,' she said. 'Tell you what – I'll ring the accountant's and leave a message for him. I think I could do with a drink myself.'

'Aye, that's the ticket,' Geordie enthused. 'We'll drink to poor old Henry and to the new start for Robby.'

'Aye,' Jan agreed. And they both began to laugh.

They reached the pub to find the regulars already in residence. Geordie went up to the bar to order while Jan crossed to the phone, taking coins from her purse. She dialled the number and waited for the ringing tone to end. Shoved a coin home in the slot.

'Mr Symbols? May I speak to Robby Box? Oh. Well, can I leave a message? What? I don't understand, Mr Symbols. You sent Robby a letter. I read it only this morning. You didn't? But ...' Realization sank like a knife into her heart.

Her eyes grew wide, then screwed tight shut on the forming tears as she whispered, 'Oh, my God! Robby! No ... please, please. I ... I ...' It was an effort of will to force her vocal cords to form the words, 'Thank you, Mr Symbols.'

She let the phone drop, features frozen in shock. She was oblivious of the tears coursing freely down her cheeks as she leant against the wall with her life, her hopes, her dreams in ruins around her. Geordie looked across to where she stood, shoulders heaving helplessly, and the smile faded from his face.

'Jan?' He hurried to her, ignoring the curious stares of Kipper and Ferret and the others. 'Jan, luv? What's the matter?'

Her reply was dragged from a deep, grief-filled pit. 'Take me home, please, Geordie.'

The black cab halted outside Jan's house and Robby stepped onto the pavement. He opened the gate and walked towards the door as it opened to reveal a grim-faced Geordie.

'Wotcha, mate. All right?' Robby frowned as Geordie closed the door and positioned himself before it like a sentry. 'Hey! Don't close it.'

'I shouldn't go in if I were you.' There was no smile on the Newcastle man's face and his voice was cold. 'I don't think you'll find the welcome to your liking.'

'Eh?' Robby was puzzled. 'What you on about?'

He moved towards the door. Geordie moved to block him. 'Hey, what's goin' on?'

'Yeah,' said Geordie in the same ugly tone. 'What is goin' on, you bastard?'

Geordie's manner told Robby that something was badly wrong. 'Has something happened to Jan?' There was genuine concern in his voice. 'Look, get outta the way, Geordie.'

'Don't make me lay you out, bastard!' Geordie stood immovable. 'She knows!'

Ice sent chilly shock through Robby's insides. 'She knows? Knows what?'

'All that.' There was contempt in Geordie's voice now and

196

he stared at Robby as though seeing his old friend for the first time. 'Gotta get the money quick to pay me tax! You no-good bastard! You just couldn't be straight with the girl, could you?'

The ice cramped Robby's belly. He felt sweat form cold on his face and neck. A sour taste filled his mouth. 'Oh, no,' he whispered.

'Oh, yes!' Geordie grated. 'Now if I were you, pal, I'd just turn around and piss off! The girl's in there breakin' her heart on account of you. And it's the last time! OK? No more – you're done here. You're through.'

Cold became heat as Robby stared at his friend. He didn't understand. None of them did. What else could he have done? And he was doing it for Jan, wasn't he? Anger protected him from guilt.

'Now mind your own business, mate. It's got nothin' to do with you. Out of me way.'

He moved to pass Geordie again, but suddenly his coat was seized in two work-hardened hands and he was spinning round, staggering off balance as a roundhouse right mashed his lips against his teeth and lights exploded over his vision. He felt a sharp pain in his back and the clatter of tumbling dustbins, then he was looking up at Geordie from amidst a litter of spilled rubbish, blood salty in his mouth.

'Now there's more where that one came from,' Geordie warned him. 'An' I'm in just the right mood to dish out a few more.'

'You berk!' Robby climbed awkwardly to his feet, spitting blood. 'I don't want to ruck with you, Geordie. So piss off out of it an' mind your own business.'

'You just don't understand, do you?' Geordie's voice was menacing, his fists clenched ready to strike again. 'She don't want to know, OK? You're not welcome. You thick git!'

Robby ignored the warning, heading for the door again. Geordie side-stepped and hit him low in the belly, doubling him over with bile threatening to spill from his gasping mouth. The bigger man grabbed the coat again and turned him to face the fist that slammed against his chin, sending him flying back along the path to crash heavily on his back.

'The first was from me,' Geordie snarled. 'The second, from Jan. An' that last one was from Debby. Now d'you get the message?'

It was written on Robby's face. He rolled onto hands and knees and shook his head groggily as Geordie stormed through the gate. It banged shut and Robby used it to lever himself upright as Geordie climbed into his van, shouting through the window, 'You gambled an' lost! You're a mug, Robby. A loser. A first-rate mug of a loser!'

Robby strained upright as the old van pulled away. 'I'll show you!' he yelled. 'I'll bleedin' show you. All of you!'

He turned to face the house. Debby's face showed at a window, staring down at him with an expression of contempt and anger and loss. Their eyes locked, then Debby shook her head and let the curtains fall, cutting him off.

'Jan!' he shouted, his tone anguished. 'Debby! Please! Let me … I can explain it all. Jan!'

There was no answer. No movement. The curtains remained still, the door closed. Robby wiped his mouth. Rubbed at his aching belly. Still there was nothing. Numbly, he opened the gate. Went through it. Closed it. Halted, turning to face the building again. Hoping.

There was no hope and again anger came to his defence. He reached into a trouser pocket to yank out a Yale key. He stared at it. Then back at the blank, unyielding windows. His jaw throbbed and he could feel blood trickling from his nostrils. He hurled the key along the path.

'I'll show you! I'll show all of you!'

Alone again, Robby Box staggered away.

CHAPTER FIFTEEN

Friday. The night of the Big Deal. The night that dreams come true. Robby, his face still showing the effects of Geordie's handiwork, was at the bar of the Railway Arms, dressed neatly in suit and tie. Joan was with him.

'So you haven't seen her?' she asked.

'Not for three days.' Pain showed in Robby's eyes, escaping past the deadpan expression. 'I've tried phoning, but ... I'd rather not talk about it if you don't mind, luv.'

'I did hear say she and Debby were going out to Aussie to see her mum an' dad.'

'She's been goin' on about that for a long time.' Once more Robby dismissed the impossible: things were going to turn out right. In the end. 'She'll not go.'

'So sure?' Joan's smile was part-curious, part-inviting.

'I'll get a result tonight an' then all my troubles will be over,' he replied, voice confident. 'I'll be home an' dry. I'll get her back.'

'What if you don't?' Pragmatically.

'I will.' Positively.

'I meant, get a result,' Joan amended. 'What if you lose?'

Robby looked at her as though she had just asked him to levitate: suggesting the impossible.

'No. Tonight's my night. I've waited a lifetime for it. It's as though I've spent all these years in all those tinpot spielers rehearsing for it. I'll not come away a loser.'

Joan studied his face, seeing blind determination, total faith. She was about to speak, but Denny More swaggered in to ask if Robby was ready.

'Yeah, I'm ready.' He drained his orange juice and grinned at Joan. 'Bye, luv.'

'Good luck.' Joan's smile was open now. 'And Robby? If the worst should happen ...' She shrugged. 'My shoulder's wide and like blotting paper.'

Robby looked back at her and nodded. 'Thanks, luv.'

He turned to follow More out of the pub. Then halted as Geordie appeared in the doorway. They stared at one another. Denny More said, 'We ain't got all night, pal.' And Robby nodded, going out past Geordie as the Newcastle man stepped aside as if avoiding a plague carrier. Robby heard the gang greet him, their warmth emphasizing his own loneliness. Then he shrugged, dismissing them all: the big game lay ahead and after that everything would be fine. He followed More into the night.

The five men waiting for Robby in Frank Aldino's place were of five different nationalities. Aldino was short and muscular, with a thick neck and a bullet head; Brookman was tall and tanned and very American; Lafe Hemmerson, the Finn, was tall and thin and so fair he might have been an albino; Henk Van Kessel, the Dutchman, was big and bluff, with a ruddy face and pale blue eyes; the German, Dieter Bernhardt, was built like a weightlifter, his hair cropped short on a square, heavy skull. Each one was different, yet each bore a marked similarity to his companions: their eyes were sharp, calculating and impenetrable, giving nothing away. Poker players' eyes. Robby kept his own face straight as he was introduced, not letting the awe he felt overwhelm him. These were the finest players in the world – and he was one of them. He was invited to sit down with them and play poker. It was a dream come true. And it was going to be a dream with a happy ending. He could feel it. He was going to walk out with sixty thousand pounds in his pocket, and when he showed Jan the money, she would forgive him. Understand why he had done it. For them. So that they could make a decent start in the straight life. It would be his last serious game. A glorious, magnificent farewell to the gambling life. And after, when people talked about the great players, about Brookman, Bernhardt, Hemmerson, Van Kessel, there would be another name: Robby Box. Yeah, they'd say, Robby Box walked out that game with sixty grand in his sky. A real poker player. And he lived happily ever after.

Robby felt good as he sat down and put his money on the table.

'Right, gentlemen, here we go.' Hal Brookman began to deal the cards. 'Ace to bet.'

Each man got one card face-down, one showing. Robby showed an ace. He put fifty pounds on it. One by one, the others followed suit, until Brookman said, 'Yes, and raise fifty.'

The third card was dealt. Robby got another ace. He checked his hole card: the king of Hearts.

'Two hundred.'

The others went along with him and Brookman dealt again, giving Robby the king of Spades. Two pairs: aces over kings.

'Still those lovely aces to bet,' Brookman said.

'Yes.' Robby's face was deadpan. 'Three hundred the bet.'

To his left, Aldino shook his head. 'Not here.'

Bernhardt and Hemmerson dropped out, but Van Kessel called. Brookman smiled and folded, dealing the last card. Robby got the three of Hearts, the Dutchman, an ace, which gave him aces and nines showing. He said, 'Five hundred,' staring at Robby's expressionless face.

Robby said, 'Called and raise. Up another hundred.'

Almost four thousand pounds sat at the centre of the table. Van Kessel looked at the money, then at his cards. After a while, he shrugged and threw in his hand. Robby hauled the pot to his side of the table. Brookman smiled and said, 'First blood to Bobby.'

Aldino said, 'Easy, ain't it, Bobby-boy.'

Casually, Robby said, 'Win some, lose some.'

'Winning's the easy bit, son,' Aldino murmured. 'It's the losin' that hurts.'

Robby laughed as he stacked the winnings neatly by his elbow. It was going as he knew it had to go. Aces in the first hand: a propitious start that was going to get better as the night went on.

The night went on. Money changed owners across the table. Players lost; players won. Men dropped out to freshen up, to take a drink and returned to the game. Darkness gave way to light. Brookman opened the curtains, letting in the day. It changed nothing: the game continued.

'Know how you feel, Bobby,' Aldino sympathized as Bernhardt took Robby with an ace-high flush.

'Didn't think he had it,' Robby said through a yawn. 'Hurt me bad.'

He glanced at his diminished pot and decided to clean up. He went into the bathroom and splashed cold water on his face. Lack of sleep and the tension of the game put shadows under his eyes; nervous excitement kept him hyper-active.

'Well, Bobby-boy?' Aldino joined him. 'How d'you like the big time?'

'It's different, I'll say that.' Robby towelled his face, wincing as he touched his sore lip. 'Those guys know their poker.'

Aldino chuckled. 'Well, of course they do. How you doin'?'

'Started well.' Robby shrugged.

'So did the Titanic, son,' Aldino remarked.

'I'm down about six grand,' Robby allowed.

'Ouch!' Aldino exaggerated a wince. 'Sorry you came?'

'No.' Robby shook his head, his tone confident. 'I'll turn it around. It goes like that sometimes.'

'Yeah.' Aldino zipped his fly. 'Word of warning, son? When players like this see a man runnin' low on the old ackers, it's instinctive to them to push. Know what I mean?'

'A spieler's a spieler,' Robby shrugged. 'It's the survival of the fittest. Has to be that way.'

'That's right.' Aldino smiled. 'Well, let's go get 'em.'

Robby grinned back and opened the bathroom door.

The morning passed. Became afternoon. The light began

202

to fade. The big game went on, its duration taking a toll of the players. Chins sprouted stubble, eyes grew red. It was as much a test of physical endurance as of skill with cards: twenty-four hours of non-stop concentration. Of calculating chances; out-guessing; bluffing; taking losses; sometimes winning. As the lights of the city began to come on outside, Robby found himself playing alone with Hal Brookman, his stake badly down. Brookman was showing a possible royal flush: the ten, jack, queen, and ace of Diamonds. Robby was showing three kings and a ten. The king of Diamonds was not part of his hand.

'Well, son, just thee and me again.' Brookman flashed his dazzling smile. 'I've bloodied your nose on the last few finals, eh?'

'Like I said – you can't win 'em all.' Robby didn't smile back. 'Your bet.'

'Mmm, so it is. OK.' Brookman remained affable, glancing at his opponent's pot. 'Looks as though you've got a slight cashflow problem there, son. What you got? About seven hundred? Seven-fifty, maybe?'

'Make your bet,' grunted Robby, holding his deadpan expression despite the tension gripping him.

'OK, son.' The American remained imperturbable. 'Just to show you I'm not a hard man, I'll call your five hundred and up it by only two. How's that?'

'Always a gentleman, you,' Aldino remarked as Brookman pushed seven hundred pounds to the centre of the table.

'Of course,' smiled the tanned man. And to Robby, 'Well, son?'

Robby looked at the immaculate teeth and the cold eyes. 'Called,' he said, defiantly. 'And raise another hundred.'

When he put his bet on the table, the notes left at his elbow amounted to no more than fifteen pounds. Aldino smiled and shrugged at Brookman. The American frowned.

'OK. Called.'

Robby watched him put eight hundred down and smiled triumphantly, turning his hole card. It was a ten, giving him a full house, kings over tens. Brookman glanced at the hand, then at Robby. Irritation showed momentarily in his eyes. He turned his own hole card. It was the king of Diamonds.

The king of Diamonds. Plus the ace, the queen, the jack and the ten: the royal flush.

For an instant that filled the future, Robby stared at the cards. A hand clamped tight on his insides. His heart palpitated, his throat clogging so that he held his breath as the instant went on and on and on. He closed his eyes, his mouth filling with the bitter taste of dead dreams. The sour bile of lost hope. Brookman said, 'I said you were out of your class, son,' in the same conversational tone.

There was nothing Robby could say, except, 'Thanks for the game.'

It came out slow and strangled as he jerked awkwardly to his feet, not wanting to meet the indifferent eyes of the watching players. He snatched his jacket, his remaining fifteen pounds. Lurched to the door. Behind him, Brookman glanced at Aldino and shrugged.

'Right. Whose deal?'

The game continued.

Robby Box no longer existed.

Outside, the street was empty. Dark. Robby put one foot in front of the other. Repeated the process: an automaton. A numb, lost wanderer. His eyes were wide and red, beard stubble dark against the ashen pallor of his skin. His breath came in long, ragged gasps, quickening as the full enormity of his loss hit him. Ten thousand pounds blown out. Everything he had saved. His future blown away on the turn of a card. Geordie, Dick Mayor, his friends outraged. Jan lost. The hand clenching his insides balled tighter and he staggered against a tree as vomit climbed the tunnels of his stomach to fill his throat and explode from his mouth. His shoulders heaved and suddenly his legs had no strength. He went down heavily on his knees, bracing his hands against the ground as his head hung and the spew flooded out. He had no idea how long he crouched there. Time ceased to exist. There was only the vomit and the voice inside his skull that boomed over and over, *You blew it. You blew it all. You blew everything.*

When the contents of his stomach were gone and only dry heaves tore at his throat, he lifted his head, wiping his eyes. He wrapped both arms around the tree, clutching the bole, tears running down his face to mingle with the puke smearing his chin. He sobbed as he wailed, 'Oh, Jan! What have I done? God! What have I done?'

And the same mocking voice answered him: *You blew it.*

Red-eyed, staggering like a drunk, Robby Box crashed through Jan's front gate. He tottered up the path to hammer on the door. When there was no answer, he put his mouth to the letterbox and began to shout.

'Princess! Please! Let me in!'

From beside him, a voice said, 'The lady isn't there any more, I'm afraid.

Robby turned, squinting at the man who stood there, nervously watching the dishevelled man still holding the letterbox open.

'What d'you mean, not here any more?'

'She, er, sold the flat. She and Debby have gone to live in Australia.'

You blew it all.

'No!' he moaned, shaking his head wildly. 'No! She can't have! You're lying! She told you to say that, didn't she?'

'No.' The neighbour took a step back, as though afraid Robby might turn on him. 'They left about half an hour ago for Heathrow, I swear to you.'

For a moment, Robby stared at him in blank incomprehension, not able to take in the words. Not wanting to.

You blew everything.

'No!' He spun away, hurling himself down the path. 'Jan! You can't!'

'I was going to leave at the end of this term anyway, Mum. So missing the last few weeks of school are hardly going to make any difference.'

205

Jan turned a wan face to her daughter, envying Debby her youthful resilience. 'No, I suppose not,' she sighed. 'I wanted you to stay on, though. You know that, don't you?'

'Yeah. But it would've been a waste of time.' A new life in Australia loomed ahead of Debby: the past was fading. 'I want to get out and about. To work, have my own money and that. I bet you were the same when you were my age.'

'Yes.' A faint smile creased Jan's lips. 'Yes, I was. And it doesn't seem that long ago, either.'

'Well, there you are then.' Debby gestured towards the counter of the coffee bar. 'C'mon, I'll buy you a drink.'

'Oh, will you now?' Despite herself, Jan's smile brightened as she studied her daughter's eager face.

They got their coffees and found a table, joining the anonymous bustle of the airport as they waited for their flight. The past few days had taken a toll, and Jan was grateful for the momentary respite. Their neighbour had agreed a price on the house and Jan had left the details to be sorted out by her solicitor, who would transfer the proceeds to Australia. The furniture had been sold off and her bank account cleared. All ties with the past were severed, the most important cut by Robby. All Jan wanted now was to forget. She started as the tannoy announced, 'Quantas Airways are pleased to announce that flight nine eight six, London to Sidney, is now boarding at gate ten.'

'That's us!' Debby shrilled. 'Oh! I'm all excited!'

'Yes, so am I.' Jan smiled, catching Debby's enthusiasm. Then saw the girl's face cloud. 'What's the matter?'

Debby's eyes were wide. No longer with excitement, but with something almost like fear. Jan turned, following her gaze, and felt the smile freeze on her mouth as she gasped, 'Oh, God!'

A few feet away, Robby stood. He was haggard, his chin unshaved and his eyes red with dark purple shadows. Stains decorated his shirtfront and tears ran unnoticed down his stubbled cheeks. His mouth moved as though trying to form words that refused to pass his lips. Softly Jan said, 'Why did you have to come? Why, Robby?'

She closed her eyes and took a deep breath. Forced

herself to stand up and walk towards him, not knowing if the pain inside was anger or regret. Knowing only that she had to face him.

'Why did you come here?' she asked, her voice teetering on the brink of hysteria. 'I didn't want this. I didn't want this!'

'Princess ... I ... I ...' The words came slowly, pain-wracked through the tears. 'Please don't go.'

'It's too late for that, Robby.' Dully; fighting the pain. 'I love you, Princess.'

She fought the tears and lost, but her resolve remained. 'Oh, Robby. Don't. Please. I can't handle this.'

'There's so much to say, Princess. You can't just go. Please? We have to talk.'

'No. No more talk.' Jan shook her head as the tannoy spoke again, repeating the boarding call. 'There's nothing left to say. Except goodbye.'

'No! Not that!' There was a plea in his voice. Raw emotion. He shuddered. Looked down at his feet as though too hurt to meet her own tear-filled eyes. 'I'm sorry, Princess. I wanted so much for us. So much! I did it for us.'

Jan shook her head again, forcing the words out. 'No, Robby. You did it for you. You can't keep away.' She stared at him, hurt by his obvious grief. 'What happened?'

'I tried for us!' he moaned.

'No, you *gambled* us, gambling man. We were the stakes. It was our future. It'd always be that way with you.'

Robby forced his head up. Forced himself to look into her eyes.

'No, Princess ...'

'Yes, Robby.' Definitely; bitterly. 'It would. I can't handle it any more. I've been the joker in the pack too long. You've lost all your money, haven't you?'

'I don't care about that, Princess!' He shook his head. Hopelessly; helplessly. 'I need you! I know that now.'

She stared at him through her tears, wanting to put her arms around him and tell him, *Yes, Robby, and I need you. I love you. I loved you all along.* But she didn't because she

207

knew it was not the answer: he had held their future in his hands and chosen to gamble it. Their future on the turn of a card.

She said, 'Goodbye, gambling man,' and turned away.

Robby cried, 'Jan, Princess!'

She halted, turning again to face him.

'I'm sorry, Robby.'

Debby rose from her seat, crying as she ran to Robby and reached up to hug him. To kiss his cheek. 'Take care, Robby,' she whispered. 'Take care.'

She moved back, picking up her dropped bag. Rejoining her mother. Robby watched them, frozen. Not knowing what to say. Not knowing what to do.

You blew it all. You blew everything.

Jan turned in the direction of the boarding gates, then paused. For a moment, hope glimmered in Robby's soul as she stared at his face. Then she reached up to unfasten the gold necklace he had given her so long ago. And borrowed back to pawn so many times. She tossed it to him.

'You'll be needing this, I expect.'

Robby caught the necklace. Held it as Jan and Debby and his future walked away.

Robby Box was alone again.